GET MORE OF MY BOOKS FREE!

To say thank you for buying this book, I'd like to invite you to my exclusive *VIP Club*, and give you some of my books and short stories for FREE.

To join the club, head to adamcroft.net/vip-club **and two free books will be sent to you straight away! And the best thing is it won't cost you a penny — ever.**

Click here to join the VIP Club

Adam Croft

For more information, visit my website: adamcroft.net

I see you.

You don't see me.

That's just the way I like it.

I know every line on your face, every angle of your jawbone, every twinkle in your eye. I know you better than you know yourself. Because I knew you long ago.

You won't remember me. Not yet, anyway. But I will remind you. I fully intend to make sure you remember.

And then things can be like they were before.

When we were happy.

1

My fist connects with his skull and he snaps his head back, almost losing his footing. It's a perfect punch, and I surprise even myself.

I see the look in his eyes as he lurches forward, keen not to lose momentum or allow me the overall advantage. It's a look that tells me he's got something up his sleeve. He goes for me, leans into the punch, his balled fist missing my face by millimetres.

I don't have time to register what's going on. Before I've noticed him reversing his lean, his leg's up and heading towards the side of my head. My momentum from the dodge has kept me moving, and there's nothing I can do.

I brace, and time slows.

My head rattles, the sound goes dull and I taste blood. Every part of my skull feels immediately stunned and my eyes feel like they're on fire. I see the black edges start to appear around the sides of my vision, realise I'm going to lose consciousness if I don't get down on the floor quickly. But if I get down on the floor, it'll all be over.

I need to try and fight on.

My legs take that decision out of my hands, turning to jelly as I'm forced to hit the deck. My body relaxes almost immediately, and I see his feet walk up to me, see his shadow move as he leans down over me, feel his breath on the back of my neck as he places a hand on my shoulder.

'You alright, Alice? Sorry. Been saving that one for a while. Didn't expect it to be so brutal.'

'I'm good,' I say, my voice sounding alien to me.

Martin takes his hand off my shoulder and offers it to me. I take hold of it and he hauls me to my feet.

'Between you and me,' he whispers, whilst catching breaths, 'I think it's a bit fucking stupid putting men against women. But maybe that's just me. I feel dreadful every time I make contact. Can't get my proper game in, you know what I mean?'

I nod, then quickly wish I hadn't. It only makes my head ache more.

He's right, though. It's only because so few people attend these classes any more that we have men fighting women. People round here would rather spend their evenings watching TV than kickboxing.

Martin takes off his protective gear and heads towards the bench. The velcro rasps through my skull as I loosen the belt strap on my head guard and take it off, my head feeling instantly cooler.

'Right, that seems as good a place as any to leave it for

tonight,' Simon says, addressing his small and dwindling group of pupils. 'Remember next week we've got a later start. Eight-thirty, alright?'

I know from experience that at least another two people will use that as an excuse not to turn up next week. I doubt whether the classes will still be running at Christmas. That thought makes me sad. Even though I know there'll be other kickboxing classes around, there's something quite special about this one. Apart from only being a short walk from my house, it does have other added advantages.

'You sure you're alright?' Simon asks me, once the others have headed off towards the changing rooms.

'Yeah, I'm fine,' I say, smiling.

Simon smiles back. It's a warm, pleasant grin that says *I'm comfortable. You can trust me.*

I can't say *comfortable* is something that usually appeals to me, but there's something different about Simon's style of comfortable. Friendly-casual, perhaps. I guess all teachers have to have that about them.

'You'll be here next week?' His Australian lilt and habit of using rising intonation at the end of sentences means I'm not entirely sure whether it's a question or a statement.

'Yeah, I'll be here,' I reply. *When have I ever missed a lesson?* 'It's a shame it's a bit later, actually, because I was going to ask if you fancied a drink after. Only there's this new bar open up the road, and, y'know,' I say, running out of steam.

'That'd be cool,' he replies, in a non-committal way that

doesn't tell me whether he genuinely means it or is just going through the motions.

'Or perhaps tonight, if it's not too short notice?' *Bad move*, I tell myself immediately. *Too desperate.*

'Ah, I can't tonight. Got things planned already. Week after next, maybe?'

'Sure,' I reply. *If the classes are still running by then.*

It always seems to take me longer to walk home from the leisure centre than it did to walk there. I don't know if it's because I'm more tired afterwards, because I've not got the lesson to look forward to or because everything seems to take longer in the dark. It seems longer, too, because I know I'll be going home to an empty house.

Sure, Kieran wasn't there all the time, and he never technically lived with me, but knowing that I had someone to spend the rest of the evening with was always a comfort. That ship has sailed, though. He couldn't handle me, and I sure as hell couldn't handle him. Nutcase and Tedious doesn't have the same sort of ring as Bonnie and Clyde.

I try not to think about it too much. The more I do, the more it upsets me. If there'd been any specific incident that either of us could put our finger on, it would have been much easier. But to me, it was pretty clear the relationship was over. I just wish he'd taken it half as well as I thought he might.

The steps up to my front door often ice up at this time of year, so I'm extra careful as I walk up them. The leaky gutter means that water drips onto the steps then freezes, making the whole place a deathtrap for two or three months of the year.

I put my key in the lock and open the front door. As I step inside and close it behind me, I feel my heart jump in my chest. Not a lot, but I notice it.

There's a sense of unease, a feeling that something isn't quite right. I tell myself I'm being daft; I'm going to have to get used to coming home to an empty house. After all, it was my decision to break up with Kieran. Can't have your cake and eat it, girl. I walk into the kitchen and put the radio on, listening to the soothing bass tones of a Simply Red song I semi-recognise, as I pour myself a glass of wine from the fridge. The first of a couple, I fear.

2

Work's chaotic at the moment, and I'm finding myself having to get into the office earlier and earlier all the time. The only problem is that I'm so knackered by the time I get home I find myself drinking more and more each evening, too, and that doesn't fit well with early starts.

There's a horrible taste in my mouth that only comes the morning after drinking white wine – almost like the alcohol vapours have seeped up from my lungs overnight – and I lean over to take a mint out of the packet. I'll brush my teeth once I'm up and have had breakfast, but at least this'll make me feel a little more human. While I'm there, I prise one of my fluoxetine pills from its blister pack and slug it back with a mouthful of water before crunching the mint.

Mornings are lonelier now than they were before. Generally speaking. It has its upsides, though. It's better than having to wait to use my own bathroom, or getting downstairs to find the kitchen work surfaces covered in crumbs. There are some things I don't miss one bit.

My morning routine doesn't end when I leave the house, either. Even though I've already had a small bowl of cereal at home, there's no swaying me from my morning pastry on the way in to work. One of my colleagues introduced me to a new patisserie on the high street a few months back, and I've been in there every day since. And today's no different, as I find myself going through the motions, walking in through the door and smelling that familiar smell of freshly baked pastries. The woman behind the counter smiles as she spots me join the back of the queue, packages up my pastry and sets the coffee machine running. By the time I reach the front of the queue, I'm ready and waiting with my £4.90 — I've got the right change today — and we go through our usual daily routine of asking each other how we are, even though we don't even know each other's names. It's reassuringly familiar, though.

I leave the shop and turn right, in the direction of the office. I don't even see him there until it's too late.

'Shit! Sorry,' he says, placing a reassuring hand on my upper arm as he bends down to pick up the pastry packet from the pavement. 'My fault. I wasn't looking where I was going.'

'Honestly, don't worry,' I reply, as I take the pastry from him, being careful not to spill my coffee too.

'No, really, it was my fault. Let me buy you another one.'

I shake my head. I just want to get to work. 'It's fine. It's packaged up so it'll be alright.'

'Nonsense,' he says. 'It'll be a bag full of crumbs now. Let me buy you another one. Please. I insist. I'll feel dreadful all day if I don't.'

He looks me in the eye in a way which makes me think I'll feel like a complete shit if I say no. If he wants to buy me another pastry, why not?

'Alright then,' I say. 'If you insist.'

Back in the shop, the queue has died down, but we still have to wait for a minute or two.

'I wasn't even paying attention out there,' the man says, still going on about it.

'It was an accident,' I reply. 'It happens.'

'I know, but it's still my fault. I've had my head in the clouds for the past few days and I should've been paying attention. Relationship break-up,' he adds, giving me information that I didn't ask for.

'Sorry to hear that.'

The pastry replaced, we leave the shop and I thank him.

'Oh, just a second,' he says, putting his hand on my arm again – not in a creepy way, but a reassuring one. 'I told myself in there I wasn't going to mention it, but I thought I should. No regrets, and all that. I run a modelling agency, just down the road here. I mean, I'm a photographer by trade, but I've got a lot of friends in the fashion industry and I quite often do a bit of talent spotting for them, if you see what I mean. I don't mean to be rude, and I hope you're not offended, but you've got fantastic bone structure and a great figure.' He hands me a business card from his back pocket. 'Just in case it appeals. You know. No pressure or anything, but I think you'd be great. It's good fun, and some of the people I've referred have gone on to make great money. Just a thought.'

He shows me his friendly smile. There's something in the way he said it. Something reassuring. But now really isn't the time or place for me to be thinking about a change of career.

'Thanks,' I say. 'I'll bear it in mind.'

'Sure. Give me a call or a text if you fancy it, alright? No charge, naturally. There are some places who make money by charging people for photos. Between you and me, they just throw them in the bin. The only time I make money is the referral fee I get when my contacts take on a model I've referred to them. So you've got nothing to lose.'

'Sounds good. I'll give you a call,' I reply, not really having any intention of doing so, but wanting to get to work.

We go our separate ways, and I walk up the high street in the direction of the office – with a spring in my step that surprises even me.

3

Mandy and I try to meet once a week if we can, usually after work and usually in one of the cocktail bars in town. We've been pretty good at keeping in touch regularly since school, and I think there's an unspoken truth that we both try our best to keep it that way.

We've always been pretty close, but I think it's one of those friendships that's matured in recent years. I've found myself feeling comfortable telling her almost anything. She knew I was going to break up with Kieran even before he did. To be perfectly honest, I think she probably saw the warning signs earlier than me. She's good like that. She always knows the right thing to say or do. And that's why I plan to ask her about that weird encounter with the photographer guy earlier this morning – Gavin Armitage, according to his business card – and whether she thinks I should take him up on his offer.

I've been thinking about it all day. On the face of it, it

seems a bit weird to go up to a random woman on the street and ask her if she'd like to become a model. But then isn't that how these things are done? After all, the people working in the industry know what sort of look they're after. If they see someone who they think would be a good fit, why not? Headhunting's done in almost all industries — it's a large part of my job, after all — and where else would you find potential models than out in public, where there'll be a greater number of people?

Having said that, it still doesn't feel right. It's not *me*. Men have always considered me attractive, I guess, but I've never even thought about using my looks to my advantage. I've always seen that as a bit demeaning. After all, there's far more to me. The thought of posing in a seedy photography studio for some guy I don't even know doesn't really appeal to me all that much. But then again, neither does spending the rest of my life in HR, struggling to deal with management's constant reshuffling and 'restructuring' of departments. Being paid to tell people they're being made redundant is never nice, particularly with Christmas just round the corner, and I don't want the job to desensitise me to people's real lives.

I make a promise with myself that I'm going to turn my thoughts to happier subject matter, and I enter Zizi's Bar with a smile on my face. I spot Mandy sitting on the other side of the room — she always tries to grab one of the booths — and wave to her, gesturing to ask her if she's got a drink. She holds up two glasses — margaritas from what I can tell — and beckons me over.

'We actually got here in time for happy hour,' she says as

she hugs me and hands me one of the glasses. 'Two for the price of one.'

'Bonus,' I reply, shrugging off my coat and scarf. 'So, how've you been?'

'All good here,' she says, as she does every week. 'And you?'

Some people might see that as dismissive, even nosy. *You don't give, you don't get*. But I know Mandy. This is her way of saying *Don't worry about me. I'm more worried about you.*

'Yeah, I'm alright,' I reply. 'Well, y'know. Getting there anyway.' Even though I had plenty of time to come to terms with the breakup of the relationship, I still feel bad knowing that Kieran saw it as a bolt from the blue. I feel bad for him. 'I'm keeping busy with work. That all helps.'

We chat for a little while longer, and soon find ourselves on our third cocktail. I feel my stomach rumbling and think about heading home for dinner. But there's something I need to speak to Mandy about first.

'I meant to say. I had a bit of a weird experience earlier,' I say, before recounting what happened.

Mandy raises an eyebrow. 'Seriously? People still do that?'

'Well yeah, I guess so. I dunno. It just seemed a bit odd. I wasn't expecting it.'

'Isn't that just one of those things to make money? I mean, they charge you two hundred quid or whatever for the photos, then do nothing with them?'

'Apparently not. He doesn't charge a penny. He gets his

money from his clients whenever they take on one of his models.'

'Weird. Must just be a perv then,' Mandy says.

I force a smile and flick my eyebrows upwards before taking a sip of my drink.

Mandy's silent for a few moments before she speaks again.

'You're thinking about it, aren't you?'

'About what?'

'About going down to this bloke's studio and having photos done.'

'Nah. Like you said, he's probably a pervert or something. And even if he isn't, I doubt anything would come of it.'

I look out across the bar and do a bit of people-watching for a moment or two. Out of the corner of my eye, I can sense Mandy looking at me. She doesn't say anything for a little while, but I can tell she wants to. I also know it won't be long before she does say something. She's never been particularly good at keeping her mouth shut when she's got something on her mind.

'Why don't you give it a go anyway?' she says. It wasn't what I was expecting.

'What do you mean?'

'The photos. Why not go down and get some done? What's the worst that can happen?'

'Christ knows.'

'I could come with you if you want. If you're worried.'

Yeah, that's all I need – Mandy flipping out and attacking the poor guy because he dares to shake my hand when I turn up. She's never been the most forgiving or patient person I know. Don't get me wrong, she's got a heart of gold. But there's no stopping her when she's got a bee in her bonnet about something. She's protective, and that's a good thing, but I do worry sometimes that she could take it too far.

'Nah, it's fine,' I say. 'I'm not worried. I just don't see the point.'

She considers this for a moment. 'The point is it might do you good. Let's face it. You've been pretty grumpy since breaking up with Kieran.'

Mandy's Honesty Dart hits the bullseye once again.

'No I haven't,' I say, perhaps a little too defensively.

'Trust me, you have. I'm not saying you did the wrong thing, not at all, but I'm saying you might want to have a backup plan if you catch my drift. It might make you feel better about yourself.'

I don't know whether I should feel affronted or not, but I think I do. 'I don't need to feel better about myself,' I say.

Mandy raises her eyebrows momentarily and puts the straw to her mouth before taking another mouthful of her cocktail. 'Alright. If you say so.'

The most infuriating thing about Mandy isn't her faultless honesty; it's the fact that she's always right.

4

I wasn't quite sure what to expect when I phoned Gavin this morning, but it was a bright — if chilly — Saturday dawn and I woke up feeling much more chipper than I'd any right to. I guess Mandy's words had been playing on my mind all night, and sleeping on it had helped me realise that there was no use moping around. So what if nothing came of the photo shoot? So what if it turns out to be a wasted day? What else did I have planned for today other than sitting about the house watching TV programmes I've already seen on Netflix?

Before I called him, I decided it'd be a good idea to do a bit of research. It's not that I don't trust Mandy's instincts, but it just seemed wise to find out a bit more about this guy before going down to his studio. I typed 'Gavin Armitage photography' into Google, and his website was the first result on the page. I clicked through to take a look at his website.

It looked professional to me, even though I don't know much about websites. I navigated to the *About* page, which didn't have much information about Gavin himself, but went into detail about his approach to photography and modelling in general. He seemed to use all the right words: *professional, bespoke, holistic*. Words that don't really mean anything, but convey positive connotations to potential clients. And I had to admit, it worked on me too.

I browsed through the image gallery on his website for a while, looking at some of the photos he'd taken and was very impressed. He clearly had an artistic eye, and none of the shots were lewd or even provocative. They were classy. I spent another few minutes looking through his Flickr account, which contained most of the same photos plus a few more, then decided I would take the plunge and call him.

He told me he had a pretty free afternoon, and that I could pop down any time after lunch if I wanted. Nothing too formal – bring a few changes of clothes and send him a text before I leave. The casual nature of the whole thing appealed to me. Nothing formal, no pressure. Just pop in and get a few shots done, see how it goes. When you spend your life having days that are completely regimented and organised down to the last minute, that sort of sudden spontaneity can appeal quite a lot.

I wonder how long I've been secretly longing to break out of that disciplined and systematic routine and be a little more spontaneous. I imagine it might be longer than I think. Was that why I started to feel as though my relationship with Kieran was breaking down? Was it becoming a little too regular? Was my brain telling me that I needed to have at least *something* in my life to excite me? Something that didn't consist of lists, schedules and appointments?

We even used to book our date nights a week or two in advance. If we wanted to spend time together we'd have to fit it around work, my kickboxing classes, his rugby socials. Perhaps it was all a little too clinical.

There's nothing clinical about Gavin Armitage's photographic studio, though. I look up at it as I reach the address he gave me on the phone earlier. 86b Reynolds Street. I've never even noticed this building before, even though I must have walked past the end of the road plenty of times. At first glance, it reminds me of a smaller-scale version of the building they use for the TV series *Dragons' Den*. It's all large leaded windows and exposed brickwork; an homage to the style of the old Victorian workhouses. I don't know if it's an original building or just built in that style. Architectural history was never my strong point. Either way, it looks pretty impressive.

I ring the only buzzer on the door. I don't hear anything, but I imagine a buzzing noise going off somewhere deep in the depths of the building. A few seconds later, I hear a click as the door unlocks. I give it a push and step inside.

As I close the door behind me, Gavin appears at the top of the stairs with a beaming smile on his face, his shirt sleeves rolled up to reveal a chequered tartan pattern on the insides of the cuffs.

'Sorry, I wasn't being rude. The intercom doesn't let me talk back for some reason. I can either unlock the door or not unlock the door.' He shrugs. 'Come on up. I'm just getting everything organised. Won't be a few moments. Tea? Coffee?'

I follow him up the stairs as he disappears round the corner, telling him I'd love a cup of tea.

The studio itself looks smart, in the organised-chaos sort of way that I imagine all artistic workspaces look. You would expect even the most organised painter's studio to be covered in blobs of colour and smears of oil paint, or a writer's desk to be piled high with stacks of paper. Gavin's studio is no different, except it's filled with desks covered with assorted lenses and bits of kit I couldn't even name.

There are huge white umbrellas erected in various places, as well as white, blue, green and black sheets stretched over frames. There are a number of huge black plastic cases in the shape of Smarties tubes. I have no idea what any of it's for, but it looks impressive.

'Don't mind the mess,' he says, as if reading my mind. 'I promise there's some sort of logical pattern to it all. If anyone tided it up I'd be lost.' He smiles and hands me my mug of tea. 'So, have you ever done anything like this before?'

'No, nothing,' I reply, fully expecting him to come out with something corny like *I'm surprised. Good looking girl like you*. But he doesn't.

'Well there's nothing to worry about. The best advice I can give is to stay relaxed. All sorts of people will give you different tips and tricks, but everyone's different. The only thing I'd say is relax and don't think of the camera. If you do, like if you've got to look at it or whatever, pretend it's a person. If we're going for a sexy look, pretend it's someone you really fancy. If it's a more sullen look, pretend you're talking to a funeral director and booking your nan's cremation. You know the sort of thing.'

I laugh. I have absolutely no idea what he means, but at the same time it seems to make perfect sense. No-one likes an awkward photo.

I show him the clothes I brought with me, and he picks out a few he thinks would be good for the shoot: a short red and white polka-dot dress, a tiger-print maxi dress and a pair of jeans and a jumper.

'You'd be surprised how many places are going for the casual look at the moment,' he says. 'I'm glad you brought these with you, actually. I meant to say don't just bring smart and sexy stuff. Looks like you've got more of an eye for this than you think.'

I'm not quite sure what to make of that – I know Mandy would see some sort of insult hidden in Gavin's comment – but I also know that he was actually giving me a compliment.

I spend the best part of an hour and a half at the studio. There are shots standing, sitting and lying down. Even lying down isn't just lying down, apparently. There's lying on my back with my head tilted sideways towards the camera, there's lying on my front with my hands propping up my head from under my chin, there's lying down flat on my back with him stood over me, shooting the camera downward, my hair sprayed out all around my head like a fan.

'I think that'll probably do,' he says, as he finishes taking the last photo of me standing with my back flat against a mock lamppost, my head pointed sideways toward the camera with a sullen look on my face. 'That should give us something for most of the big players anyway.'

'So what do you need me to do? Anything? Or do I just wait to hear back from you?' I say a few minutes later as I'm changing back into my usual clothes behind a screen.

'Yeah, I'll send a few of the best shots through to you over the next couple of days if you give me your email address. I should ask that people don't use them for their social media profiles or whatever, but to be honest I don't mind as long as you put my name down as a credit. Other than that, the hard work's all mine now,' he says, smiling.

I write down my email address on a piece of paper and hand it to him. Then, with a spring in my step, I leave.

5

We wouldn't normally bother going out on a Saturday night after meeting up for drinks in the week, but it's Mandy's birthday tomorrow and I promised her we'd go out for a few drinks to celebrate.

Zizi's is much busier tonight than it was last night, and it quickly becomes clear that we're not going to be able to get a table. There are some stools left at the long rectangular bar, though, so we decide that'll do for now. It's not the sort of place people tend to spend the whole evening, so there'll be a table free at some point.

Once we've ordered our drinks, Mandy elbows me on the arm – almost making me yelp.

'Don't look now, but you-know-who's down at the other end of the bar.'

'Who?' I ask, instinctively looking in the direction she'd just told me not to look. It's Kieran. He doesn't see me, but I see him. The first thought that crosses my mind is the slightest flash of anger and jealousy that he seems to be having a good time. And why shouldn't he?

'Looks like he's having fun,' Mandy says, in her characteristic way that makes it seem like she's reading my mind.

'Good,' I reply, trying to sound pleased for him. 'He's entitled to. He's a free and single man.'

'Doesn't look too cut up, though, does he?'

I find myself wanting to defend him. 'He's a bloke, Mand. He's hardly likely to sit sobbing onto his mates' shoulders, is he?'

I look over at Kieran again, just as he looks up and makes eye contact with me. Even at this distance, I can see what he's feeling. And it's not just the outer layer of male bravado. I need to get a grip, though. I'm not the sort of person who makes a decision and goes back on it. I wouldn't last five minutes in my job if I was.

I'm sorry, David. The current restructuring means that your role is no longer required. We'll keep your details on record, though, if anything else should come up in the future.

But it's nearly Christmas. I've got a family.

Okay, no problem. As you were, David.

Do I get a little pang of regret every time I have to deliver those words? Of course. I wouldn't be human if I didn't. But I've got a job to do. And anyway, it's evened out by being able to give jobs to other people. The Lord giveth with one hand...

But there's nothing I can give Kieran. We had all that. We had the good times, and it was time to come to terms with the fact that they'd reached their end.

'Fuck,' I say, reaching for my glass and taking a huge slurp.

Mandy looks over and sees Kieran walking towards us.

'He'd better not start any trouble,' she says. 'If he does I'll lump him one.'

'Mand, chill out. He's not like that. He probably just wants to say hi.'

'Yeah, well you seemed really enthusiastic about that a second ago.'

'That's different. I wasn't expecting to see him,' I say, almost forcing a whisper as Kieran reaches us.

'Hi Alice,' he says. 'Alright Mandy?'

'All good here,' Mandy replies, before burrowing her face in her margarita glass. I give her a look that says *Grow up* and make apologetic eyes at Kieran.

'We're out for Imran's leaving do,' he says to me, before explaining to Mandy. 'He's off to Australia for a year on Wednesday. Doing some travelling with his girlfriend. You out celebrating your birthday tomorrow?'

I smile a little. It's so typical of Kieran to remember his ex-girlfriend's mate's birthday. In a way, he was almost *too* caring and considerate. That sometimes came across a bit weird, though. I still remember the first time we met. His chat-up line involved telling me how he was sorry to stare at me, but he had to do a double-take because I looked like his sister. Hardly a classic.

'Just a couple of quiet ones,' I say. 'At least that's always our intention.'

Kieran laughs and Mandy forces a smile. It infuriates me

when she gets like this. It's almost as if it was *her* relationship that broke up and not mine. I know deep down she's only defending me and looking out for my best interests, but I'm a big girl now. I can look after myself. Besides which, she always gets the wrong end of the stick and sees threats and dangers where there are none.

'Well, I don't want to get in your way,' Kieran says, clearly sensing Mandy's mood. 'Just wanted to say hi and find out how you are. Didn't really fancy an evening of awkward glances and trying to pretend we hadn't seen each other.'

I laugh, as if that had never been on the cards. 'Honestly, it's fine. I hope you have a good evening.'

Kieran smiles, wishes Mandy a happy birthday for tomorrow and goes back to join his friends.

'At least that cleared the atmosphere,' I say, trying to make conversation with a clearly-pissed-off Mandy.

'If you say so.'

'Come on, Mand. It would've been far more awkward if he hadn't come over. He's trying to make the peace.'

'He's trying to get back in your pants.'

I give Mandy a look that tells her I'm not going to stand for any comments like that. She seems to back down a little. Or so I thought.

'If you want to get back with him, why don't you just get on with it?'

'Because I don't,' I say, looking her dead in the eye.

She looks down at her drink again.

'Could've fooled me.'

6

As expected, the quick couple of drinks turned into a pretty heavy night. Kieran and his friends moved on to another bar about half an hour after he came over to speak to us, and I figured it was going to make my life a lot easier with Mandy if we just stayed put at Zizi's. Unfortunately, Zizi's is a cocktail bar, and not a particularly expensive one at that. A few 2-for-1 margaritas later, and I was starting to realise it would be heavier than planned.

I'm just glad I didn't have much planned for today. A lazy Sunday in front of the TV is about all I can manage.

I roll over and pick up my mobile phone from the bedside table, as I always do when I wake up. Part of me worries that it's a little sad that this is the first thing on my daily routine, but that's modern life.

I got to bed pretty late, so the only thing showing on the screen is a text from Mandy letting me know she got home safe. Oops. I probably should have stayed up until that came through, but it's a bit late now.

I put my phone back on the bedside table and think about going downstairs and getting coffee. Again, it's part of my daily routine, but coffee's the last thing I want when I wake up with a raging hangover. Water and sleep is all I want right now. Having said that, a massive fry-up dripping with fat wouldn't go amiss.

My phone vibrates on the beside table and I pick it up again. It's an email from Gavin. The subject line is *Early shots*. I open the email. There's no text; just a succession of photos from yesterday. I reckon there must be a dozen in total. I open the first one. It looks pretty good, actually. It's a shot of me sitting backwards on a chair, leaning on the back of it with my hand under my chin, propping my head up. Nothing original in the slightest — and I remember groaning inwardly when he asked me to do it — but it actually looks fantastic. I swipe the screen to move on to the next photo, and the one after. They're both shots of me in the red and white polka dot dress, one where I'm standing face-on, my hands spread and up to the sides of my head as if in despair, and another of me looking down at the camera. I remember Gavin lying on the floor while he took that.

I carry on swiping through the photos, smiling at the quality of them. He's actually made me look pretty natural. After swiping through a few more, one shot in particular catches my eye. Anyone else might think it was a lovely naturally-posed shot. But I know for sure that I didn't pose for this one.

It's an arty black-and-white shot of me behind the changing screen, standing in my bra and knickers, holding the bottom hem of my red and white polka dot dress, which is on a hanger, hooked over the top of the screen. I'm holding it out, as if checking for marks. I don't remember doing it, but it's definitely me.

But how did he take this photo? He never came behind the screen. There's no way I would've let him anywhere near me while I was changing.

My mind starts racing ten to the dozen. Was it some sort of CCTV shot? I doubt it. The quality of the photo is far too good. It looks perfectly set up, just like his other photos. Except there was no camera there. Just a bare brick wall. I'm sure of it.

My head's pounding from last night's excesses as it is, and I can't quite figure out what this is all about. I tell myself I'm just being daft. I went to get some photos taken and I got some photos taken. Yes, he took one of me when I didn't realise, but was that the whole point? Was he trying to get some natural shots too? Even so, taking candid photos of women in their underwear isn't right, surely? It certainly doesn't feel right to me.

Maybe he's just having a joke around. *Caught you!* Or perhaps it's all about nudging me towards something else. *Have you ever considered being an underwear model?* Either way, I don't feel comfortable with it.

I decide not to bother replying to his email. My head's not in the right place at the moment and I don't want to say something I'll regret. I'm not the sort of person who thrives on confrontation. I prefer to take a step back, pretend it never happened and move on.

Sometimes that's easier said than done, though. Seeing Kieran last night proved that point. Then again, there's nothing wrong with needing a bit of time and space to catch your breath and move on properly, is there? I don't think anyone could have expected me to instantly not give a shit.

My head's pounding and that big greasy fry-up is starting to feel even more appealing. I pull myself out of bed and get dressed, trying desperately to shake the feeling that – hangover aside – something feels very, very wrong.

7

By now you'll be wondering. You might even be panicking. For you, this is just the beginning. For me, this is the midpoint. This is where we're fully into the woods and realise we have to find our way back out. Which way we go is entirely up to you.

I've been working on this for a while, you see. The first time you saw me wasn't the first time I saw you. That morning outside the patisserie wasn't your first morning there, and it wasn't mine either. But how many times did you notice me? You've walked past me practically every day for the past fortnight and you didn't even know it. As far as you were concerned, until I stopped you and spoke to you I wasn't even a human being. I didn't even have a life, a name, a personality. I was just another passing figure. A nameless, faceless form. I didn't have a history or a future. I didn't have troubles or triumphs. I didn't have the slightest impact on the world. Not on your *world, anyway.*

But we all walk around in our own universes, don't we? We keep everything internalised. Everything is about us. That woman you walk past in the street lives a normal life in a normal house with a normal husband and normal kids. She's Mrs Average. How are you to know she's got a Nobel prize? And that old man sitting on the bench, leaning on his wobbly walking stick? Just another pensioner, eh? Goes out in the morning, buys a paper, goes home and watches shitty daytime TV while he does the crossword. Maybe pulls up a couple of cabbages from his vegetable garden. Wouldn't think he was one of Britain's most prolific un-caught serial killers, would you?

You don't think about these things. None of us do. But we are all you. And you are all of us. That huge problem in your life? We've got those too. The big event you're looking forward to next week? Take a look at mine. Your impact on the world is as small or great as you want it to be, but that doesn't diminish mine.

Here's a secret that'll blow your mind: the world doesn't revolve around you.

You think it does, though, don't you? If there's one thing I've learned by watching you all this time, it's that you're self-centred. That's not the same thing as selfish. Sure, you put money in charity tins. Of course, you occasionally let the little old lady step into the queue in front of you. Yeah, you gave up your seat on the bus for a pregnant woman. But you didn't even think to help her off with all the shopping bags, did you? Who was the little old lady? Someone's grandmother?

Someone's sister? And I bet giving that money to charity sure felt good. It meant you didn't have to think about what those poor African children go through every day. Didn't have to feel guilty. Just chuck a pound coin in the pot and it's all forgotten. Viva Africa.

There's too much of it in this world.

She always taught me that. I can almost hear her voice when I remember those words. It stuck with me, indelible on my consciousness ever since.

She was a great woman. I thank the 1960s for having her as a teenager. If she'd grown up in the 1980s, as I did, all she would've known is greed, jealousy and envy. How on earth did her generation manage to lose everything they'd worked for? Why did they turn their backs on peace, love and harmony?

That dollar sign is mighty appealing.

It disappointed me when I found out what you were like.

No. Not disappointed.

Devastated.

It was all looking so promising. Your eyes. That line of your jaw.

Don't kid yourself that you're the only one. You're not. It's a distinctive look, but it's not rare.

Truth be told, I don't remember much about her. Only snippets. Just the odd flash of a vision. But it's enough. Enough to see the likeness. Enough for me to want to find out more. In the hope that her vision is still alive, that her hopes and ambitions for a better world didn't die with her.

It's easier than people think, hope. There's always the

chance, the fleeting possibility, that it might actually happen. That's what you live for.

That's what she lived for.

So I live in hope. Hope that you might see the light. Hope that things might be different.

Because she almost changed the world.

And we could change it too.

8

The weather forecast reckons there'll be rain today, but I can't see it happening. Either way, I'm not going anywhere. My hangover's still raging and the huge fried breakfast has made me feel even more tired.

The photos have been playing on my mind ever since I got up, no matter what I've tried to do to distract myself. Deep down, I know there's only one thing for it. It isn't going to be pretty – hell, it's going to be like throwing a lit match at a box of fireworks – but I need to call Mandy and talk it over with her. She might not be an expert in diplomacy, but she's rarely wrong.

She'll know something's wrong as soon as I call her. Although we're close, we don't tend to phone each other for the sake of it. There'll be the odd text here and there, plus our weekly catch-ups at Zizi's. That tends to do us fine. A phone call tends to mean something's wrong.

I bear this in mind as I call her, and try to sound as chirpy and confident as possible. That's not easy, though. My head's pounding and my stomach's churning.

'Morning!' I say, as she answers the phone. 'How's things?'

'Feels like someone's driven a pitchfork through my head. Other than that, can't complain. You sound bright and breezy.'

'Fake it til you make it,' I reply. 'I've tried water and grease. Next on the list is sleep.'

'So what's up?' Mandy says, cutting straight to the chase.

'Not much. Just wanted to say hi,' I reply. She'll see right through that, I know. So I jump straight in. 'Listen, you know that photoshoot I went on yesterday? Well the guy sent some images through by email this morning. Just a few early ones so I could see how they came out. They're good photos. Really good, actually. But one of them was a bit... Well, weird.'

There's a pause for a moment as Mandy takes this in. 'What do you mean "weird"?'

'I mean, like, a photo of me standing in my underwear. Behind the screen. Away from the camera.'

'What, you mean like a Peeping Tom shot?'

I swallow. 'I guess. Something like that.'

'Fucking perv,' she says, the venom in her voice clear.

'I dunno. I don't think he is. Honestly, he was the nicest, most polite and least pervy person I've ever met. I don't know what this is all about, but that's not it. I thought maybe it was an accidental shot, and he put it there to make me think about doing underwear modelling or something. To be honest, there wasn't anything said about not taking photos behind the screen. It was all pretty casual and friendly.'

'Jesus Christ, Alice. Will you listen to yourself? You don't need to *say* anything about not taking photos of women getting changed. It's common sense. What's his name and address?'

'Mandy, don't.' I say this a little more firmly than I usually would. It does the trick, though.

'So what now?' she asks. 'Are you going to ring him and find out what it's all about?'

I sigh. 'And say what? "Why did you take a photo of me in my underwear?"'

'Yeah. Why not? You've got a right to know.'

If truth be told, I don't want to rock the boat. The rest of the photos look great. If there's a chance of getting some modelling work, why not? Besides which, Gavin didn't seem like the sort of person who was trying anything on. He took a hell of a lot of photos yesterday. And then I went out and drunk a hell of a lot of cocktails. I can't even say for certain that I didn't pose for the shot. It's highly unlikely, but not impossible. It wouldn't be the first time mixing alcohol with antidepressants had caused me memory blanks.

'It's probably just an innocent mistake,' I say. 'A misunderstanding.'

'Misunderstanding my arse. He's a man, Alice. It's what men do.'

'I dunno. He seemed fine to me. And I've got a pretty good built-in twat radar.' I decide against pointing out that Mandy's is far too sensitive and needs adjusting.

'Wait. Run me through this again. You say you just randomly bumped into him in the street?'

'Yeah. I'd literally just come out of the patisserie. The door hadn't even closed behind me. So no, it wasn't deliberate before you start that.'

'Hey, I didn't say a thing. Only asking.' I can almost visualise her raising her hands in the air in mock surrender. 'And what, he randomly asked you if you fancied doing some modelling?'

'No, he apologised profusely for me dropping my pastry, went inside and bought me another one.'

'Then asked you if you fancied doing some modelling?'

I sigh. 'Something like that. Look, it wasn't weird or anything. Yeah, alright, it wasn't an everyday conversation, but it's not like he followed me down the street and forced me to talk to him. Besides which, I called him. Not the other way round.'

'And what did he say? You didn't give him any personal details, did you?'

'No, nothing. Apart from my email address.'

'Which has your name in it, right?'

'Yeah, but come on. Alice Jefferson isn't exactly a unique name, is it? And anyway, you're overreacting. He's a photographer, not a serial killer.'

'He's a perv, though,' Mandy replies, before realising she shouldn't have. 'And what do you know about him?'

'His name. Where he works. The fact he's had a relationship breakup recently.'

'He told you that?' She sounds like a detective who's uncovered a clue.

'Yeah, but don't go getting all excited. He mentioned it in passing. It was his excuse for walking around with his head in the clouds. And before you ask, no. He didn't come on to me, he didn't ask if I had a boyfriend and he didn't try to tease any sort of information out of me. So no, it's not jealousy or revenge.'

Mandy is silent for a moment. When she speaks, she speaks quietly. 'I didn't say it was, Alice. I was only asking, and you got defensive over it.' There's a pause before she speaks again. 'You're worried, aren't you?'

9

It's Tuesday morning. I flaked out after speaking to Mandy on Sunday and went straight to bed. I woke up about eight-thirty that evening, thirsty and needing the toilet. I knew I should eat, so I made myself cheese on toast and went straight back to bed.

It's taking me longer to deal with hangovers the older I get. Mixing alcohol with my pills doesn't help, either. I always seem to end up with a day or two of feeling mentally shitty. They say drinking alcohol with anti-depressants isn't advisable at all, so I'm definitely not doing myself any favours with the amount I've been drinking recently.

Yesterday was better. Mondays tend to be dire work-wise. Everyone's in a foul mood and nothing seems to go right. As Mondays go, though, it wasn't bad at all. I left work with a smile on my face, feeling better about the world. The incident at the weekend had more or less vanished from my mind.

It put me in a great frame of mind for today, too. The Tuesday morning was bright and crisp — my favourite part of winter. I don't mind the cold one bit as long as it's still sunny, with that biting chill in the air that makes everything seem much more positive.

The office is quieter than usual. Sandra's on holiday, seeing her family in Germany as she does every year in early December. Stefan is on a training course in Derby and Khurram is flitting backwards and forwards between delivering staff appraisals and performance reports, and nipping off for a cheeky cigarette at every given opportunity.

I'm completely on my own when the email comes through.

I try not to make a habit of using my mobile at work, but there's no-one around at the moment so I don't see the harm in it.

It's an email from Gavin. This time there's no subject line.

I open the email, my heart starting to skip a little as I'm reminded of all the weirdness at the weekend. It seems to take an age to load, the little spiral in the middle of the screen spinning and turning, trying to tell me that it's loading.

When the pictures finally load, it takes me a moment to digest what I'm seeing. The first photo shows me leaving work last night. I recognise the bobble hat, scarf and coat immediately, but it takes a couple of seconds before my brain can accept that it's a photo of me. I'm in full focus, clearly walking quickly as the background and everything else is blurred. But why the hell has Gavin been taking photos of me leaving work?

I swipe the screen and move on to the next photo. I recognise the surroundings straight away. It's Zizi's Bar. The reed-effect backdrop to the bar and the neon pineapples are a dead giveaway. But the focus of the shot is on me and Mandy sitting at the bar. It only shows our backs, but it's clear as day that it's us.

I swallow and blink as I try to take in what I'm seeing. What the hell's going on?

My head starts to spin and my hands are shaking. I hear the phone clatter on my desk as I drop it, and I start to get the sensation of an electrical buzzing in my brain. It's one I know immediately. I didn't take my fluoxetine this morning. A shrill, piercing tone starts to become apparent in my ears and I squeeze my eyes shut to try and force it out.

I walk over to the water dispenser and pour myself three glasses in succession, throwing each one down my gullet and swallowing, the ice cold water mixing with large air bubbles, making my chest hurt for a few seconds.

I sit back down and go to reach for my phone, but I don't think I want to look any further.

It takes me a minute or two, but eventually I pick the phone up again and swipe the screen. The photo keeps bouncing back from the edge, indicating there aren't any more to view. I put the phone back down and sit back in my chair.

I can hear some sort of commotion from outside the office. It sounds as if someone's having an argument. I can't hear the words, though, and the whole thing just forms part of the background noise. I barely register it.

But the sound of an email pinging through on my work computer might as well be the sound of a nuclear bomb detonating. It jolts me back into the here and now, and I lean forward and use the mouse to open the email.

I make a small choking noise as I see who the email is from.

It's from Gavin.

On my work computer.

To my work email address.

I open the photo in the email. It's another shot from the studio. Nothing pervy, nothing I didn't know about. It's one I posed for. But the photo itself isn't what's worrying me.

I didn't tell him where I work. I said nothing about my job, nothing about my life. So how has he managed to not only take a photo of me leaving work, but also get hold of my work email address?

I feel an icy chill run down my spine. And that's when I realise I'm deep into something serious.

I just don't know what.

10

I try not to panic. But I need answers. I need to find out what the hell's going on. I pick up my mobile, go to my calls list and see his number in my *Recents* list from Saturday morning. I tap the number and put the phone to my ear.

It seems to take an age to connect, but eventually the phone starts ringing. It rings and rings, but there's no answer. No voicemail, nothing. Just the constant repeating ring.

I hang up the phone and put it back down on the desk. A few seconds later, I pick it up again and redial the number. The same thing happens. It rings and rings.

I can feel myself getting short of breath and I know I need to stay calm. Having a panic attack now isn't going to do any good. There's no-one in the office to help me if I start to hyperventilate and getting worked up will have no benefits.

I try to tell myself all these things, using the coping mechanisms and strategies my therapist taught me, but I feel like I'm fighting a losing battle.

I close my eyes and concentrate on my breathing. In through my nose, hold it for three seconds, out through my mouth. In through my nose, hold it for three seconds, out through my mouth. I feel my arms on the armrests of my chair, listen to the sounds in the room – the whir of the computer fans, the humming of the central heating system – and try to ground myself in the here and now.

My breathing starts to steady and I manage to get myself to a point where I know I'm probably not going to have a panic attack. But I still need someone – need something – to tell me what the hell's going on.

I dial the other number in my recent calls list and pray that Mandy isn't too busy at work to answer. To my relief, she answers on the fourth ring.

'What's up?' she says, sensing something isn't right.

I take a deep breath and tell myself not to babble.

'I got some more photos. From Gavin. But they weren't taken at the studio.'

There's a couple of seconds of silence as Mandy tries to take this in.

'What do you mean?'

I swallow. 'One was a picture of me leaving work. The other one was of us in Zizi's on Saturday night.'

Mandy's on the verge of yelling now. 'What the fuck? What the actual fuck?' I hope my silence tells her that I don't need any convincing. What I need is a friend who can help me. 'But how? You didn't see him there, did you?'

'No. The picture's of our backs, but it's definitely us. And the one of my leaving work looks like he took it from across the street, but I don't know how he knew where I was. I didn't tell him where I worked. I didn't tell him we were going to Zizi's.'

'Shit. Has he been following you?'

I sigh. 'I don't know. It looks like it. I'm scared, Mand.'

This seems to bring her back down to earth. 'I know. But you can't be scared. He's just a dirty little pervert who thinks he can intimidate you. We need to make sure he knows he won't get away with it.'

I have no idea what she's proposing we do, but right now I'm glad I didn't tell her his surname or where his studio is. Knowing Mandy, she'd be straight down there with a baseball bat.

'Alice, you have to call the police.'

My heart sinks. 'I don't want to get involved with all that. I don't want any trouble or hassle. I just want it all to go away.'

'What, and you think he's going to stop because you ask him to? This guy's clearly deranged, Alice. If he's the sort of person who follows women around taking photos of them, who knows what else he could do? Look, call the police, give them his name, phone number and address and they'll sort it out. Please.'

I think about it for a few moments, but I know there's no decision to make. There's only one option. As usual, Mandy's forthright but making complete sense.

'Okay,' I say. 'I'll call them.'

11

My hands are shaking as I ring the police. I don't think I've ever rung them before.

I decided to ring 101, the non-emergency number. It doesn't seem to warrant a 999 call. There's no immediate emergency, and to be honest I don't want the drama.

The woman on the other end of the phone is professional and calming. I guess she has to be. That's her job. I tell her everything I can remember, going back to the first time I met Gavin on Friday. I tell her about the patisserie, about him approaching me, me going into the studio. I tell her about the weird underwear photo, then the photos I received from him today. I make a point of the fact that I did my research on this guy, and that everything seemed legit. I tell her I'm worried, that he knows where I work and where I go out socially. I think she hears the panic in my voice, and she tells me in a reassuring manner that she'll log the details and get a local officer to call me to arrange taking a statement.

Within an hour, I get a phone call from PC Jason Day, who tells me he's been assigned to look into my report. He asks me if he can come and see me. I'm about to tell him I'm at work at the moment and that it'll have to be later, but I have a different idea. My mind is all over the place right now and there's no way I'm going to be able to get any work done. I tell PC Day I'll be home within the hour, and he can meet me there.

I email Khurram to let him know I've gone home ill. He'll pick the message up at some point, I'm sure. Then I head home, taking an extra glance across the street as I leave, now paranoid that someone is following me with a camera.

True to his word, PC Day arrives shortly after, the sound of the doorbell jolting me even though I was expecting it. I usher him through to the living room and sit down, before realising I've not offered him a cup of tea. Fortunately, he says no.

He asks me to tell him what happened, right from the beginning. Every time I tell the story I feel more and more daft. How did I not spot the signs from the start? Why didn't I tell him I wasn't interested? Pure vanity, that's why.

I tell him the whole story, and he writes it down almost word for word, stopping me occasionally to check some details or specific wording. When I can't think of anything more to say, he stops writing and looks up at me.

'So his full name is Gavin...?'

'Armitage,' I reply.

'What does he look like? Approximate age, height, build?'

I try to think. 'Just... Normal, I guess. He had dark hair.

Short, but not shaved. Still enough length that it was curly. But not floppy, if you see what I mean. A natural tight curl. He was probably about... Forty, maybe? Difficult to say. Taller than me, but not massive. Slim to average build.'

PC Day nods and writes this down. 'And what about his ethnicity?'

'White, I think.'

'You think?'

'Yeah. I mean, with his hair and things, I wondered if he might have like a Moroccan grandad or something, but yeah, white.'

I decide to try and keep things simple. I feel like I'm confusing him.

'And this studio of his. 86b Reynolds Street?' He looks at me for confirmation. I nod. 'What can you tell me about it?'

I wince as I realise the first thought that comes to mind. 'The intercom doesn't work properly. It's up a flight of stairs. Iron railings. Open brickwork. A large room, bare floorboards, big windows but some of them had blinds down over them. I suppose it was so he could control the light.'

'And what sort of equipment did he have?'

'Loads of stuff. General camera gear, I guess. I didn't know what most of it was, but it looked like a proper professional setup.'

PC Day nods again as he writes. 'And you've never seen this man before or since?'

'No, just outside the patisserie on Friday and at his studio on Saturday.'

'But you'd recognise him if you saw him again?'

'Definitely,' I reply. 'No doubt about it.'

He seems to consider this for a moment. 'So how come you didn't recognise him taking photos of you outside work? Or at the bar?'

PC Day's question catches me off guard. 'I don't know. I didn't see him. I wasn't looking for him.'

'But would you not have noticed someone pointing a camera at you?'

I start to feel like I'm being interrogated. I tell myself he's just trying to get all the information he can, trying to get to the bottom of this for me. But I can't help how I feel. I swallow and try to control my breathing.

'In the photo of me leaving work it looks like he's on the other side of the street. And in the bar we were facing the other way. I wasn't exactly expecting to see him in either place, so why would I be looking out for him?'

PC Day says nothing. Instead, he picks up my mobile phone from the coffee table and flicks through the emails again.

'Can you forward these to me?' he asks. 'You'll need to keep the originals as well. We might need the tech people to have a look at them in case they need to trace them.'

'Yeah, course,' I reply. I watch him as he copies down Gavin's email address from the screen onto his notepad.

'Here's my card. If anything else happens, call 101 and let us know. Unless it's an emergency of course, or you're in any danger. In that case, always call 999.'

I swallow and nod. How do I tell him I already feel like I'm in danger?

12

I felt calmer after speaking to the police on Tuesday. After a while, I mean. I didn't know what to expect, didn't know what their plan of action would be. I presumed it would be very little, particularly as I'm not even sure a crime has been committed. Sure, I feel harassed, violated. But is that a crime in itself? I don't know. All I know is the police seemed to take it seriously and that's what matters most. It put my mind at rest more than I expected it to. Just knowing that *somebody* knows who this guy is. That helps. That there are eyes on him. That the authorities know I'm in some sort of danger. I feel less alone. But that doesn't mean I'm comfortable.

Mandy keeps suggesting we go down there and confront him. I keep telling her I don't think that's a good idea. I've made out that I lost Gavin's business card and don't remember the address of the studio or his phone number. I don't know if she believed me or not, but I don't care either way. I don't want any confrontation. I want the whole thing to go away. I want to forget about it all.

I don't think I've ever been any good at handling tricky situations. I know. That sounds like a bizarre thing to say when my job involves ending people's careers, but it's true. I've often wondered whether I took that job because a part of me was yelling to get over my fears. For me, detaching myself from the situation helps. I try not to think about their families, their unpaid bills. I just look at the facts, the figures. I think about how it'll benefit the company, and a part of me tries telling the rest of me that it'll give the person a chance to find a job elsewhere. Potentially a better job, for a better company, where they'll be happier. Where their families will be better off and their bills will get paid. I know I'm kidding myself, but it's the only way I can reconcile what I'm doing.

I realise how much nervous energy I've still got every time my phone rings or a text message comes through. I look down at my phone and see Kieran's name on the screen. The fact that my heart sinks a little tells me everything I need to know. If I was at all conflicted as to how I felt about him, that involuntary reaction has put paid to any doubts.

'Hi,' I say as I answer the phone. I try to keep my tone neutral.

'Hi. How's things?'

I see. Friendly chat, is it? 'Yeah, not bad. You?'

'Yeah I'm alright,' he replies, unconvincingly. 'Well, sort of anyway. I've been thinking.'

Here we go.

'Listen, Alice, I know what you said about not feeling like

we were going anywhere, but I never really knew what you meant by that. I thought we were good together.'

I try to mask my sigh. 'We were. But sometimes you just get the feeling that things haven't got a future.'

'I don't.'

'No, but I did. And it might be news to you, Kieran, but a relationship involves two people. Not just one.' I feel bad the moment I stop speaking. He didn't deserve that, but I can't help feeling frustrated that he's making me out to be the bad person here. 'Look, I'm sorry, alright? It wasn't anything you said or did, and it wasn't because of anyone else. I just looked forward a few years and didn't see us there. We had a great time, and you're a great guy, but there wasn't a future.'

Kieran stays silent for a moment or two before speaking. 'I can change.'

I sigh again, and this time there's no doubt he hears it. 'I don't want you to change, Kieran. You don't need to change anything. We can still... Look, I think we both need to move on.'

'You were about to say we can still be friends, weren't you?' Kieran says, as I sense a bite of venom in his voice. 'Got any more clichés to throw out there? "Go our separate ways"? "It isn't you, it's me"?'

I don't reply to that. It's unlike Kieran to get worked up about anything. But when he does, giving him a second or two usually leads to an apology.

'Look, I'm sorry Alice. I'm just a little bit... y'know? It took me by surprise a little. Maybe I should have seen the signs. I dunno. Maybe it was my fault.'

If I didn't know him better, I would think he was playing the guilt trip card. 'It wasn't anybody's fault. It's just one of those things.' I cringe as I hear myself speaking yet another cliché. Fortunately, Kieran doesn't pick up on it.

'I just... Can we try again? Please. I know we can make this work.'

He catches me by surprise. Kieran isn't the begging type, and I didn't expect him to come out with this.

'I don't think so, no,' I reply. 'I've made my mind up, Kieran. I'll let you know if it changes, but I don't expect that it will.'

I don't want to hurt him. He's a great guy. But he needs to know that it's over. I feel like an utter bitch for having to be so firm with him, but he just doesn't seem to be able to take no for an answer.

'So it's totally over?' he asks, after a good ten seconds of silence.

'Yes,' I say quietly. 'It's totally over.'

13

I don't know whether it was Kieran's phone call last night that put me on edge, but I was awake for most of the night, worrying and panicking, my heart rate increasing with every noise I heard. I lost count of how many times I jumped out of bed and peered through the curtains every time I heard a car stop on the road outside.

I didn't go to the kickboxing class this week. I couldn't face it. I feel bad now, especially knowing that Simon is disappointed at the dwindling attendance figures. I'll send him a text at some point today to apologise and promise I'll be there next week.

I thought I was doing alright, thought I was dealing with it all. But now I realise I was just trying to push it to the back of mind, as I always do.

There's no way I can face going into work today, so I call in sick. I don't even need to try and sound tired and groggy – I reckon I must've had two hours' sleep at the very most.

After I've called work, I make another phone call; one I now realise I needed to make a little while ago.

I haven't been to see Maisie Haynes in a while, and part of me wonders whether she'll still remember me. She must see so many people every day, I doubt she can recall everyone she's had through her door.

I'd put off that call to Maisie for far too long. The doctor promised me the medication would help and I was hanging on for the morning I'd wake up feeling better. The morning I could stop taking my pills and all would be better. But now I know that was unrealistic.

When I'm like this, I feel like I'm drowning. I can feel the water creeping up over my nostrils as I flap and splash about, doing nothing much but at least feeling like I'm trying. The medication was my set of inflatable armbands. It allowed me to bob around in the water, keeping my head just above the surface. Safe, unless an armband were to burst. If a massive prick came too close, for example. The sessions with Maisie were different. They were swimming lessons. A long-term method of changing the way I do things. Lessening the danger in the first place. I'm still not a great swimmer, though, and the armbands give me extra comfort. Sometimes I forget how to swim.

The waiting room looks strangely familiar, but then again I suppose it should. Nothing much has changed. The same posters are on the walls: a phone number for the Samaritans, a collage of good mood foods, three steps to remaining calm in an anxious situation. The furniture's the same, too: a laminated chipboard table with a selection of books and magazines on top of it, surrounded by five large eighties-style beige chairs. No arms, but covered in a horrible soft plastic vinyl which is either too cold in winter or too hot in summer.

Fortunately, I don't have to wait long. The waiting room is empty when I arrive, and within a couple of minutes Maisie calls me through.

My first worry is how much this is going to cost. It sounds silly, I know. My initial round of sessions were covered by the NHS, but this time I decided to self-refer. The last thing I wanted was anything going on my medical record.

Maisie immediately puts me at ease. 'It's been a long time,' she says, sitting down in her chair and gesturing for me to sit opposite her. 'How have you been getting on?'

I take a deep breath, exhale, then tell her.

'Generally, not bad. Pretty good I guess. But lately I've been having some problems. Work has been stressful. And I went through a relationship breakup recently. The silly thing is, it was completely my decision but I still feel dreadful about it. I can't even put my finger on why. I guess because he was a nice guy, but that doesn't really mean much. I think I just feel like I've taken a step back, like every time I have something good I run away from it.'

Maisie smiles. 'Do you remember when you came to see me before and we talked about Imposter Syndrome?'

I nod. I remember her saying it's actually quite common. Certain people, when things are going well, are beholden to their brains trying to right this sudden dissonance. The person doesn't feel like they have a right to be happy or successful. Their mind tells them their success is down to pure fluke – not hard work – and that someday they'll be found out to be a fraud. It's almost as if they're afraid of happiness. Time and time again, they push away loved ones, overruled by this internal sense of not deserving to be loved or admired.

'Do you think that might be at play again?' she asks.

'It's possible.'

I remember all the things we talked about before. About how I used to be a very accomplished pianist for my age. My parents were thinking about taking me out of mainstream school and putting me through a musical academy. There was talk of scholarships, of trips to New York under invitation from academy programs. And then, overnight, I decided I didn't want to do it any more. Piano wasn't for me. I wanted to play basketball instead. Why? Because I knew I wasn't any good at basketball. My success with the piano scared me. I remember feeling an overwhelming sense of pressure. Even as I think back, I can feel my chest tightening, my breath quickening.

'And are you still taking medication?' Maisie asks.

I nod. 'Fluoxetine.'

'How do you feel about that?' she says, looking down at her notes. She's remembered me saying I didn't want to go on Prozac. How I was scared when I found out what fluoxetine's more common name was. I'd told her all the horror stories people had told me, or I'd read online.

'It's become a part of me now,' I whisper.

'What about side effects?'

'No, nothing,' I reply. Truth be told, after reading some of the stuff about Prozac online, I didn't even look up an official list of side effects. I didn't want to. I'm a firm believer that you see what you want to see. The last thing I wanted is a checklist in my mind, so I could panic every time I sneezed, yawned or scratched my nose.

We sit in silence for a moment or two before Maisie speaks again. 'So why have you come to see me today? Do you need my help with something?'

It sounds silly, but this is a question I don't really know the answer to.

'I'm not sure. I just... I haven't been myself recently. A couple of things have shaken me. And generally I just feel like I'm plateauing. I'm not going anywhere with my life. I feel like I'm slipping again. And I know that last time I came to see you a lot of stuff started to make sense. I made some changes and started to think and feel differently. So I guess... I dunno. I guess I thought that if I came back to see you again, you might be able to do the same thing for me now.'

She nods. 'Do you remember when you first came to see me? The very first session? I mentioned that I'm able to give you the tools and information to change whatever you want to change, but the desire to do so needs to come from within you. You are able to help yourself far more than I or anyone else can.'

I think about this for a moment. I hate feeling like this, but I still don't know if I have the energy or the willpower to drag myself out of it. Besides which, there's the panic attacks, the anxiety, the thoughts... If my mind is constantly playing tricks on me, do I have the fire to fight it with? That's a question I don't know the answer to.

My phone rings in my pocket. I apologise to Maisie and tell her I'll put it on silent. As I look at the screen, I see the call is from a withheld number. Immediately, an icy chill runs down my spine and I feel my breathing start to quicken.

And that's when I know I need all the help Maisie can give me.

14

I feel brighter when I leave Maisie Haynes's clinic. Not better, but brighter. As if there's a light at the end of the tunnel. It's still a damn long tunnel, and there's a lot of stuff to get past on the way, but at least the end is visible.

As I walk back towards the bus stop, I feel my phone vibrating in my pocket. Only faintly, but enough for me to realise and reach for it. When I look at the screen, I see the withheld number is calling me again. This time, I decide to try and put some of Maisie's tips into action. I take a deep breath as I run through the possibilities.

Who could it be? Absolutely anyone. But what's the worst option? Potentially, that it's Gavin Armitage. Is that likely? No. If the police have been speaking to him, I'm the last person he'll be calling. Besides which, I haven't heard anything since Tuesday. That's three days. Would he be stupid enough to call me? I doubt it. But what if it is him? I'm in control of the call. I can hang up. I can report it to the police. Can he hurt me over the phone? No. Not physically. And as soon as I heard his voice I'd hang up anyway, so his power is limited. I could go straight to the police station from here, and I'd be safe.

Running through that logical progression of worst-case scenarios in my mind helps ground me, and I decide to swipe the phone and answer. The overwhelming likelihood is that it won't be him anyway.

'Hello?' I say, trying to make myself sound bright and confident, but failing miserably.

'Hi, is that Alice Jefferson?' the voice says. I recognise it immediately.

'Yes, hi.'

'Hi, Alice. It's PC Jason Day. We spoke on Tuesday when I came to your house.'

'Hi,' I say again, for the third time.

'I just wanted to ring to give you an update, really. We've been having a look at the details you gave us. Can you confirm the spelling of Gavin's name for me please?'

I spell out his name and surname, as it was written on his business card. I can still see it in my mind's eye. Every letter, every crease, every printed pixel.

'Yeah, that's what I've got written here. Only we can't seem to find any record of anyone locally with that name. Then again, he might use a different name for his work. Sometimes people do. You don't know him by any other name?'

'Uh, no,' I say. As if I wouldn't have bothered telling them if I did. 'That's all I know.'

'Okay, not to worry. I've sent an email to the address he emailed you from, and I've tried calling him on the mobile number you have, but I've not had anything back yet. We'll see how things go over the weekend. It was Saturday you went in, wasn't it?'

I tell him yes, it was.

'Well maybe he only works weekends or something. Anyway, don't worry. I'll keep trying. Give me a call if you hear anything else, alright?'

'Hang on,' I say, trying to keep PC Day on the line. I can't quite make sense of any of this. 'Have you been to his studio? He might be there. That's the only other thing I have.'

'Not yet,' he replies. 'We'll do that if we don't get any response within a day or two.'

I struggle to believe what I'm hearing. 'So you just sent an email and tried phoning him? Seriously? This guy's been stalking me and taking photos of me leaving work. And you haven't even been to the one address we have for him?'

There's silence for a couple of moments. I can almost sense PC Day squirming awkwardly.

'It's never easy in a situation like this,' he says. 'I don't want to use the old "budget cuts" line, but everything goes through a process of grading and prioritisation. If we thought you were in immediate danger, we would've been straight down there and Mr Armitage would be in custody now. The fact that we haven't is probably a good thing. It means we don't think you're in any immediate danger.'

I lean back against a shop window as I try to take this in.

On the face of it, it should sound encouraging. *Not in any immediate danger*. Surely that's a good thing, right?

It should be.

The only problem is, I'm not entirely convinced he's right.

15

As I turn the corner into my street, I recognise the car parked outside my house straight away. It's one I haven't seen for a while, but it's unmistakeable. The black Audi is getting on a bit now, but it still looks the same as the day they drove it off the forecourt, thanks to my dad spending three hours every Sunday morning cleaning, drying and waxing the thing. It's that sort of effort that made me never want to own a car.

The car doors open in unison as I approach, my mum climbing out of the passenger side and trotting towards me with her arms outstretched, a sympathetic smile on her face as she envelops me in her fake-fur hug. Dad stands stoically at his side of the car and tries to look pleased to see me.

'What are you doing here?' I ask, hoping I don't sound too shocked or ungrateful. I barely see my parents these days, and it's not like them to turn up unannounced.

'We were passing in the car, and we decided – I decided – we should probably pop in and see you,' Mum says, making it sound more like an obligation than a desire. I know that isn't true, though. Dad's the one who tends to hold back a little more. If it was up to Mum, they'd see me every week.

'Shall we go in?' Dad says. 'Bit nippy out here.'

'Uh, yeah. I'll put the kettle on,' I reply, leading them up the steps to my front door.

They've only been here once or twice before, but even so, every time they do come Dad acts as if he's never set foot in the building in his life. He steps around deliberately, his hands clasped behind his back, looking up at the walls and ceiling as if he's ambling through an art gallery. Mum scuttles through to the kitchen and makes herself at home.

'So how are you keeping?' she says, as she pulls out a chair at the kitchen table and sits on it. 'We haven't been very good at sticking to those weekly phone calls, have we? I know I haven't.'

'No, I know. Sorry,' I say. I immediately wonder why I'm apologising. I've got nothing to apologise for. My parents and I have gradually drifted apart over the years, and that's no-one's fault. We're all very different people.

I feel dreadful saying it, but neither of my parents were great for me when I was going through my lowest periods. Dad couldn't handle it full-stop. He made all the usual noises about it not being a 'real' illness, about needing to occupy myself with something, or needing to 'snap out of it'. Deep down, I think he's scared. He didn't want to admit it was a real illness, because that would have meant his daughter was ill. And what parent wants to admit that?

Mum, on the other hand, tried to be helpful but in all the

wrong ways. I felt smothered and claustrophobic, feeling as though I was constantly fighting off phone calls and messages checking up to make sure I hadn't topped myself. She was always emailing over links she'd found online to various articles espousing natural remedies or 'mood boosters', as if all I needed was to boost my mood a bit. She was trying to help, I know, but it was too much. I didn't want her involved; I just wanted her to *know*. I felt she had a right to know. After all, dealing with my illness was one of the reasons I had to leave home. Making my own way in the world, independent of my parents, was a huge part of learning to live with myself — in more ways than one.

'How's work?' she asks. I instinctively look at the clock and realise it's mid-afternoon. On any other day I'd be at work right now, but I'm not. Mum and Dad would have known that, too. So why were they waiting outside my house, as if they were expecting me to return at any minute?

'Yeah it's fine,' I say. 'I'm not in today, though. Obviously.' I hold Mum's gaze for a little longer than I usually would. She picks up on my unspoken question.

'Alright. We came through town on the way up here and we saw you at the bus stop. We didn't want to pull over and startle you, so we thought we'd wait at your place until you got back.'

Didn't want to *startle* me? This strikes me as a pretty odd way of phrasing it. That's not the first thing that comes into my mind, though.

'But I thought you said you were passing? Wouldn't it

make more sense to come off the bypass and in at the edge of town, rather than all the way round and through the town centre? I mean, unless you were coming here straight from your place, of course, in which case coming through town would've made more sense.'

Mum's silent for a moment. Dad realises he might as well come clean.

'Your mum wanted to come and see how you were doing. I told her that you'd call if you needed us, but she wasn't having any of it.'

Mum seems affronted at this. 'Well no, that's not quite true. And anyway, what's wrong with me wanting to pop down and see you?' She aims this more at Dad than at me.

Something still isn't quite right, though. Even if they were making a special trip, why would they come down on a Friday afternoon when they knew I'd be at work? Unless they knew I wasn't.

'So who told you I was off work today?' I ask, leaning back against the counter with my arms folded across my chest. I stay silent and wait for an answer. It's Dad who finally speaks.

'Kieran's been worrying about you. He got in contact with your mum a few days ago.'

That wasn't the answer I was expecting. I'm not quite sure what to say. 'Right. Why?'

'Because he's worried about you,' Mum replies.

'But what's that got to do with me not being at work today? What is he, psychic?'

Dad sighs. 'She at least deserves the truth, Linda.' He looks at me. 'Kieran's been in touch with one or two of your work colleagues too.'

I realise I'm standing with my mouth open. 'What the hell? What gives him the right—'

'He's worried about you, Alice,' Mum says. 'Not about you splitting up, but...'

The look Dad gives her tells me that they weren't meant to know about this either. Mum stands and comes over to me, placing a hand on my arm to placate me.

'We're just looking out for you, sweetie. Kieran cares for you and he wants to make sure you're alright. Regardless of anything else. When your colleague mentioned to him that you weren't in work today, he let me know, just in case there was anything we needed to worry about.'

Great. So now everyone's been talking about me behind my back, conspiring to keep an eye on me, make sure I'm not going loopy or posing a threat to myself or anyone else.

I try to remain calm, keep my voice level.

'There isn't anything anyone needs to worry about. I took the day off work because I had an appointment in the middle of the day and yes, I really couldn't be arsed to go in for an hour or two either side of it. And yes, I phoned it in this morning as a sick day because I forgot to book it off in advance. Alright?' I know I'm telling a small lie, but that seems like nothing compared to the deception of them creeping around behind my back for God knows how long.

I can see tears starting to form in Mum's eyes. 'Alice, we—'

'Now, if you don't mind,' I say, 'I've got plenty to be getting on with.'

16

My head feels foggy and muzzy as I roll over and look at the alarm clock. It's ten to nine. I never sleep in this late, even on a Saturday. I realise the pent-up stress and anxiety from Mum and Dad's visit yesterday – not to mention the visit to Maisie – probably didn't mix all that well with the bottle of wine I consumed in front of the TV last night.

I've still heard nothing further from PC Day or anyone from the police. But today's Saturday. It's one week since I called Gavin Armitage, one week since I went to his studio and had the photos taken. Like PC Day said, maybe he only works weekends. Perhaps he's got another job, too. He might be right. I doubt it, but he might be. Either way, I know Gavin works weekends.

With my state of mind as it currently is, I know exactly what I intend to do today. My mind's made up. I'm going to go down to his studio and confront him, ask him why he's been taking secretive photos of me and why he feels the need to operate under a false name.

A small part of me tells me this is a stupid thing to do. What if he's dangerous? I have half a mind to text Mandy and let her know I'm going there, in case something does happen. But that means I'll have to give her the address of Gavin's studio, in which case I can almost guarantee her going down there and making a scene. She's far more likely to do something stupid, whereas I only want answers.

Before I can even think about what I'm doing, I've grabbed a large kitchen knife from the block in the kitchen and zipped it up in my handbag. What if I get stopped by the police? But then, why would I? I'm not exactly the sort of person who's likely to be subjected to a stop-and-search. Either way, I decide that the risk of things turning nasty with Gavin is higher than the odds of the police stopping me on the way there.

The cold air hits me square in the face as I open my front door. I head down the steps towards the street, faster than usual, and my foot slips a little on the icy step. The jolt of adrenaline is enough to stop me dead in my tracks.

This isn't me. I've never wanted to confront anyone over anything in my life. It's not how I operate. I prefer to bury my head in the sand or avoid any sort of situation which might provide confrontation. So what am I doing, heading off to the studio of a man I barely know, whose name I know to be false, who's been stalking me, complete with a kitchen knife in my handbag? On the face of it, it's sheer madness. Yet it feels absolutely right. I need to know who this man is. I need to know what's going on.

I start walking again, quicker this time, almost marching in the direction of Gavin Armitage's studio. The bitter wind whips around my neck, and I can feel my earlobes turning numb. But none of it bothers me in the slightest. I'm like a homing missile, my focus on one place and one place only. I see nothing else.

When I get to 86b Reynolds Street, I pause for a moment and then press the buzzer. I don't know how long I stand there. Probably only a couple of seconds, but it feels like hours. I press the buzzer again, then step back towards the edge of the kerb, looking up towards the first-floor windows. It's dark inside, but then it would be. It's a photographic studio. When I was here last week, most of the windows were covered up.

I step back towards the door again and peer inside. It's just the same corridor and staircase I saw last week. There aren't any lights on in the corridor. I don't recall if there were last week either, though.

I jam my finger against the buzzer again, pressing it and pressing it repeatedly, harder and harder.

I give up.

I close my eyes and lean back against the outside wall.

I hear a click.

'Can I help you?' says a voice — female, croaky. Old.

I spin around and look back at the door and see a short woman, probably in her seventies, peering out from behind the main door to 86b. She's wearing a dark pink blouse with a blue tabard over the top of it.

'Uh, yes. I'm looking for Gavin Armitage. The photographer from upstairs?'

The woman shakes her head and goes to close the door again. 'Sorry, I don't know anyone by that name.'

'No, you might not,' I say, stepping forward and putting my foot in the doorway so she can't close the door. 'He uses different names. But he's the guy who runs the photographic studio.'

She studies me for a few seconds. 'Are you a police officer?'

'I'm investigating him,' I say. 'Is he in?'

'There's nobody in, I'm afraid. The company downstairs only work Monday to Fridays, but they don't do anything to do with photography. They're architects. I'm just the cleaner for the building.'

'And what about upstairs?' I ask.

'Nothing.'

I blink. 'What do you mean nothing?'

'Nothing,' the woman repeats, as if this explains everything. 'There isn't anyone upstairs. There hasn't been for months.'

'No, I mean upstairs here. Those stairs,' I say, pointing. 'The photographic studio. I was here last week and it was there then.'

The woman curls her bottom lip over and shakes her head. 'I don't think so, love. There's nothing up there.'

I feel my heart hammering in my chest. 'Uh, can I take a

look?' I ask, stepping inside the doorway as I say this, giving the woman no option.

'If you like. But I'll need to come up with you,' she replies, as if she's going to provide the necessary security muscle needed.

I take the stairs two at a time. When I get to the top, I can't quite believe what I see.

There's nothing there.

17

You're going to be trouble. I know it. In truth, I've known for a little while, but I hoped I wouldn't need to resort to anything extreme.

Why couldn't you just play along? It didn't need to be difficult. A small tweak to the way you think. A slight alteration of the mind. All you needed to do was get outside your box and embrace the possibilities.

She would've done. She would have been the first one to open her mind. And that's the litmus test, you see. This is how I know if you're worthy. And you're very quickly starting to prove that you're not.

Going to the police was a very, very bad idea. Did you think I wouldn't know? Did you really imagine that even though I could find out everything about you, permeate every cell of your life, I wouldn't know you'd made a phone call? That PC Jason Day had visited your house on Tuesday afternoon? You must think I'm stupid.

No. You must think you're clever.

Because that's what happens on TV and in the films, isn't it? You go to the police, they catch the bad guy, everyone lives happily ever after. They're there to help you, aren't they? Except sometimes there isn't anything they can do. Sometimes, the police don't hold the power. Sometimes, there is only one person who can help you.

I could have helped you. I still can, if you'll let me. Will you let me?

I can show you how things should be. I can provide enlightenment. There's a spark that can't be left to die. A soft orange glow that stayed long after the flame had been so cruelly extinguished.

It won't need much. Some tinder, a bit of oxygen and a lot of determination.

I'm prepared to give you another chance. I know you won't let me down. I know it's you. I know it's you.

You're the closest anyone has come. You're going to need more work, but it's the sort of work that only you can do. I can guide that horse to water, but I can't make it drink. You need to see it. And I need to keep showing you.

I don't want to do anything drastic. I'm not like that. But everyone has their limits. Mine are a lot further along the line than most people's. She taught me that.

That's what I remember most about her: her compassion. So forgiving. Even when people did the most horrible, unspeakable things, she'd always find a way to hold no malice. She'd try to understand, try to reason as to why people might feel compelled to do these things. She apportioned no blame. She was a fucking modern day Jesus. And you know what? I see that in you too. You have a peaceful soul. But you hang on to too much. You don't even realise it.

We used to go dancing in the meadow. Yes, it's exactly as it sounds. We'd go down late on summers' afternoons and she'd take me by the hand and we'd dance among the daisies and the buttercups. She'd hum an imaginary tune. Sometimes she'd sing it. And I'd sing along too. And we'd have the time of our lives. Sometimes a group of boys would be watching. Sometimes we'd get looks and stares from people who just didn't understand. But she never once had a bad word to say about them. 'They can't feel it,' she'd say. 'One day, I hope they will.'

One day, I hope you'll feel it too. Because that's all I want for you. I want you to feel the love, the peace, the tranquility flowing through you. To take yourself to a higher plane, above all the poison this world has to offer. That world isn't for you, Alice. You're better than that. You're destined for better things.

You can do what she couldn't. There's a legacy there to be had, and the sad thing is you don't even know what it means. I'm a realist; I know you'll never truly understand. How could you? You never knew her. But as long as you understand what it means to me, *and as long as that understanding fills you with a fire in your belly and a love in your heart, I know I'll have done my job properly. I'll have fulfilled my promise. I'll have done my bit.*

I just have to make you realise. I have to show you. And to do that, I'm going to need a slight change of plan. I didn't want to have to do it this way, but you haven't left me with much choice.

I know you'll forgive me in the end.

I know you'll realise I'm doing this for you.

I know you won't let me down.

18

I don't even know how I got home. I must have wandered the streets in a daze. It's not the first memory blank I've had. Sometimes, when I go through stressful situations, my mind tends to try to protect me. At least that's the way Maisie put it when I first saw her.

I'm still struggling to make sense of exactly what it all means. The fact that Gavin Armitage's studio is no longer there is worrying enough. That he could clear everything out inside a few days and disappear is unlikely, but still possible. What worried me the most is what the cleaner said.

There isn't anyone upstairs. There hasn't been for months.

Except I know for a fact there was someone there last week. Gavin was there last week. And he hadn't just moved in that morning, either. The whole place was kitted out as a full photography studio. He would've needed days to set it up and days to take it all down. There was no way the cleaner could've not known about it.

Unless.

Unless.

The alternative doesn't bear thinking about. And it's not possible. There's no way on earth I could have imagined the whole thing, invented it in my mind. There's no way at all. I was there. I spoke to him. I told Mandy about it. I recognised the inside of the building when I went back there. How could I do that if I'd never been there, if I'd imagined the whole thing?

By midday, I'd managed to regain enough mental control to realise that I needed some help. I've felt like this before – the crushing realisation that I can't even help myself, that I need something extra. My local GP surgery isn't open at weekends, so I spent the rest of Saturday and the whole of Sunday at home, mostly in bed, with my phone switched off and the TV on in the background to try and block out the thoughts.

I didn't expect to be able to get an appointment when I phoned up this morning, but I figured it was worth trying. Mondays are the worst days to try and get an appointment. I don't know if the receptionist had access to my medical notes or whether she sensed something in my voice, but when she came back from putting me on hold for a minute or two she'd miraculously found an appointment for me to see Dr Onoko within the hour.

I've seen Dr Onoko before. He's the only doctor who seemed to understand, who wasn't just interested in getting me out the door and getting the next patient in. He's not a major fan of meds; in fact, he was the first person to suggest I go and see Maisie. I owe him a lot. And now I need his help again.

Behind his beaming smile, I sense a slight undercurrent of worry, as if he wasn't expecting to see me again. I guess all doctors hope you're not going to come back with the same recurring problem, as it indicates a level of failure on their part.

I tell him all about the way I feel right now, which isn't easy as I'm not really sure myself. He looks at me with his head cocked slightly, nodding as I speak. I don't tell him any details about the last week or so – at least not about the photos, anyway. I don't see that it's relevant, and I don't want to sound mad – as ridiculous as that might sound, having come to the doctor to effectively tell him I think I'm going mad.

He listens with great interest as I try to describe my feelings after the relationship breakup with Kieran. I'm quick to tell him that I don't want to get back with Kieran, that it was my decision, and that the overriding feeling is probably that of guilt. I briefly mention that I think I've been having blackouts and hallucinations, and, unsurprisingly, this is what he picks up on.

'Can you describe it to me?' he asks.

I think for a moment. I need his help, but at the same time I don't want to overdramatise it. I'm fairly sure my worries and anxieties are coming from within myself as opposed to anything else. I just need to learn how to control them.

'Well, there was one two days ago. Saturday morning. I

was faced with a situation that didn't make any sense. I don't want to go into the details, but it was something that challenged everything I believed. Something that made me question my own sanity. And instead of reasoning, I just kind of shut down. I don't even remember getting home.'

'And what about the hallucinations?'

'That's the bit I don't really know about. I feel silly even saying the word, but I don't know what else to describe it as. There have been a few times where I've thought things were the case but they weren't.'

Dr Onoko picks up on my verbal hedging and tries to elicit more details. 'Are we talking visual hallucinations? Auditory ones?'

I shake my head. 'I know it sounds stupid, but I really don't know. Neither I guess, sometimes both. I think it's more my brain inventing situations to try and make sense of things. I really don't know how to describe it. All I know is sometimes I get confused. My mind runs away with me. And when I can't make sense of the world I panic and everything goes blank.'

'And what do you think causes it?' he asks. His tone is friendly. I think he can sense that I might have my own theories.

'I don't know, but I wondered if it might be the medication. I know that sometimes some meds can do weird things. Either way, I'm not in a great place right now. They aren't working. I think I need to change them.'

He nods. 'I'll be honest with you. Hallucinations and blackouts aren't really known side effects of fluoxetine. That said, everyone reacts in different ways so it's possible. If you don't feel you're improving or that the medication is working, we can look at changing it. That might well help with your symptoms, too. The only slight problem is that you can't just stop taking the fluoxetine. We need to gradually reduce your dosage, as otherwise the side effects could be much worse. Some of them can be quite severe.'

'And what about the new medication?' I ask. 'Can we introduce that at the same time?'

'It depends what it is. Sometimes, yes. But I think considering your circumstances we need to have a careful look at what's out there and what'll be best for you. You can't take any MAOIs at the same time as fluoxetine, though. They're monoamine oxidase inhibitors. They react really badly with SSRIs like fluoxetine.'

I remember the acronym from when I was first prescribed it. A selective serotonin reuptake inhibitor.

'It could be that your body has got used to the fluoxetine, and that it's not effective any more. Besides which, the potential side effects you're experiencing mean it's definitely worth reviewing. We could try another SSRI, like sertraline.'

'Isn't that the same class of drug?' I ask.

'Yes. It works in a similar way. But crucially it's a different drug. In terms of side effects, anything involving anxiety tends to be lower. You should find you have fewer panic attacks and spikes of anxiety.'

Right now, I'll take anything. 'Okay. We can give it a go.'

I leave the surgery feeling a little more hopeful. Dr Onoko didn't give me any magic cure, but then I guess he can't. The sooner this all goes away, the better. If I had the money I'd book a last-minute holiday. Recharge the batteries. But I don't. So I'm just going to have to keep on fighting.

Fighting against myself. Fighting against the possibility that my mind is playing tricks on me, that I'm imagining the whole thing with Gavin. But it isn't possible. I keep going back to that same key point: that there's no way I could have recognised his studio again this Saturday if I hadn't been there the week before. How else would I have known what it looked like? And then...

Yes. That's it. There *is* something. Something I can use to prove — if only to myself — that I'm not imagining this. I start to walk more quickly as I pull my mobile from my pocket and call the police.

19

Fortunately, PC Day is at work and they're able to put me through to him. I don't have my crime reference number to hand and I don't much fancy recounting the whole of the last week's events to someone new. I need PC Day, and I'm lucky to get him.

'I'm on my way home now,' I tell him. 'I've got the original business card that he gave me last week. That has his name, his phone number, the address – everything. There might be something you can use,' I say. I don't know what, but it's got to be worth a shot. His mobile phone number must be registered in his real name, for a start. Or maybe there's some fingerprints they can get off the card. Can you get fingerprints off paper? I don't know.

'Business card? You didn't mention a business card the other day,' he says.

I try to think back. Did I mention it or not? I can't see why I wouldn't have done, but I can't be sure.

'Oh. Sorry, I forgot,' I say, immediately realising how feeble this sounds.

'The information on the card, this is all information we already have isn't it?' PC Day asks.

'I dunno. Possibly. But it's in black and white. It's the actual card he gave me. You might be able to get fingerprints or DNA or something. Or see if he gave one to anyone else. I don't know. All I know is it's the only physical item I have from him.' I've started to realise that his method of emailing me the photos was probably quite clever. No physical printing, no DNA, no fingerprints. So why would he take a risk with a business card? 'Did you get anything from the emails?' I ask.

'Nothing that we can use, according to the notes. Says here the Gmail address is anonymous. We could get onto Google for IP addresses, but that might only narrow it down to the general area. And anyway, these companies are notoriously strict when it comes to things like that. Unless we're talking serious crime, they're unlikely to give us anything. There's a note that says the IT forensics people looked at something called the EXIF data?' PC Day says, making it sound more like a question than a statement. 'Says here that the footprints had been scrubbed. I guess that's tech speak for removing all the evidence.'

I sigh. I vaguely recall hearing something about EXIF data at some point. As far as I know, it's the digital meta data encoded within an image, which can tell you the camera it was taken with and possible even the GPS coordinates of the original image.

'But the business card could help, right?'

'It certainly wouldn't hurt,' he replies. I detect a note of optimism and hope in his voice. 'All I'd say is don't touch it, though. Just in case they can do anything with it forensics-wise. I'll see if we can get someone out who can retrieve it properly for you. Can I call you back on your mobile?'

'Yes, yes,' I reply. I can feel the lactic acid building up in my legs as I power-walk up the high street in the direction of my house. 'I'll be home in a few minutes.'

I say goodbye to PC Day and end the phone call, just as I turn right at the Chinese takeaway into Pearl Street. As I round the corner, a large figure appears in front of me. All I see is the big black Puffa jacket with the scarf tucked inside it as I scream and feel the pain of the adrenaline shooting through my chest.

The arms grab me, and an icy blast surges through me. Every fibre in every muscle is yelling for me to run, to get out of there, but I can't.

'Woah, easy there. You alright, love?' the man says. I look up at him through my foggy eyes, my heartbeat hammering in my eardrums.

'Sorry,' I say, unable to find any other words. 'Sorry. I was just...'

'No problem. Didn't mean to startle you.'

I swallow, sweep a stray lock of hair back behind my ear and carry on up Pearl Street, feeling the eyes of the man in the Puffa jacket looking at me, thinking I must be some sort of mad woman.

But now I know I'm not mad. And now I know I can prove it.

20

I fumble with my key in the lock as I try to open my front door. My hands are numb with the cold and my body is still trembling from the adrenaline surge a few moments ago.

Finally, I get the door open and I step inside, feeling the instant enveloping warmth of the central heating. I kick my shoes off and make my way through to the kitchen, where I left Gavin Armitage's business card, pinned to the fridge by a magnet I bought on a weekend away with Kieran.

As soon as I step into the kitchen, something feels wrong. I can't quite put my finger on it, but I get the sense that my mind is telling me things might not be quite as they seem. Almost as if it's preparing me for the inevitable; something it already knows is about to happen.

My heart catches in my throat as I look at the fridge. I walk over to it and run my hands across the white vertical surface, just to make sure. Just in case my eyes are playing tricks on me. I see the fridge magnet as clear as day, the well-endowed cartoon figure of the early 20th-century blonde busty seaside-going woman winking at me, the message *Get me back to Blackpool!* emblazoned on the small chalkboard she's holding. Kieran and I both joked about how tacky it looked at the time. So tacky, I had to get it.

And now, it's all I can see. The rest of my vision is fuzzy and clouded. It's almost as if I don't need to see anything else. I can see the magnet, and I can see what it's not holding to the fridge.

I look down at the floor, hoping that I'll see it there, but knowing in my heart of hearts that I won't.

It was definitely there. I don't know when, but it was. Was it this morning? Possibly. I can't say for sure. But it was definitely here. I have no doubt about that. I know I wasn't imagining it.

I get down on my hands and knees and look under the fridge. I slide my fingers under, but all I find is crumbs and a couple of defrosted peas. I wipe my hand on my jeans and stand up again.

I can feel my heartbeat starting to race, and my breathing is quickening. I need to try and regain control, but I know that's going to be difficult. Right now, all I can think is the worst.

Maybe I took it off the fridge and put it somewhere. I don't think I did, but how can I be sure? What if I did it straight after I got back from the studio? I don't really remember getting home, so how would I know? It makes sense that I might have come back home and gone straight for the business card, particularly if I'd been doubting myself.

I go over to my microwave and take the stack of papers off the top of it. Kieran was always on at me about not keeping paper on top of the microwave, saying it was a fire hazard. When he left, it was one of the first things I reinstated. One of my first acts of regaining control.

I start to work my way through the pile, riffling through the papers before going back and removing one sheet at a time, convinced that I'm going to find the business card here. I turn over a letter from the optician, inviting me to book my next eye test. Then a credit card statement. Then a piece of junk mail I kept for no good reason. I keep going, turning each sheet, expecting that each one will be the last one. But as I get further and further through the pile, I begin to realise it's futile.

I open each of the kitchen cupboards and drawers in turn, searching through for any sign of it — any flash of white card — but there's nothing.

In the living room I take the cushions and throws from the sofas, I lift ornaments, I search under furniture. The longer I go on, the more certain I am that I'm not going to find it, the more agitated and anxious I get. I can hear myself sobbing as I search. I don't know how long I've been making that noise for, but I've only just become aware of it.

I *know* it's here somewhere. It has to be. The alternative doesn't bear thinking about.

I head into the kitchen and grab my laptop off the side. I open the lid and will the machine to load faster. Eventually, it does, and I open a browser window and start typing Gavin's name into the address bar. The browser remembers his website and autocompletes the address for me. I hit Enter, and wait a second for the site to load.

All I get is a grey screen with a message saying *Safari Can't Find the Server*. In a panic, I type 'Gavin Armitage photography' into the search bar, and hit Enter. The Google search results load quickly, but I immediately see exactly what I feared might be the case. There is no Google search result for Gavin Armitage's photography studio. It isn't there.

21

It's not often that you hope to God you're going mad. And I really, really do. At least that way it means this is all in my mind. It's a far better thought than the alternative – that I'm being stalked by a man who'll never be caught, a man who's retreated into the darkness, a man who's been in my house and tampered with my stuff.

By now I'm fairly certain I'll end up losing my job. As it stands I've got two options: I can either keep taking days off – as I have again today – and end up being fired, or I can go back into work and do something stupid that ends the same way anyway. I can't even trust myself right now, so I don't see how anyone else will be able to.

I spent the rest of yesterday and most of the night swinging dangerously between emotions. At first there was sheer frustration and helplessness. Then came the feeling of being completely and utterly petrified that I was losing my mind. I managed to talk myself round, tell myself there was a logical explanation. But the only explanation was that someone else had moved it. That nudged me towards anger and feeling violated. The truth of the matter, though, is that no-one has a key to my house except me. Kieran did have one, but he gave it back before he left. I hesitate to say 'moved out', because he never properly 'moved in'. Not on paper, anyway.

I had to ring PC Day back and explain that I couldn't find the business card. I'm not sure what he made of it, but I figured it was better than having the police come out and me tell them they'd made a wasted journey.

I started to realise that I don't feel fully safe here. I don't know whether that's because I feel insecure in the house or because I'm more worried about myself. Earlier this morning I decided I needed to at least do something to put my mind at rest. I summoned up the courage to call a locksmith.

It sounds daft saying I had to summon up the courage, but it's true. Every time I reached for my phone I felt fear. I didn't want to speak to anyone, didn't want to risk the confrontation. What confrontation could there be from a locksmith? None. But try telling my brain that.

He arrived two hours later and replaced the locks on my front and back door. I told him I'd got rid of a nuisance housemate and wanted to make sure he didn't have access. I was amazed at how quickly it was all done. Within three or four minutes he'd replaced both locks and wanted seventy quid for the privilege. I reasoned that it was a small price to pay for peace of mind.

I still can't shake the feeling, though. And that's what makes me think it might be coming from within me, rather than an external force. I can feel myself on the edge, and I know I need to step back. I need some sense of routine, of normality, of sheer, downright ordinariness.

As if on cue, my phone rings. It's Kieran.

For the first time in a long time I see his name on the screen and don't feel complete and utter dread. As long as he's not ringing to beg me to get back with him, I don't mind. He might take my mind off things for a while.

'Hi,' I say as I answer the phone.

'Hi Alice.' He pauses for a moment. 'How are you?'

'I'm alright,' I lie. 'You?'

'Yeah, I'm good.' There's an awkward silence – the sort of awkward silence he only does when he wants to say something but doesn't know how. 'I saw you yesterday. You were walking up Pearl Street. I was in the car, so I couldn't say hi, but you looked really... stressed.'

Yeah, that's what it is. Stress.

'Oh. I'm fine. Just had a bad day.'

I hear Kieran swallow. 'You looked like you were panicking over something.'

'I'm fine. Honestly. Just a bad day.'

'At work?' he asks, the words laden with hidden meaning.

'No. I wasn't at work.' There's no use in lying. He saw me out in town during work hours. 'I was off sick.'

'And today too?'

'Yes. And today too.'

'Oh right. Hope it's nothing too serious.'

I close my eyes. 'I'll be fine, I'm sure. Just need a couple of days off.'

There are another few moments of silence as Kieran tries to work out what to say. I can tell what he wants to say, but he's doing his usual thing of trying to do it with tact. I also know he'll fail miserably.

'You know I'm here for you, don't you? That if you need to... I dunno, talk or something... I'm here. As a friend. As whatever. It doesn't matter. I just... I don't like seeing you like this. You're a great person, Alice, and I want you to be happy. If I can help in any way, or do anything, just shout. Alright?'

I feel my eyes misting up, and I swallow.

'Yeah. Alright.'

22

I know Kieran's call yesterday was meant to comfort me. I know he means well. But all it did was cement in my mind that I must be going mad. It's one thing worrying about myself, but the constant stream of people telling me they're worried about me isn't doing me any favours. Mandy, Mum, Kieran. I don't have anyone else in my life. Not really. Other than the kickboxing class. And if I don't turn up to that this week, there might not be a class left. It might even be a good way to take my mind off things for a couple of hours, release some pent-up energy and frustration. But energy isn't something I've got in plentiful supply right now.

I went back to work today. I guess part of me worried that I wouldn't be able to get away with constantly taking time off, that sooner or later I'd need a doctor's note, at which point they'd either find out there was nothing wrong with me or it'd be put down to depression or some bollocks. I can't see that going down too well. Besides which, it'll probably do me good. I know that sitting around the house and moping isn't going to help things.

Losing myself in work enabled me to forget everything for a few hours. I stuck to the admin side of things, replying to all the emails I'd missed, processing performance review reports and crunching some data. I even offered to do the admin for the rest of the team. They were more than happy to oblige, particularly as everyone hates doing admin. If there'd been any doubt in their mind about me going mad, that would have put paid to it. But today, it was perfect for me. It didn't need any great mental exertion, nor did I have to deal with people. I just got my head down, went through the paperwork and ticked off the hours on the clock.

By the time I came to leave, I was feeling much calmer. Not that I was particularly agitated before, but my mind was much more relaxed; not skipping from thought to thought, worry to worry. It's not like me to fixate on a particular thing like that. Usually, I bury my head in the sand and try to get away from whatever it is that's worrying me. But this isn't quite so easy.

The cold crisp air on the walk home is helping to clear my mind, too. I would, perhaps, even go so far as to say I'm starting to feel a little more positive about life. If I can put the whole episode with Gavin and the photos behind me, and trust that the police are on the case — perhaps have even scared him off — I'll be much happier.

I decide I'm going to enjoy my evening. I'm going to have some me time, and I'm going to try and ensure that doesn't involve alcohol. I might even go for a run or do some exercise in the house. The endorphin rush will make me feel even better and I'll feel a little less guilty about missing the kickboxing class last week.

I step inside my house and close the door, the reassuring and familiar smells coming to me instantly. I walk into the kitchen and switch the kettle on. I get milk from the fridge, pausing for a moment to look at the magnet from Blackpool. I smile and shake my head. Learning to laugh at myself will help. I mislaid something. So what? People do it all the time. Acceptance means I can start to think clearly.

Once I've made my tea, I walk through to the living room and sit down on the sofa, feeling the cushions envelope me as the mug warms my hands. I think about lighting the fire tonight. Maybe after I've gone for a run I'll get some logs from the wood chest and cosy up.

And that's when I look up at the mantelpiece. On it are three photo frames. I know the images like the back of my hand. One, on the left, has a picture of me and Mandy, a shot taken in a nightclub almost ten years ago, but still one of my favourite pictures of us. The frame on the right is a picture of Milo, the family dog when I was younger. He died a few months before I moved out. The photo in the centre is a portrait frame, whereas the others are landscape. It's a photo of me in my university gown, having just received my degree.

But that's not the photo that's in the centre right now.

The picture that's in the centre right now is one of the photos Gavin took at his studio last Saturday.

One of the photos I've only ever viewed on a screen.

One of the photos I've never printed out.
In a frame I've never changed.
He's been in my house.

23

You intrigue me.

Who changes their locks but doesn't worry about how secure they are? If you're going to swap one Kwikset deadbolt lock for another, don't bother. You'd be better off replacing it with a handle. At least there's a small chance your burglar might turn the handle the wrong way then give up.

Having your lock at more or less waist height is a pretty stupid idea, too. Have you got any idea how easy it was for me to walk up to your door, ring the doorbell, use my body as a shield while I spend a few seconds picking and raking the lock, then step inside your now-unlocked door whilst greeting an imaginary you?

The truth is, most people think their homes are secure. Most people are wrong. So you locked the door. Big fucking whoop. I've got a few pieces of metal in my pocket that'll sort that out in well under a minute. Sometimes even less. Now, if you had an alarm system things might be different. But you don't. I know you don't, because I know more about the structural setup of your house than you do by now. You might want to get that back door sorted, too. It's so bumpable it's unreal.

You've got a nice house. Just a shame you clearly don't give a shit about it. Or maybe you don't mind the idea of people coming and going. I hope you don't, anyway. I'd hate to offend you.

I wanted you to know I was here. Sure, I could have left you a note. I could've smashed a window, too, or bumped your back door. But that'd leave a definite, provable trace. After all, who's to know you didn't put that photo in the frame yourself? It's a photo you have a copy of. I know. Because I sent it to you.

No-one will believe you. You know that. And I know that. And that's important. Because this isn't about anyone else. This is about you and me. And I need you to see that. I need you to see that I'm everywhere. I'm the grey man. I'm everybody. I'm the people you pass in the street, the passengers on the bus who might as well be blobs of colour for all you see or care. Don't you see that? Don't you see that it's your own ignorance and self-centred attitude that has become your downfall? Nothing has happened that you couldn't see. If you wanted to see it, that is. But you didn't.

I love that I can watch you. I love that I can see you. I love that I know where you are at all times. You're a creature of habit, Alice. Habits involve patterns. And patterns are predictable. You are predictable. You never know what you might love about me if you could see me, too. But I'm willing to bet you probably wouldn't even recognise me again if you saw me in the street. How often do you even look? How much attention do you pay? Not much. I know that already. But I think it's time to test those limits. I think it's time for me to go further.

Because you need to see me, Alice. You need to be able to enjoy this too. And one day, sooner or later, you will realise your true calling. You'll reject this life of habit and routine, this soulless existence you call living.

And then you'll discover what it really is to live.

24

I don't know what to do, where to go. Home was the only place I felt vaguely safe, but that's been destroyed, torn apart by the realisation that he's been here.

There's no doubt in my mind. I didn't swap that photo over. I've never had a physical copy of the picture; only a digital version in my email inbox, from when Gavin sent it. I don't even own a printer; I do all my printing at work. Wait. No. I definitely didn't print it out at work. Today's the first day I've been back in. If I'd printed it when I was last at work and swapped it over in the interim, I would have spotted it before now.

It's strange how your mind plays these tricks on you. I'm lucid enough now to know that it's only doing so to protect me. Because the alternative – that he's been in my house and has done this purely to scare me – is too much to bear. It's easier to assume I'm mad, right? That I somehow printed the photo out, put it in this frame and then forgot about it.

My heart lurches as I remember the business card on the fridge. Is that how that disappeared, too? I tell myself that's not possible. I've had the locks changed since then, and there's no way in hell that photo was on the mantelpiece like that this morning, never mind any earlier.

He's been here today.

The thought makes me feel sick. I run upstairs and check my cupboards and drawers, making sure nothing has been taken. I know in my heart of hearts he's not a burglar – just a creep – but I still feel the need to check.

The fact that he hasn't taken anything doesn't make me feel any better. It wouldn't be the loss of material possessions that'd matter; it's the feeling of complete violation, of someone having entered your safe place. That's what gives me the sickest feeling in the pit of my stomach.

I don't know which way to turn. It's an indescribable feeling. To have nowhere to feel safe, no person you can trust. To feel so alone.

I try to tell myself I'm not alone, that there are people I can trust. I can trust Mandy. I can trust my mum and dad. Can't I? I can even trust Kieran. Good old dependable Kieran. I tell myself this is the case, but I don't believe it. Even though I know none of these people are responsible – I know it's Gavin Armitage because I've seen him and spent time with him – it still doesn't help those feelings of suspicion. When the threat is unseen, and could be lurking round every corner, your whole concept of trust goes out the window.

I do the only thing I can do. I pick up the phone and call the police.

The officer seems sympathetic at first, perhaps because he can hear the terror in my voice.

'Sorry, you'll have to slow down a bit,' he says. 'Did you say someone's been in your house?'

'Yes. Gavin. He's been here,' I explain between breaths, trying not to hyperventilate.

'How do you know?'

I take a deep breath and hold it for a second, trying to slow my breathing. 'The photo. There's a photo on the mantelpiece. He's changed it. He's put the photo from the shoot in there.'

'And what makes you think it was Gavin?'

'He's the only person who has them. Who else would do it? I didn't do it.'

'Okay. And does anyone else have access to your house? Does anyone have a key?'

'No. No-one. I had the locks changed recently as well. I'm the only person who has a key.'

'Right. Is there any other sign that someone's been in the house? Anything stolen? Signs of forced entry? Broken windows?'

I think I would have noticed a broken window at this time of year. 'No. Nothing,' I say.

There's a couple of moments of silence as the officer thinks about how to phrase his next question. 'Have you had any guests round recently? Anyone who might have done it for a practical joke?'

I shake my head, even though he can't see it. 'No. No-one has come round. The last people who came over were my parents, but I've changed the locks since then. No-one else has been in since.'

'And the photo wasn't there earlier today?'

'No,' I say, trying to sound certain even though I'm not. I don't remember specifically looking at the mantelpiece this morning, but I'm sure I still would have noticed it – even if it's been like that for a day or two. Right now, I don't care. I just want someone to come out here and make the place safe, to put my mind at rest. Even if they're investigating something that turns out to be nothing, I don't give a shit. It's peace of mind. I need to feel safe. 'Please. Can someone just come out and have a look? He's been here. I know he has. There's no other explanation.'

I hear the officer take a deep breath on the other end of the phone. I imagine him weighing up the odds in his mind, trying to work out whether ignoring a potential breaking-and-entering outweighs the chance of me being some crazy woman.

'We'll get someone out this evening,' he says. 'In the meantime, is there anyone you can call to be there with you? To make you feel safer and more reassured.'

I think for a moment. I could call Mandy. Or my parents. But there's nothing they'll be able to do. The only people who can help me are the police. 'No,' I say. 'There isn't.'

He pauses for a moment before speaking. 'Alright. I'll try and arrange for someone to be there as quickly as possible. I can't grade it as an emergency situation, you understand, but we'll do all we can.'

I let out the breath I didn't realise I was holding. 'Thanks. Thank you.'

25

The police officer who turns up seems friendly enough. She's a woman in her forties, I estimate. Probably in the police as a second career. She doesn't have the world-weary look of someone who's been in the force for twenty years.

'Is it just the two external doors you have?' she asks.

'Yeah. Front and back.'

'To be honest, I can't see any signs of forced entry. No damage from crowbars or jemmies or anything.' She walks around the house checking the windows as she speaks. 'What about window locks? Do they all lock from the inside?'

'I think so, yes. I can't see how anyone would've got through one from outside.'

'And they were definitely all closed when you left the house?'

'It's December,' I say, deciding she probably doesn't need an in-depth explanation of the local climate at this time of year.

'I know. But you'd be surprised. Sometimes people open their bathroom window or whatever, then forget to close it.'

'I didn't,' I tell her. 'It was closed when I got home, too. So unless he came in through the window, closed it behind him and is hiding under my bed right now, that's not how he got in.'

Even saying those words frightens the life out of me. I hadn't even considered the possibility that he might still be in the house. I know deep down that he isn't. Of course he isn't. But even thinking about it shoots a deep terror right through me.

The officer looks at me, can sense that I'm still very uncomfortable to say the least.

'Mind if I take a look around upstairs? Just in case there are any signs of entry there.'

I gesture limply towards the stairs.

After a few moments she calls down. 'Is the loft space shared?'

'No,' I call back up. I have friends who live in terraced houses, in which the loft space is continuous. Mine's completely bricked up between my house and next door, though. As far as I'm aware it was built like that.

'Mind if I have a look up there?' she says quietly, peering around the corner of the living room door, making me jump. I hadn't even realised she'd come back downstairs.

'No, go on,' I say. 'There's a chair in my bedroom, in front of my dresser. I use that to reach the hatch.'

I hear her footsteps as she walks into my room, picks up the chair and plonks it down under the loft hatch. A few seconds later I hear the sound of the ladder sliding down before she goes up into the loft, presumably carefully, on the off-chance that someone's waiting up there for her. I'm not worried, though. She might be a middle-aged woman, but I've absolutely no doubt she could kick the shit out of even the biggest burglar.

After a couple of minutes I hear her back on the landing, pushing the ladder up into the loft space and closing the hatch.

'Can't see any signs of entry anywhere,' she says, as she jogs back down the stairs. 'It's an odd one.' She walks over to the mantelpiece and looks at the photo frame. 'You've not touched it, have you?'

I shake my head. 'Not since I found it like that. That's the last thing I want to do.'

'Alright. Might be some fingerprints on it, but I wouldn't hold out much hope. If someone's managed to break into your house without any signs of forced entry and without needing a key, I doubt they'd be stupid enough to leave fingerprints. Especially not at this time of year. Wearing gloves in the middle of winter isn't exactly a marker for suspicion.'

She leaves the room and walks into the kitchen, where she uses her radio to ask for someone to swing by with evidence bags. I take this to mean that they're not going to send out a forensics team to dust the photo frame and the house for fingerprints in situ. To me, that says they're not treating this as seriously as they might otherwise do. My heart sinks.

'Someone will come round to retrieve the photo frame,'

she says. 'I can't do it myself as I don't have the right gear. It all needs to be signed off and everything. Cross-contamination and all that. Needless to say, don't touch it until they get here.'

I nod. 'What about other things? I mean, can I touch other stuff? Or will they want to...'

'I'm sure that'll be fine,' she replies, a little too confidently for my liking.

'Won't they be dusting for fingerprints or anything?'

She averts her eyes from my gaze. Only briefly, but enough for me to notice. 'I wouldn't expect so, no.'

I leave it a second or two. 'Why?'

'Honestly? Unless there's been any sign of forced entry, they're unlikely to treat it as breaking and entering. Entering, maybe, but that's not illegal. And at the moment we can't prove it even happened at all.'

There's a look on her face that says *I wish I'd phrased that a bit better*. I can tell she doesn't believe me. And why would she? She doesn't know me. All she knows is I've reported a guy stalking me — a guy who doesn't exist on any records, whose photographic studio isn't where I said it was — and now I'm convinced someone's been in my house, even though there's no evidence for it whatsoever, other than my deluded, paranoid mind.

'What's the medication for, Alice?' she asks.

My head snaps towards her, perhaps a little too quickly. The question caught me by surprise.

'Hmmmm?'

'The tablets. I wasn't prying, but when I went to get the

chair to go into the loft I saw the packets on your dresser. Fluoxetine and sertraline.' The fluency and familiarity with which she reels off the names tells me she knows exactly what they're for. There's no use in lying.

'I went through a rough patch a little while back. I needed help to keep my head above water. But I'm alright now.' I hope my face looks convincing. I also hope she didn't look too closely at the prescription dates on the labels.

She nods. 'Alright. If you do struggle again, there are lots of places that can help you. I know I'm no doctor, but I know people who've been there. Medication isn't always the answer.'

'He had a website,' I say, trying to divert the conversation and desperately prove to her that I'm not going mad. 'I was on it a few days ago, and when I checked back again it was gone. He was on Google and everything, but now nothing.'

She glances at me in a way which makes me feel uncomfortable.

'Seriously,' I say. 'I can give you the website address. You can check to see who it was registered to, can't you?'

She raises her eyebrows slightly. 'I suppose we can, yes. The tech boys will be able to, anyway.'

I give her the website address, and she notes it down. I'm starting to feel very uncomfortable, so I try to speed up the conversation and bring it to an end.

Once she's gone, I feel slightly relieved. The feeling of being under suspicion in my own home is one I don't want to repeat. But it's not her fault. The truth of the matter is I no longer feel safe here. I no longer feel safe anywhere.

26

I watch the police car disappear up the road, the exhaust fumes creating a dirty cloud behind it in the cold winter air. As the fume cloud quickly disappears, I put on my shoes, step outside and lock the front door behind me.

I ring my next-door-neighbour's doorbell, wait a few seconds, then hammer my fist on the door. It's no use. They're clearly not in.

I jog across the road, looking both ways as I do so, and knock on the door of the house directly opposite mine. An old couple lives here. I don't know their names, but I know it might take them a little longer to get to the door. As it happens, they're there in seconds, no doubt having been watching the police car outside my house and ruminating on how the neighbourhood's gone to shit.

'Hi. I'm Alice, I live over the road,' I say, gesturing weakly at my house. 'I was just wondering if you'd seen anything odd recently. Anyone trying to get into houses. A man, maybe?'

The elderly gentleman's brow furrows, and his wife appears from around the living room doorway and hovers behind his shoulder.

'I don't think so. Why, is something wrong?'

'Has there been a break-in?' his wife says, before I can answer his question.

I quickly decide that all evidences points to 'yes' and that, in any case, having my neighbours on extra high alert isn't going to do me any harm at the moment.

'Yeah. Looks like it,' I say.

'Oh dear. We've never known anything like that around here,' the woman says, before her husband adds: 'When was it?'

Good question. 'Earlier today, we think. It's not as straightforward as it sounds, unfortunately. It looks like whoever got in managed to do so without breaking anything. They might've forced the door or picked the lock. We don't know yet.'

I amaze myself at how calm I manage to sound. I've never been any good at hiding my emotions or putting on an act, but even though all I want to do right now is break down and cry, I'm managing to not only hold it together but to sound steady and completely unruffled.

'Oh. Well I haven't seen anything unusual,' the man says. 'How about you, dear?'

She shakes her head. 'No, nothing.'

'Well thank you anyway,' I say, forcing a smile and turning away.

The woman calls to me as I'm halfway down their front

path. 'You know where we are if you need anything, alright dear?'

I force another smile and nod, before I continue my walk down their path, tears now starting to run down my cheeks. The kindness of strangers.

I stand for a moment at the side of the street, wishing I knew my neighbours better. I've never spoken to any of them before in my life, apart from the occasional wave. How many of them can I seriously expect to be looking out for my safety when I can't even be bothered to say hello to them, or pop round and introduce myself? I guess we're all guilty of breeding insularity and at the same time expecting to be able to carry on as normal.

I try the next house along, but again there's no answer. How can everybody be out? Surely there must be someone still at home. Somewhere.

But as I look around me, the houses all seem to converge into one. Everything's spinning and I suddenly feel very woozy. I just about manage to put my hands out and brace myself against someone's front wall, before everything turns black.

27

'Alice? Alice, can you hear me?'

The first thing I feel is a splitting headache. I instinctively reach up to check, recognising that I'm lying on the cold concrete slabs and trying to work out whether I hit my head. There's a thick blanket over me, a coarse material like the sort of thing you'd put in the back of an estate car for a muddy dog to sit on.

'It's alright, you didn't bump it,' another voice says. I recognise them as the man and woman from the house opposite mine.

As my eyes come back into focus, I see a pair of feet entering my field of vision, walking towards me. I look up, following the line of the legs, and just about make out the face of a blonde woman who I don't recognise, but who looks at me and walks past without affecting her stride.

My first response is anger. I'm clearly lying on the pavement in the middle of December with a rug over me, with two people attending to me. Why the hell would you not stop? What sort of human being would walk on past? How would she feel if it was her?

'Sorry,' I say to the elderly couple. 'I think I fell.'

'You passed out, dear,' the woman says.

'We saw you,' the man adds. 'You've been out for a few minutes.'

'Have you had much to eat today, dear?'

I nod and tell them I have, but the truth is I don't remember. I'm not even entirely sure what day it is.

'I'll go inside and phone an ambulance,' the man says.

'No, no.' I try to get up, but the woman pushes down on my shoulders, keeping my backside firmly planted to the paving slabs. They're cold, and I want to stand. 'Please. It's fine. It happens sometimes. I've got medication, but I was so tied up with the break-in that I forgot to take it. If I can go back home and take it, I'll be fine. Honestly.'

The man looks at me, and then at his wife, unsure whether to believe me.

'Honestly,' I say again. 'If you call an ambulance you'll be wasting their time. It's my own silly fault for forgetting to take my tablet. I'll go back and take it, and I'll be fine.'

'What is it, dear? Blood pressure?' the woman asks.

I grunt and grumble as I try to get to my feet. They try to help me, but their lack of strength isn't doing much.

'Yeah, something like that.'

'You know where we are if you need us, alright?' she says, the same way she did when I walked away from her front door a few minutes ago — or whenever it was. This time, though, I'm not emotionally affected. I just want to get home. I want to crawl into bed, put the duvet over my head and imagine none of this ever happened.

'Thanks. I appreciate your help.'

My legs feel light, like feathers. Jellied feathers. I try not to let any of this show as I make a point of confidently crossing the road, ignoring the pounding in my skull and the nausea rising up from the pit of my stomach. As I get to the other side of the road and my front gate, I turn and smile at the couple, who are still standing at the side of the road, the man with his arm around the woman's waist. She lifts her hand and waves at me.

I fumble with the key in the lock, my hands trembling and shaking, but eventually I get back inside, close the door behind me and let everything out.

28

I do the only thing I can do: I call Mandy. I need someone to speak to, someone I can trust, someone I can depend on. I need to lay it on thick, though. If I try to hide how insecure and anxious I feel, Mandy will be her usual over-the-top aggressive self, which won't help. I don't need to know how much she wants to kick his head in or what she's going to do to his testicles. I need her to be there for me, to comfort me, to tell me everything's going to be alright.

'Hey Alice. What's up?' she says as she answers the phone. I can hear a lot of noise and commotion in the background. It sounds like she's in a bar.

'Are you at home?' I ask, knowing damn well she isn't.

'No, I'm away with work in Plymouth. Why's that?'

'Oh. No reason,' I say. I struggle to hide my disappointment.

'Is something wrong? Has something happened? I can come back,' she says. I can now hear that she's had a couple of drinks, too, so I find that very unlikely. It's a hell of a walk from Plymouth.

'No, nothing. Well yes, but I can tell you whenever you're back home. It's nothing urgent. Honestly.'

'I can come back, Alice,' she says again. 'I'll get on a train or something. If you need me I'll be there.'

I close my eyes and try not to cry. For all her hard-arse attitude, Mandy's an absolute gem. She's the only person I can completely rely on at all times.

'Honestly, it's fine. I'll tell you all about it when you're back.'

'I'll be back tomorrow,' she says. 'Afternoon time probably.' There's a pause. 'Is it Kieran?'

'No, no. It's probably nothing. Honestly. You know how I am at the moment. Things just affect me. I thought maybe if you were home I'd pop over, but there's really nothing urgent.'

'You sure?'

'Sure sure.'

'Well make sure you pop over tomorrow,' she says, after an audible slurp of her drink. 'We'll sort out details later, yeah?'

I force a smile through one corner of my mouth.

'It's a date.'

Just speaking to Mandy made me feel a little more comfortable. At the time. With the phone call over, though, I'm back to feeling alone again. I need human companionship.

Before I even realise what I'm doing, the ringing tone of the phone sounds in my ear just before Kieran answers.

'Hey,' he says. 'You alright?'

'Not especially. Bad day at work. Listen, I really need someone right now.'

I don't know why I've called him. And I don't know why I'm saying what I'm saying. But I'm not stopping myself either.

'Sure. So what, do you want to go out? Get a drink? I've not eaten yet.'

I think about this for a moment. Do I really want to be going out in town? No. Especially not with Gavin seemingly able to snap pictures of me in bars. I just want to hide away somewhere, where no-one can find me. And I don't want to be here at home. I don't feel safe.

'Can I come to yours?' I ask. I know it might come across as rude, but right now I don't care.

'Course you can,' he replies. 'Do you want picking up?'

Kieran lives on the other side of town. It's not an easy place to get to without a car.

'I'll call a taxi,' I say. 'See you soon.'

I call a cab, then throw together an overnight bag. I haven't told Kieran I'm staying yet, but I figure I'll drop that one on him when I get there. I'll tell him something about the boiler going. I really don't want to go into any details about Gavin or the photos.

I look around to see if there's anything I want to bring with me. The thought of leaving the house makes everything seem vulnerable. What if he comes back? What if he starts going through my stuff, taking things? I can't possibly take all my belongings with me.

I take out my phone and quickly tap out an email to PC Day, using the email address on the card he gave me when he first came over. I let him know I won't be at home tonight because I don't feel safe here. I figure this way I've put it in writing and covered myself should anything else happen while I'm gone. I doubt it will, though. He didn't touch anything but the photo frame. He's after me, not my stuff.

The thought makes me shudder.

I hear a beep from outside, and peer round the curtain. The taxi's waiting for me. I raise a hand to acknowledge its arrival, grab my overnight bag and lock up the house.

I feel completely exposed on the journey to Kieran's. I watch every car, every person, every window with suspicion. Gavin could be anywhere, just lurking, watching. I feel sick at the thought. Every time the car behind us turns off into a side road, I relax a little more, feeling the tension release from my shoulders.

When we finally arrive at Kieran's, I pay the driver, get out and ring Kieran's buzzer on the main door to the block of flats. Even something so small and insignificant as using an intercom system again sends shivers down my spine.

I hear a click as Kieran picks up the phone. 'Come up,' he says, before hanging it up again, the front door buzzing to let me know it's now unlocked.

A few moments later I'm in Kieran's flat. It's only the

second time I've been here. The first time was to drop off some stuff he left at mine after we broke up.

He knows better than to ask how I am, and instead asks if I'd like a drink. 'Tea? Coffee? Wine? Orange juice? Water?' he asks, casually throwing wine into the middle of the mix in the hope that he won't feel like he's pressuring me into drinking on my medication, but that the mention won't be conspicuous by its absence either.

'I know it's bad, but I really could use a drink right now,' I say, making it obvious which one I want. 'One of those days.'

Except it isn't one of those days, is it? It isn't the sort of day most people will ever have, never mind one they'll have regularly. But how can I tell Kieran that? I can't.

We sit down and watch TV for a bit. I don't know how much wine we drink. It's not enough to feel drunk as such, but I can definitely sense myself feeling more relaxed and less anxious.

'So,' Kieran says, as if he's been avoiding the question all night. 'What happened today?'

I look down at the floor. 'I don't want to talk about it.'

He pauses for a moment. 'Alright. No problem. But you know I'm here for you if you want to talk, okay? Always.'

I didn't realise how close I was to the edge until he said that. And I can tell from the way he said it that he means every single word. Before I know what's happening, I can feel the tears rolling down my face as Kieran comes over and embraces me in a hug.

'Hey. It's alright. Don't worry. It's alright,' he says, his warm hands rubbing my back.

I pull my nose back from his shoulder, feeling the side of my face rub against his, the stubble reassuringly familiar. My mouth finds his, and it barely leaves it for the rest of the night.

29

Kieran has many faults, but he always knows how to make people feel comfortable. When I woke up in his bed this morning I was expecting it to be awkward. But he's already downstairs, making coffee and breakfast.

'Morning. You want something to eat?' he says, in a way which sounds friendly and comforting, yet not *are we back together now?* I think even he knows that isn't on the cards. At least I hope so.

'I'll be alright,' I say. 'I'll grab something on the way into work to eat there. I'll be late otherwise.'

The atmosphere takes on an awkward feel.

'Listen,' Kieran says. 'I don't want you to feel that we have to—'

'No, I know,' I reply, putting on my boots and scarf.

'I just didn't want you to think that I—'

'It's fine, Kieran. Honestly. We're both adults. I'm sure we'll manage.'

The truth is probably even harsher than that, though. The fact of the matter is that I have bigger problems on my plate right now.

I consider popping home on the way to work to change, but the thought fills me with dread. If I'm honest, I'm petrified as to what I might find. I'd rather just sit out the day at work, wearing the same clothes I wore last night. I couldn't care less about showering. I just want to get out of here and keep away from my house for as long as I can. I certainly don't want to go back there alone.

I need Mandy around. She should be on her way back from her work trip this morning. I know the company car she was given has built-in hands-free, so I decide to give her a call.

'Yo yo,' she says, as she answers my call. 'How's it hanging?'

'Bit chirpy for this time of the morning aren't you?' I reply.

'So would you be if you'd had a night's kip on that hotel bed. It was like sleeping on a fucking cloud, Alice. Seriously.'

I decide against telling her about the bed I slept in last night. 'You on your way back then?'

'Yep. And get this – no work, either. Nigel marked up that none of the team will be in today because most of them are heading on to meet with a client in Gloucester on the way back. Lucky ol' me wasn't invited, but they've still marked me down as away on work business. Full pay, motherfucker!'

Sometimes I wonder how Mandy managed to even get a high-paying job like the one she has, never mind how she manages to keep it. I can only imagine she takes on a completely different personality when she's at work.

'Nice,' I say. 'So you're free later?'

'Free as a... free thing,' she says, before yelling 'Cunt!' at the top of her voice. 'I fucking knew he was going to do that.' I hear a blast of her horn followed by the roar of her engine. 'Learn to fucking indicate! Sorry, Alice. Where was I?'

'You're free as a free thing,' I say, choosing to completely ignore her road rage.

'Yeah. Yeah. So what do you want to do?'

'I don't mind. I just want to get out of the house.'

There's a moment of silence as Mandy makes the connections in her brain. 'Is this about last night? When you called?'

'Yeah. It is. Listen, I don't want you to go mad, alright? I'm telling you this because I want you to know and I want your support. Your emotional support, I mean. I don't need you trying to fight fights for me.'

'Depends who I'm fighting.'

'Mandy, I'm serious.'

'Alright, alright,' she says. 'No fighting.' I can tell she means it.

I take a deep breath. 'When I got home from work last night, I went into my living room. I keep three photos in frames on my mantelpiece. One of them had been changed. Someone put one of the photos Gavin took of me in there.'

It's quiet as Mandy digests this. 'Someone?'

'Well, yeah. The only person who had those photos is Gavin. Apart from me, I mean, and I didn't put it there. I never even printed any of them. I wanted rid of them after he started sending those weird ones.'

'Wait. So you're saying he's been in your *house*?'

I take a deep breath. 'Yeah. I think so.'

'Fucking hell, Alice.'

'I know. So I don't really want to be at home right now.'

'What, did you go to the police? What are they doing about it? They need to fucking find him and, I don't know, kill him or something.'

'Slow down,' I say. 'Yes, I went to the police. And I don't know what they're doing about it. A woman officer came out. I've got a crime reference number.'

Mandy sounds incredulous. 'A crime reference number? Yeah, that'll stop him dead in his tracks, that. Listen, you don't need to go home. You can come and stay with me. They might not be taking you seriously, but I am.'

'Thanks, Mandy,' I say. I don't think I can stay at hers long-term, but it might be an option until all this blows over. Until I feel comfortable staying in my own home.

'But you need to get back onto them. You need to make them take you more seriously.'

I sigh. 'How? I can't tell them what to do. I guess in their eyes there's no physical risk to me, so they haven't prioritised it.'

'No *risk* to you?' Mandy says forcefully, her voice straining. 'He's been in your house!'

'I know.'

I can't work out how to tell her that I sense the police don't believe me, that they think I did it myself.

'Listen, Alice. You need to get down to that police station and demand to speak to someone. You've got to make them take you more seriously.'

'I've got to get to work,' I say. 'I'll think about it.'

'No. No thinking about it. Seriously, Alice. I've got a bad feeling about this. You need to get to that police station. Now. If you don't, I will. I'll never forgive myself if you don't and something happens to you.'

For the first time, I sense real danger and worry in Mandy's voice. It's not like her. I realise that I need to take control.

30

I ring work to let them know I'll be late in. I don't offer any more information. Sometimes other things have to come first.

When I get to the police station, I'm surprised by how small it seems inside. I imagine there are corridors of back offices and things that I can't see, but the public-facing area is tiny. It feels clinical, and the counter-to-ceiling bulletproof glass does seem rather drastic.

I pass a piece of paper with my crime reference number through the slot at the bottom of the screen. A grumpy, middle-aged Afro-Caribbean man looks up at me. There are perhaps a dozen desks behind him, with a couple of officers milling around, one or two on the phone.

'This is my crime reference number,' I say. 'I'd like to speak to a detective.'

'Okay, do you have an appointment?' the man asks, the tone of his voice implying that he knows damn well I don't, and I'm not going to get one either.

'No. There's been some new developments, though, and I'm really starting to worry. I need to speak to someone.'

'Can you tell me a bit more?' he says, reading something off his computer screen. I presume it's the case notes he's got from my crime reference number.

'I've got a stalker,' I say, using the word for the first time. 'And he's going to weirder and weirder lengths to frighten me. He's been in my house while I was at work. I don't know how, but he has. And I'm too scared to even go back into my own home.' I can hear my voice cracking as I speak, as I verbalise my fears for the first time. 'I think he's trying to harm me. I think he's going to hurt me, physically.'

'Okay, I can get an officer to call you if that helps. If you have more information that isn't already on here, they can log that and—'

'Please. I need to speak to someone now. I need to speak to a detective.'

The officer shuffles in his seat and leans forward towards the glass barrier. 'Ma'am. There are certain procedures in place that we have to follow, I'm afraid. All reports and threats are graded, and the response we make is according to that perceived threat. If you—'

'Please,' I say again. 'Please. I'm finding it difficult to put into words, but I think there's a serious and imminent threat to my life. Please, just give me five minutes to speak to someone.'

He looks at me for a moment, presumably trying to work out whether I'm a fruitcake. He picks up the phone next to him, presses a couple of buttons and waits for an answer.

'Yeah, hi. There's a lady at the front desk who wants to speak to someone from CID. It's with reference to an ongoing case. She says there's been a development. I don't have full info, but it could be an Osman.'

I don't know what he means by an Osman. I can only assume it's some sort of police slang.

He replaces the receiver on the phone.

'Someone'll be down in a moment. Take a seat.'

I do as he says. The crime prevention posters on the walls seem designed to scare. I'm sure they're meant to warn and reassure, but in my current mental state they do nothing of the sort. I try to keep my eyes on the brown tiled floor instead.

It's almost fifteen minutes before a woman finally comes down and introduces herself as Detective Inspector Jane McKenna. She looks like the sort of woman who takes her job far too seriously. Right now, that's exactly what I need.

'Sorry for the wait,' she says. 'I had to look at the case notes and familiarise myself with everything. Saves you having to tell me the whole story from the start. Under normal circumstances we get a bit of warning,' she says, in a way which most people might not spot, but tells me this situation is in no way conventional. Not only that, but she doesn't appreciate it either.

She takes me through a security door, down a corridor that's windowed on one side, showing the desk-bound officers hard at work on the other side. She guides me through into a small room, which I presume must be an interview room. It looks more like the sort of places you see on TV, where they interview suspects rather than witnesses.

It's only a small station, though, so I assume it's all they've got.

'So you mentioned that there've been some new developments since you last spoke to an officer,' she says, glancing down at some printed papers.

'Uh, yes,' I say. 'The man, Gavin Armitage. He's been in my house. He put a photo in a frame on my mantelpiece. No-one else has those photos. Only him and me. And I'm the only person with a key to my house.'

'You told our officers this already, though, didn't you? It says here we attended the scene yesterday.'

I sigh. 'I know. But I just... I don't think she took me seriously. She kept going on about the fact there was no sign of forced entry, and that I could have made a mistake. But I know I didn't. I know.'

'Our officers do have to consider every possibility, Miss Jefferson. I'm sure you can understand.'

'Yes, I know. But I know what happened. That photo wasn't there yesterday morning. I don't even *own* a copy of it. I've never printed any. I don't even have a printer!'

I can feel myself getting more and more worked up, and I try to calm my breathing.

'Are you okay?' McKenna asks. 'Do you want a glass of water?'

'I'm fine,' I say. 'I just... No-one seems to be taking me seriously.'

'We take all reports of crime seriously, I can assure you. But we also need to work with what presents itself. The notes show no forced entry, no unlocked windows, no damage to the property. Yet you say you're the only person with a key. I'm not saying nobody believes you, of course not, but if there's no sign of forced entry we can't treat it as breaking and entering.'

I clench my jaw and try not to grind my teeth.

'I'm not asking you to treat it as breaking and entering. I'm asking you to treat it as stalking,' I say, quiet but firm. 'The website address. I gave the police officer a website address when she came over. It had his website on it, and now it doesn't. Now it's disappeared. Have they looked into it?'

She says nothing, but instead looks back at the notes for a few moments before answering me. 'Yes. We contacted Nominet, the domain registry, later that day. The domain was registered using a silent registry company. People pay them a fee to keep their details secret.'

I feel my throat constricting. 'Can't you get the details from them? Surely the police can force it.'

'Possibly. If we can prove a crime has been committed.'

My head is swimming and my chest hurts. I'm going round in circles. There's nothing I can do.

'Are you sure you don't want a glass of water?' she asks again.

'No. No I don't want a bloody glass of water. I want to be taken seriously!'

She's silent for a couple of moments.

'What's the sertraline for?' she finally asks.

I blink. 'Sorry?'

'Sertraline. The officer noted that she found a packet on the dresser in your bedroom.'

I'm now finding it very difficult to keep my calm. I can feel my throat constricting and my blood pressure rising.

'So what? What's that got to do with anything?'

'And fluoxetine?'

I look her in the eye. 'You know damn well what they're for. They're SSRIs. Anti-depressants. It means I have periods of extreme lows, where I barely function. It doesn't mean I'm loopy, it doesn't mean I'm a danger to anyone and it doesn't mean I'm a fruitcake. It means sometimes I get ill. Sometimes I don't go out for a while because I'm tired and can't face the world. Sometimes my whole body moves at half speed. It's an illness like any other. Alright?'

I realise I was ranting.

'Do you ever get hallucinations or any sort of mental confusion?' she asks, clearly trying not to sound over-patronising, but her effort means nothing. The words are still the same.

'Perhaps you need to look up what depression is,' I say.

'Oh, I know plenty. I'm trained in dealing with many different forms of mental illness, believe me. I know there are many different forms. Some make people panic and run away, start new lives. Some mean they push away the people closest to them, perhaps because they feel they're a bad person and they want others to be happy without them. Some include auditory and visual hallucinations, often the brain's way of making sense of things at a time when it's overloaded.'

'Well mine doesn't,' I say.

She looks down at her notes again.

'You started taking the sertraline fairly recently, didn't you? Within the last few days.'

'Yes.'

'It's quite common for different types of medication to interact with each other and cause side effects. Particularly if it's a form of medication you haven't taken before.'

Why is she being like this? Surely she can *see* I'm not lying. It's her job.

'I first met Gavin Armitage a week and a half before I started taking sertraline. Your officers have seen the images he took and the ones I didn't know he'd taken.'

'It's not illegal to take photos of someone without their knowledge, though. No, it's not nice. Yes, it's creepy. But it's not illegal. He hasn't taken photos on your property, has he?'

'Not that I know of. But the point is this all happened before I started the new medication, so you can't blame that.'

'It's also worth noting that we still can't find any trace of Mr Armitage. There isn't anyone by that name in the town, and there's no record of a photographic studio at the address you gave.'

'He obviously used a false name,' I say, ignoring the fact there's no record of his studio. I can't explain that bit.

'You were prescribed sertraline on Monday, weren't you?'

'Yes.'

'When did you start taking it? Morning? Evening?'

'Tuesday morning. So I was taking it at the same time as my other tablet.'

'And you discovered the photo frame had been changed on Thursday evening.'

'Yes.'

'The half-life of sertraline is twenty-two to thirty-six hours,' she says, looking at her notes.

'That means nothing.'

'Which would be round about Thursday evening,' she continues.

'It means nothing.'

'My job is to consider all possible explanations. I know some of them might be difficult to think about, but they still need to be considered and investigated. And at the moment, as things stand — from the point of view of an impartial observer, you understand — there are no signs of a break-in at your property. You said yourself you're the only person with a key. You're also on two types of strong medication. It's not for me to cast aspersions, but we need to consider all the facts carefully.'

'I'm not—'

'Now I think it would probably be best if you had some friends and family around you. I know how distressed you are, and I know you don't feel safe at home. That way you'll feel safe and there'll be someone to keep an eye on you, too.'

'I don't need someone to keep an eye on me,' I say, now weary and resigned.

'I think it would be a good idea. At least for a little while. Of course, if anything changes or if there are any other signs that something isn't right, or if you hear from Mr Armitage, do give us a call.'

I look at McKenna for a few moments, trying desperately to think of some way to get her to change her mind, but I can't. She's already made up her mind. She thinks I'm a nutter.

I nod. There's nothing else I can do. 'Thanks,' I say, trying to sound gracious but not meaning it in the slightest.

McKenna stands and leads me out of the room. She walks me back down the windowed corridor, and I glance inside at the officers working at their desks. Some are on the phone, some typing at their computers, others stand around talking. But one of the officers sticks out like a sore thumb. Because he's just standing, staring at me. There's no look of malice on his face; it's completely neutral and devoid of any expression. And I recognise the face instantly.

It's him.

31

'Someone fetch a glass of water, will you?' McKenna yells down the corridor as she hooks my arm over one of her shoulders and half-guides, half-pulls me forward down the corridor. 'Come on. We'll get you sitting down out front. It's bloody warm in here and it'll be more comfortable than sitting on the floor.'

There's a ringing noise in my ears and my chest hurts. I can feel myself hyperventilating.

'It's alright,' McKenna says. 'Nearly there now. You're going to be okay.'

I don't know what's happening. All I know is I feel bloody rough, and I don't know what just happened. I must have passed out.

We finally get to the other end of the corridor and back into the waiting area at the front of the station. As the security door starts to close behind us, I glimpse back behind me. I don't know why, but I feel compelled to. And it's then that I see the glass window again, with the officers on the other side of it. That's when I remember. That's when my breathing speeds up and I can feel my legs starting to go again.

'Woah, okay. Sit down, sit down,' McKenna says. 'Now follow me. Breathe in through the nose, hold it for a couple of seconds. Okay, now out through the mouth. And hold it. In through the nose. Hold it again. Out through the mouth.'

It's a tried and tested breathing exercise, and it's just about working. I need to try and remain calm, need to regain my composure, but I can't. I know what I saw. Gavin Armitage was on the other side of that window. He's a police officer. But how the hell can I tell McKenna this? She already thinks I'm crazy. She's latched on to this idea about me having mental difficulties and she's decided that's what's behind all this. I can't tell her seconds later that my stalker is a police officer, a colleague of hers. I'll end up being sectioned.

'Has this happened to you before, Alice?' she asks, as my breathing begins to slow.

I struggle to find the right answer. Do I say no and end up making a big thing of it, or do I tell her yes, and have her think I regularly black out and don't know what's going on?

I wave my arms. 'Uh, once or twice. A long time ago. Not really.' I try to make my answer sound vague and noncommittal, but I quickly realise it makes me sound even crazier.

'Do you want me to call you an ambulance?'

'No, no,' I say quickly.

'Tell you what. I'll fetch you a chocolate bar from the machine. Might be blood sugar. Did you have breakfast this morning?'

I go to tell her that yes, I did, but she's already walked off and left me with a male officer who's handing me a plastic cup of ice cold water. I sip it gently, feeling it lubricate my dry throat. I didn't realise how dry I was. Must have been the hyperventilating. A couple of minutes later, McKenna returns with a king-size Mars bar.

'Amount of sugar in that, you'll be dancing on the ceiling inside a minute,' she says.

I try to force a smile. All I want to do is get out of here. I can't trust any of these people. And while Gavin Armitage is through there, in the office, I can disappear a million miles away. I can vanish into the distance. If I had a passport, I would. I'd be straight home, packing a bag and getting on the next plane out of the country. Start again. Fuck the lot of it. No. I wouldn't. I wouldn't even take a bag. It wouldn't be worth the risk. Just straight in the first cab to the airport, no looking back.

But I can't. I've not been on holiday in almost a decade and my passport ran out four years ago. Besides which, if I disappeared now, who else would I be putting in danger? Would he come after Mandy? Kieran? My parents? It doesn't bear thinking about. I need to end this. I need justice. I just don't know how to get it.

I feel trapped. I can't run away, but I can't stay here either. How can I face this on my own? And if you can't trust the police, who can you trust?

All I know is I need to leave the station. Quickly.

'I'm sorry,' I say. 'I'd better get going.'

'Are you sure?' McKenna asks. 'You're still pretty pale. I'd rather you stayed until you felt better.'

'I do. I feel better already. Much better. Sorry. I've got to go.'

I stand up and immediately my legs feel like jelly. A wave of nausea rises up from my stomach, making me feel for a moment as if I'm going to be sick. It passes, though, and I concentrate hard on putting one foot in front of the other, and slowly make my way towards the door.

32

By the time I get back home, I'm feeling a bit better. The fresh air seems to have cleared my head somewhat. I feel more defiant. I'm not going to run away. I'm going to stay here and fight. Why shouldn't I? This is my home, my life. Why should I let some bloke I don't even know try to ruin it?

I can't do it alone, though. I text Mandy to confirm she's still on for tonight. I need to tell her everything, tell her that Gavin Armitage is a police officer. She might always seem like she overreacts, but I know she's a logical thinker when she wants to be. She'll be able to help me find a way out of this.

A few seconds after I've sent the text, my phone rings. Mandy does this sometimes. She's never been a fan of texting, and often tends to call in response to a text. As I look at the screen, though, I can see it's not Mandy. It's Kieran. I feel my heart rate increase. I really don't want to speak to him right now, but he knows I'm not in a good place. If I refuse to answer his calls, he'll turn up at the house. I know he's worried about me, but it's a little creepy.

'Hi,' I say, hoping I sound a lot calmer and healthier than I must have done at the police station earlier. 'How's things?'

'Yeah I'm alright. Look, I wanted to call to clear the air. After last night.'

I've got to admit it. That whole evening had slipped out of my mind after what happened at the police station today. After seeing Gavin Armitage again. As I remember yesterday evening, I can feel myself growing increasingly agitated and frustrated.

'Don't worry about it,' I say.

'Okay, cool.' I can hear him smiling. 'I just wanted to check everything was alright. Y'know. I know you haven't been well lately, and I wanted to make sure you were alright with it all. Last night, I mean.'

'Well, mistakes happen.'

Kieran is silent for a moment. 'Mistakes?' he says, almost whispering.

'Yes, Kieran. Mistakes. Things that weren't meant to happen but happen anyway because something went wrong.' The adrenaline is surging in my chest now. I'm not a confrontational person, but I can't escape the feeling that Kieran needs to hear this. I need to know he's heard it, too. We need to draw a clear line and make sure it isn't crossed. Otherwise, how long will this go on? How many months or years will we spend bouncing apart and together, never knowing where we stand, not able to move on with our lives? It isn't fair on either of us.

'What do you mean went wrong? You mean you regret it happening?'

I take a deep breath. 'Yes. Yes, I regret it happening. Alright?' I hear my voice gaining in force and volume. Kieran seems taken aback.

'So... Well, I'm sorry for asking, but why did you do it if you didn't want to? I mean, I didn't force you or anything. You wanted to just as much as I wanted to, from what I can remember. Surely you would've told me if you—'

'Just fuck off, Kieran, alright?' I hear myself yelling before I've even realised what I'm saying. 'Just *fuck off*!'

I end the phone call and sit for a moment, my throat tight. It feels like I've got a golf ball lodged in my throat. My vision starts to blur and cloud and I feel my chest heaving, hear noises escaping my mouth that I don't remember making. There's an electrical buzzing in my head and a pain in my chest that feels like I'm being stabbed through the heart. I think I'm falling to pieces, and I don't know what to do about it. I want it all to go away. I want it all to end, in any way possible. Before I know it, I'm curled in a ball, letting the pain and anguish envelop me.

The only noise that punctuates my sobs is the sound of my phone ringing again.

33

I don't even look at the screen. Not properly. Just enough to find the green *answer* button.

'*Just fuck off!*' My voice is strained and staccato. I struggle to push the words out between heaving sobs. Even with the blood rushing in my ears, I can hear quite quickly there's another noise on the line which wasn't there a moment ago. It sounds like traffic, and a passing train.

'Alice? Is that you? Are you alright?' the voice asks. I vaguely recognise it, but I can't pitch it. I pull the phone away from my cheek and wipe my eyes, trying to focus on the blurred screen. I can just about make out the name. Simon.

'Yes. Sorry,' I reply, trying to force the sobs back down. It's too late, though. There's no way in hell I can make out that I'm not upset or haven't been crying. I'm just going to have to be honest with him if he asks. Fortunately for me, he doesn't.

'It's Simon,' he says. 'From the kickboxing class.'

I cover the phone's microphone and sniff deeply to try and stop my nose running. 'Sorry, Simon. Hi.'

'I thought I'd call because I noticed you haven't been at the last couple of sessions. I wanted to check everything was alright.' He leaves that hanging in the air, the unspoken words being *I can tell it isn't, but I'm not going to ask why.* The contrast is incredible. If this was Kieran he'd be quizzing me, wanting to know why I was upset, needing every single piece of information. If it was Mandy, she'd be getting her knuckledusters on and asking me who she needed to beat up. Simon, though, is different. He's calmer. More caring.

'I'm fine,' I lie. 'I've just been ill.'

'Oh. Nothing serious, I hope?'

'No, no. Some sort of virus. A coldy-fluey type thing. I'm okay now, though.'

'Alright, great. So we'll see you next week then?'

I hesitate for a moment. I can't help it. I hope Simon doesn't notice.

'Yeah,' I say, my voice slightly choked. 'Yeah, you'll see me next week.'

'Cool.'

The line is silent for a moment. The conversation feels far more awkward than it needs to. I get the impression that Simon wants to say something else, so I let him.

'Listen, Alice, I was wondering something actually. You mentioned when you were last in about going out for a drink. That new bar you told me about. I just wondered if that offer still stands. Nothing like... Well, like that. But just to chat and catch up and get to know each other a bit better.'

I try to work out my answer quickly. I can sense how embarrassed and awkward Simon feels and I don't want him to feel like that. Part of me thinks it's ridiculous to be planning to go out for a drink with my kickboxing instructor when everything in my life is going to shit, but somehow it seems to make sense. Why can't I live at least one aspect of a normal life? Why should I let Gavin Armitage bully me into not even being able to enjoy a night out with a friend?

'Yes,' I say. 'I'd like that.' And I mean it.

The atmosphere of sheer relief floods down the phone line, closely followed by Simon's voice.

'Great! Well, when's good for you?'

I almost smile. 'I'm free tomorrow if you are?' The thought of having to spend time on my own fills me with dread, so I'm trying to cram stuff into every waking minute. I'm seeing Mandy tonight and tomorrow... Well, who knows? It makes sense to go back into work and try to take my mind off things, but I won't truly know how I feel until the morning.

'Tomorrow sounds great,' Simon replies.

'But I wouldn't recommend that new bar in town,' I say, keen to keep well away from places Gavin knows I go to. 'It's not all that great, to be honest.'

'Okay, no worries. There's a new place near me that's just been taken over. I mean, it's a pub, but they do food too. Good food. If you wanted that sort of thing, that is. Entirely up to you.'

'That sounds great.'

'I'll text you the details.'

After the call ends, I feel somewhat more comfortable. No, not comfortable. That's the wrong word. But I feel *better*. Just the thought that I might have something tiny to hold onto helps enormously. Something to take my mind off things. After all, there's got to be a decent chance that Gavin Armitage will be steering well clear of me now. I try to recall that look on his face as I saw him through the large window at the police station. Did he look scared? Shocked? Worried? I don't know. There was no emotion on his face whatsoever. I can only imagine he was stunned. He'd have to be stupid to carry on now that he realises I know he's a police officer.

Wouldn't he?

34

After I get off the phone to Simon, I resolve to get something done. I call the locksmith. Not the same one as last time. I don't fancy looking quite that stupid. I've already had the locks changed once, but it's clearly not good enough. It needs more.

He asks me if it's an emergency, and the only reply I can come up with is 'sort of'. I tell a little white lie and say that I've just moved in and that I don't trust the previous occupants. I add that the locks seem really insecure and that I'd like to upgrade them while he's here. I play the damsel-in-distress card and he agrees to come over within the hour with a selection of different options, not so subtly adding that it'll be on emergency callout rates. I don't even ask him how much that'll be. I don't care. I need it done, no matter what it costs.

To his credit, he turns up about forty minutes later. I

reckon he's about sixty, and I imagine he's been doing this job all his life.

He introduces himself as Bob, then adds, 'To be honest, I don't know why I rang the doorbell. Would've been quicker to pick this thing.' Bob points to the lock on the front door.

I don't know whether to be offended or not. That's my door. It's what's been keeping me safe the whole time I've been living here. But at the same time I realise exactly how Gavin Armitage has got into my house.

'Is it that bad?' I ask.

'These deadlocks are Mickey,' he says, and it takes me a moment to work out what he means. 'Don't worry about a key. You'd be just as well off taking a paperclip out with you. Stick a sign on the door that says "Burgle me".'

I wish he'd shut up. I get the point. The lock's shit.

'Do you have anything better you can put on?' I ask.

He takes that deep intake of breath that all tradesmen do before they're about to say *It'll cost you.*

'I have, but it won't be a quick job. You might be better off having them done on day rates. If you book ahead, I can—'

'No. No, sorry. I need it done today. Before tonight.'

'Oh, I can do it. But it won't be cheap. If you want top-notch security, most people will be better off replacing the door. This one looks fairly new, though. Christ knows why they've stuck this lock on it. I imagine the previous owners probably did it themselves, trying to save a bit of money. Stupid really, considering what they're putting at risk.'

I nod. Truth is, I didn't even change the locks after I moved in. It didn't cross my mind. In practice, the previous owners could have come waltzing back in any time they liked. Except for the fact that the old lady who lived here before me had died, of course. The state she'd left the place in – plus a timely inheritance from my grandmother – had just about made the mortgage affordable, even on my modest salary.

'What you want on here's a five-lever mortice,' he continues. 'Front and back doors, ideally. You could bump that back door pretty easily.'

'Fine. Do it,' I say, and I let him get on with the job.

I sit in the living room with a mug of tea and try to relax, but it's difficult. The locksmith's drill sounds like it's boring into my skull rather than the door, and I will him to hurry up and get it over with.

In the end, it's quicker than I thought.

'Right. You're now the proud owner of two five-lever mortices,' he says as he assiduously places his tools back in their rightful spaces in his toolbox. 'That's about as secure as you're going to get on those doors. If you're really security conscious, I can recommend a good company in town. They do CCTV, alarms and monitoring, all that stuff.'

He passes me the company's business card.

'Oh right. Thanks.' I hadn't even thought about CCTV or an alarm. They sound expensive, but what price do I put on my security right now? 'How secure would you say the doors are now?' I ask him.

'As secure as they can be. I mean, unless you're planning on adding whacking great steel deadbolts, reinforcing the door and sticking a sniper on the roof.' He chuckles. It's a throaty, sticky laugh that sounds like he's recently given up smoking. 'Seriously, though. If you're that security conscious, you can't go far wrong with an alarm and CCTV. Although, it's always worth remembering the one golden rule of security.'

He says it as if I'm meant to know what the golden rule of security is, but at the same time knowing damn well that I don't and wanting me to ask him what it is.

'What's that?' I ask, acquiescing.

'The golden rule of security is there's no such thing as security. Not *total* security, anyway,' he says, raising his index finger like a primary school teacher. 'If someone wants to get in, they'll get in. You can't stop them. All you can do is make it more difficult for them, or more likely that they'll get caught if they try.'

The thought is a sobering one. And all of a sudden I feel far less secure than I did a moment ago.

35

I meet Mandy at Bar Chico. I don't trust Zizi's any more. Not since Gavin Armitage started taking photos of me sitting inside.

I've no way of guaranteeing he hasn't somehow followed me here, either, but I have to trust my instincts. I've been much more aware of my surroundings recently. I clock everyone who's walking on both sides of the street, I know exactly who's following me and how far behind they are. I can spot someone sitting in a parked car from a hundred yards away. I think it would be fair to say the whole episode has made me paranoid, but right now that's no bad thing. It's the only thing that keeps me feeling anything like safe.

I've started carrying a rape alarm, too. I don't know what good it'll do. I'm pretty certain I'll never have to use it. After all, Gavin has never approached me directly, other than when we first met. It's not his style. He prefers to lurk in the shadows and let me know where he's been, without ever actually showing me at the time. Apart from at the police station, of course, but that can hardly be something he was in control of. Can it? No. It was my choice to go down there, my choice to speak to the police, my insistence that I wanted to put my side across to a detective. There's no way he could have known any of that in advance. The only person who knew I was going there is Mandy, and I trust her implicitly. Still, the rape alarm adds slightly to that feeling of safety.

I won't feel completely safe until Armitage is caught, though. And after finding out what I found out earlier today, that's going to be one hell of a lot more difficult than I thought. I need something. Some way of being able to convince the police that one of their colleagues is my stalker. That he's been breaking into my house. That I'm not just some mad nutter on medication who doesn't know what she's saying. But how I go about that, I have no idea.

I spot Mandy sitting in a booth on the other side the bar and I walk straight over to her. The bar's pretty empty, so I can keep a good eye on who's in. So far, everything seems safe. I sit down and Mandy immediately drops the question.

'So, what's new?' The words seem innocuous and ambiguous, but the way she says it lets me know exactly what she means.

'If you mean how did it go today, not well.'

Mandy's face drops. I can't tell whether she's disappointed for me or angry at someone for some perceived slight or injustice.

'What do you mean? Tell me.'

I sigh and lean back into the red faux-leather padded bench.

'They weren't having any of it. Not at first, anyway. But I kicked up a fuss and demanded to speak to someone senior. They sent out this detective woman, and I sat down with her and told her everything. I think she'd already been briefed, because she jumped straight to asking about my medical situation, what tablets I was on, all that stuff.'

'Are you fucking serious?'

'Yeah. Yeah, I am.'

'That's fucking insane,' Mandy replies.

'It's not the least of it,' I say.

She looks at me quizzically, clearly able to tell there's something on my mind; something else I need to tell her.

'What is it?' she asks.

'You're going to think I'm crazy.'

'Try me.'

I genuinely have no idea how to put this into words without sounding like a nutcase. 'After I spoke to the detective, she took me back out to the reception area. You have to go down this corridor, with windows all down one side. You can see desks, workstations and all that sort of stuff. There were quite a few police officers milling around. And I saw him.'

I can tell instantly that Mandy knows exactly who I'm talking about, but she asks anyway.

'Who?'

'Gavin Armitage. He's a police officer.'

For the first time since I've known her, Mandy is speechless. She just sits there, blinking at me.

I continue. 'I didn't know what to do. In the end I passed out. They ended up carrying me back out to reception.'

'Wait. I can't get my head round this. I thought he was a photographer?'

'Yeah. At the weekends, clearly. Don't you see? That's how he managed to get into my house. That's how he's been following me without me seeing him. Who looks twice at a police officer? And if you do, you only look at the uniform. He can go around taking photos of whatever he likes, whenever he likes.'

'But breaking into your fucking house...'

'He'd know exactly how to do it. If he was in uniform, who'd suspect a thing?'

'I thought you said none of your neighbours saw anyone at your place. Even a policeman.'

'No. They didn't. But if they had, it wouldn't have looked as suspicious as it would if it was a bloke in a black hoodie.'

For the first time, I think I know what the look on Mandy's face is. It isn't the look of someone who can't comprehend what I'm saying or make sense of it. It's the look of someone who knows exactly what I'm saying, and knows exactly what the ramifications are. It's the look of someone who's scared.

'You need to come and stay at my place,' she says, placing her hand on mine and looking me in the eye. 'You'll be safer there.'

I shake my head. 'There's no need. I've had the locks changed. I'd rather be at home.'

'Alice, this isn't right. Are you absolutely certain it was him?'

'Yes. Absolutely dead certain.'

'Then you need to tell the police. There's got to be something they can do. Police officers aren't untouchable. You see it all the time, being dragged up in front of the IPS or whatever they call it.'

'IPCC,' I say.

'Yeah, whatever. If you can prove it was him who was there that day taking those photos, and it's him who's broken into your house, they've *got* to do something.'

I lower my eyes.

'That's the problem. I can't prove a thing.'

36

Sleepless nights are becoming something of a regular occurrence now. Even the new door locks aren't doing much for my peace of mind. I'd ring the security company the locksmith recommended and get an alarm and CCTV installed, but I barely have a penny to my name. My credit cards are all maxed out and work are starting to get heavy about my recent absences. It won't be long before they fire me, I'm sure, but every time I think of going back in it fills me with dread.

Besides, it's Friday today. They won't be expecting me back on a Friday. That gives me three days until I'm due back in, or until I can get a doctor's note to prolong my absence. With that, they wouldn't be able to fire me. It would be illegal. Sure, I imagine they could find a way around it, but somehow I don't think they'd try that with me. Not when it's my job to hire and fire people in the first place. I probably know the rules and regulations better than they do.

First of all they'd have to discuss it with me in more detail. They'd have to offer ways in which they can help me manage work with my illness, whatever that illness were to technically be called. *Stress*, I guess. They'd only need a doctor's note after seven days off work, too. On top of that, I'm entitled to take my annual leave as sick days. And I've still got more than a fortnight left. In short, NMFP. Not. My. Fucking. Problem.

I have bigger fucking problems.

Mandy's right. I need to go to the police. But without proof, what good will it do? Are the police obliged to investigate and question someone purely on the basis of an allegation? I can only presume so. If I said someone I knew had assaulted me, they wouldn't need CCTV evidence before they went round and asked the other person for their side of the story, would they? There's always the possibility that things are different for serving police officers. I imagine they're more protected against allegations. They must get them all the time. Police brutality, racism. You hear those allegations all the time.

But then there's the other aspect. If Gavin Armitage — or whatever his name is — finds out that I now know who he is, will that make him back off? If he's spoken to or questioned and, as I imagine he will do, he manages to squirm away quite easily through a complete lack of evidence, will that be enough to ensure he keeps his distance? He'd be daft to try anything stupid after that, wouldn't he? Knowing that eyes are on him. That his name is now linked to mine.

Of course, if he's a complete psychopath it could go the

other way. It could make him think he needs to act quickly and decisively to avoid anyone uncovering anything. And, being a police officer, he'd know the right ways and means of doing that. He'd know how to doctor evidence or avoid anyone ever finding it in the first place. He has experience of both sides here, and can use that to his advantage.

Whichever way I look at it, I can't shake the feeling – the compulsion – that I need to speak to someone high up in the police and get this properly investigated. My parents brought me up to respect the police and to trust in them if I needed them. Until now, I never have. I don't want my sole involvement with the police to end negatively, whatever that might mean.

I call the station again. The phone rings and rings. As it does so, I think about what I want to say. I haven't prepared at all. Do I speak to McKenna again? Or do I accept that she thinks I'm a fruitloop and go above her head instead? What are the chances of them putting me through to a superintendent or chief constable just because I phone up and ask? Slim, I reckon.

Finally, someone answers the phone. I ask to speak to McKenna. It's the only thing I can think of saying. I'm asked what it's about, and I tell her it's an active case. I give my name. I'm put on hold for a good three minutes. Eventually, McKenna's voice comes on the line.

'Hi, Alice.'

'Hi,' I say, swallowing. 'I wondered if I might be able to speak to you again. About what we spoke about yesterday. I have some new information.'

There's a moment's silence as McKenna considers this. 'What sort of new information?' she asks.

'I don't want to sound weird, but I can't really say on the phone. But I think I know who this Gavin Armitage guy is. Who he *really* is, I mean. His real identity.'

'Okay. And why can't you tell me over the phone?'

'Can I just see you? Please?' I ask, avoiding her question.

'It's not that simple, Alice. If you have information that might be pertinent to the case then we have to—'

'Please,' I say, my voice sounding far more desperate than I'd intended. 'I can't. Please.'

This seems to trigger something in McKenna's mind. Maybe she thinks I can't say over the phone because the person is in earshot. I don't know. But she seems to pick up that it's security-sensitive.

'Are you at home?' she asks.

'Yes.' I go to add *I'm in all day*, but I don't. Half because I don't know what access Gavin Armitage will have to this call and half because I want McKenna to come round now.

She sighs. 'I'll be round before lunch, alright? I'll have a colleague with me.'

'That's fine,' I say. 'Thank you.'

I have no idea how it's going to go. I don't know how McKenna will react to what I tell her. I can guess it won't be *Right, we'll go and arrest him at once*, but other than that I'm clueless.

All I can do is cross my fingers and hope.

37

Sometimes I'm not sure what to make of you. Just when I think I know you, I realise you still have the capacity to surprise.

I hadn't expected to see you yesterday. And that's putting it lightly. But I'm impressed. You're becoming strong.

I like to think I've helped you. Would you have been so brave, so insistent beforehand? Would you have had the courage to stand up for what you knew was right, for what you understood deep down was the just thing to do? I don't think so.

And that means it's working.

I told you I could see glimpses of her in you. I knew they were there somewhere. That inner strength, that conviction. It's not something you can create. It's something that's either inside or nowhere. Most people are weak. Most people will roll over at some point and give up, particularly when things get tough. But the tougher things get for you, the harder you seem to fight.

You've never really been tested, have you? Not properly, I mean.

Until now.

And that means you've never had to find that inner strength, never had to prove to yourself that you're a warrior for justice. Oh, we all think we are. But very few of us are. We all plod on, happy for an easy life. As long as it's not happening to me, it doesn't bother me. It's someone else's injustice.

Until it does *happen to you. As you're now finding out.*

She never drew that distinction. She never cared whose injustice it was. Every injustice was her injustice. It was the world's injustice. I think you could make that leap. I can see you're starting to feel that way.

You remind me more and more of her all the time. I knew it was inside you, Alice. That Woodstock spirit.

And it's made me so happy. It's like having her back here with me again. Not holding me, not telling me she'd always be there for me. Not yet. But you're there. And that's all that matters. We can work on the rest later. It'll come. These things take time. But we're getting so close, Alice. So close. Can't you feel it? You must feel the change. We can change the world together, you and I. Because you're growing with every day. Growing stronger. Watching that happen in front of my eyes is truly illuminating. You have no idea what that means to me. Even at this distance, it doesn't matter. It's the comfort in knowing.

The comfort in realising you're never far away.
The comfort in her.

38

True to her word, McKenna turned up before lunch. Not long before, but still before. She's accompanied by a man who introduces himself as DC Brennan.

True to form, McKenna's keen to get to the point. 'So, this new information,' she says, having rejected the offer of a cup of tea or coffee on behalf of both of them. 'You think you know Gavin Armitage's identity.'

'Yes,' I say, pre-empting her asking me who I think it is, and instead feeling the need to explain myself first. 'And I know that as soon as I tell you your reaction is going to be that I'm crazy. But I need you to listen to me. I know I'm right. I've never been more sure of anything in my life. And I really, really need your help because if you can't help me then I don't know what'll happen. I haven't got anyone else.'

'I understand,' she says. I'm not sure she does. 'But we can't do anything unless you tell us who you suspect.'

'Know. Not suspect. I know it's him.'

McKenna bears with me. 'Alright. What's his name?'

I glance down at the floor. 'I don't know.'

As I look up, I see McKenna and Brennan shooting a look at each other.

McKenna closes her notebook. 'What do you mean you don't know?'

'I don't know his name, I mean. But I know who he is. I saw him. I saw where he works. I know who he is. I saw him.'

She looks at me, and just for a moment I think I see the glint of realisation in her eyes. I'm not certain. Maybe it's just hope. But I see something.

'Where did you see him?' she asks in a low voice.

I pause for a moment.

'At the police station.'

The detectives don't look at each other, but Brennan lifts his chin.

'He works at the police station?' McKenna asks.

I nod.

'Is that why you had that reaction? When you passed out? Because you thought you saw Gavin Armitage?'

'I *did* see him,' I insist. 'I didn't think I did. I did.'

'But we were standing in the corridor at the time. There was only me and you there.'

'Through the windows,' I say.

'That's the first response unit, Alice. They're all uniformed police officers.'

I swallow. 'I know. He was one of them.'

McKenna shuffles in her seat. Brennan makes eye contact

with her and I detect some unspoken words. After a few moments, she speaks.

'Alice, you know this is an extremely serious allegation you're making, don't you?'

I nod. 'I know. But if you look into it, you'll see I'm right. You need to find out where he was the Saturday before last. Or look at CCTV from outside the patisserie. You'll see him talking to me on the Friday morning.'

'There isn't any CCTV outside the patisserie,' she says. 'We already checked.'

I don't know whether to feel reassured or not. Does this means they've actually been investigating and trying to identify Gavin Armitage themselves, or was it police-speak for *There isn't any evidence*?

'Well, look at the photos. The ones he took of me leaving work and in the bar. You can see when and where they were taken, I presume. Then you can find out where he was at that time.'

'We would, but the photos weren't timestamped. They'd had their meta data scrubbed.'

I can feel myself getting more and more agitated. 'This is my point. He knows exactly what he's doing. He knows all the ways he could be caught, and he's avoiding them. That's because he knows exactly what *he'd* do. Because he's a police officer!'

'With all due respect, Alice, I'm a bit stunned. Where am I meant to go from here? I can't line up an identity parade of the male officers who work on the first response team.'

'I could have a look at pictures,' I say. 'There must be

photos of them all on file somewhere. I could pick him out straight away.'

McKenna tries to sound reassuring, but she fails. 'Alice, I can completely see where you're coming from. And I understand your frustration. Believe me, I do. But my job is to assess information that comes in and decide whether there's a credible threat to someone's safety. At the moment, we're stumbling at that first bit. At the moment, all I've got is stories. Now, I'm not saying they aren't true. But what I am saying is that I need to assess whether we can allocate resources to investigate something based on the information we receive.'

'But you've already allocated resources,' I say. 'You looked for the CCTV footage from outside the patisserie. You got the computer people to look at the images. So you must at least believe some of what I'm saying.'

'Investigations are fluid,' McKenna replies. 'Just because we've started investigating something doesn't mean that information won't come to light that means we need to scale things down.'

'You mean like discovering the suspect is one of your own,' I say, more as a statement than a question.

'No,' she replies quickly. 'Not at all. Allegations against serving police officers are an extremely serious matter. If anything, we take them more seriously than most other allegations. But it does mean they need to stand up to extra scrutiny.'

I look at her for a moment. 'This is because of the medication, isn't it? My medical history. You think I'm making this up. You think it's some sort of play for attention or something.'

'Not at all. We just need to make sure we prioritise our investigations so that—'

'No!' I yell. 'You don't get it, do you? How difficult is it? *He's been in here.* In my house. He's stood in this room, right here,' I say, jumping up and walking to the mantelpiece. 'He put a fucking photo in this frame! Did you send anyone round to take fingerprints? No. You didn't. Even after you promised me you would. You did fuck all!'

My rage quickly dissipates as the sound of the photo frame smashing against the wall makes me realise what I've done. I'm shaking. If they didn't think I was nuts before, they will now. Is there a law against throwing your own photo frame against your own living room wall? They didn't even flinch.

'Please,' I say. 'Please. I'm at my wits' end. I promise you, every word I'm telling you is the truth. Please. Just let me see those photos and I'll be able to identify him straight away. Then you just need to investigate him and this will all be over. If I'm wrong, lock me up. Whatever. But I'm not wrong. I've never been so certain of anything in my life.'

I look at McKenna, knowing she's the only one of the two that'll be making this decision. I hope I can prey on her womanly instincts. If she has any. She looks over at Brennan. He looks back at her. Neither of them say anything for a second.

'You realise it's an offence to waste police time, don't you?' she asks me.

'Yes. I know. And I promise you I'm not wasting a single second. Just let me identify him. I promise you it's him.'

She takes a deep breath – one that seems to go on forever as she takes in every molecule of air her lungs will allow.

She holds it for a second or two.

'Alright,' she says, finally exhaling. 'I'll see what I can do.' She turns to Brennan. 'We'll need to get IT to run us off the staff photos of shift officers matching Armitage's description. Anonymised.' She turns back to me. 'I'll give you a call later, alright? In the meantime, I'd fetch a dustpan and brush.'

39

I had a call from McKenna a couple of hours later, asking me to come into the police station to look at the staff photos. I didn't imagine it'd move this quickly. In my mind, there are two explanations for that: she's either coming round to the fact that this guy is dangerous, or she wants to get the whole thing over with as swiftly as possible.

I get a strange feeling of déjà-vu as I sit in the waiting room at the police station, watching the officer behind the counter and the glass screen tap away at an ancient computer. At least I presume he's an officer. He's wearing a black shirt with epaulettes. Do civilian staff wear those too? I don't know.

After about ten minutes, McKenna arrives with a manila folder under her arm and takes me through to a side room. It's on the opposite side of the waiting room from the corridor we went through last time, thankfully. I don't think I could cope with walking past those windows again, and I think she realises that.

The room is dark and oppressive, but it's still infinitely preferable to having to see that man's face again. I think anything would be. The walls are bare breeze block, whitewashed with paint that's started to turn a creamy yellow colour. There's a suspended ceiling lined with cheap polystyrene ceiling tiles. The floor is covered with even cheaper carpet tiles of an indistinct colour somewhere between mauve and brown.

I sit down on the hard plastic chair and lean forward on the hard plastic table. I can feel my heart hammering in my chest. Am I about to identify the man who's been masquerading under the name Gavin Armitage, the man who's been stalking me and making my life hell? I hope so. I hope beyond any hopes I've ever had before in my life.

'Are you alright?' McKenna asks, pausing with her hand inside the manila folder, as if teasing me.

I nod. I fear that if I open my mouth to talk I'll vomit.

She sits down as she removes the photographs from the folder. I can see already that the top photo isn't him. This relaxes me a little, although I know his picture must be in this pile somewhere.

'These are the staff photos of each of the shift officers working on the first response unit. They're the officers you saw inside the office. I want you to look at each of the photos carefully and to let me know if any of these men is who you recognise as Gavin Armitage. Alright?'

I nod again. She holds eye contact as she shoves the pile of photographs over to me.

I stare at it for a moment. I reckon there must be ten or fifteen in total. Part of me doesn't want to look through, but I do. I take the first photo off the top, discarding it, and move onto the second. I have a good look at the photo, even though I know damn well it isn't him.

As I move on to the third photo and see that it isn't him either, the door opens and a woman walks in. She's not in police uniform, but she's wearing a name badge. I can't read it from where I'm sitting, but she seems to know McKenna.

She asks McKenna if she's got a moment. She replies in the affirmative, stands and steps outside the room, closing the door behind her.

I move on to the fourth photograph, and immediately it feels as though someone's stabbed me in the stomach with an ice dagger. I recognise him straight away. There's absolutely no doubt in my mind.

Before I realise what I'm doing, I pull my mobile phone out of my pocket and try to unlock it. My hands are sweaty and shaking and the fingerprint recognition isn't working. I go to type in my PIN and get it wrong twice in a row. I force myself to calm down, then try again. This time, the phone unlocks. I jab the *Camera* icon and the screen turns black for a moment before it shows the desk in front of me. I lift the phone, wait a second for it to focus on Gavin Armitage's face, then tap to take a photo. I tap it twice more for good measure, then lock the phone and put it back in my pocket. In that moment, I know exactly what I have to do. There's only one way out of this.

Gavin's eyes stare back at me from the photo, and it's as if he's watching me. As if he knows. His image is giving me the creeps, but I try to remain calm. I try to focus my breathing. In through the nose, out through the mouth.

As my breathing starts to approach something resembling normal, there's a loud noise as the door opens again and McKenna reenters the room.

'Sorry about that,' she says.

'It's alright,' I reply, almost whispering.

'Any luck?'

I shake my head and make a pretence of looking through the rest of the photos.

When I get to the end of the pile, I force my best dejected look and glance up at McKenna. Her jaw is clenched slightly. 'Do you recognise any of them?' she asks.

I shake my head again. 'No.'

40

The truth is I need the police. But I can't trust them. They're two very different things.

The moment I saw Gavin Armitage's photo, I knew what I had to do. I couldn't risk McKenna speaking to him. There's no way he'll have left a single grain of evidence that they can use. He's too smart for that. And when the police are investigating one of their own I'm sure you need one hell of a lot of grains.

If I'd told McKenna that the fourth photo was the man I knew as Gavin Armitage, she'd have to go and speak to him. Interview him, perhaps under caution. Then he'd know that I know. He'd know his identity had been compromised. And then what? There's nothing that can convict him. Even if he didn't have an alibi for the Friday morning or Saturday afternoon, so what? Neither do I. Our alibis are each other, and they're going to trust his word far more than mine.

I *know* it was him, so any investigation into him and any rebuttal he gives is only going to work towards proving me wrong. If he can falsify an alibi or find a friend or colleague who says he was with them on those days, it's all over. He's innocent, I'm officially a nut job and he's free to do whatever he pleases. Enact revenge, perhaps. I'm already in such a precarious situation, I can't risk anything but finding complete and overwhelming evidence. Nothing I have right now is going to make McKenna believe my word over his, and he's in a prime position to discredit everything I've said.

But now I have one huge advantage. I have his image. And I think I have an idea as to what I should do with it.

I fire off a quick text to Kieran.

Are you free tomorrow night?

My phone shows me barely five seconds later that he's read the message, but I don't get the three dancing dots that tell me he's composing a reply. I visualise him sitting in his flat, looking at the text, trying to work out why the hell I'm asking him this the day after yelling at him over the phone and telling him to fuck off.

I stare at my phone for what feels like an age, but eventually those dots appear. A few seconds later, his response pops up on the screen.

• • •

Yeah. What did you have in mind? X

A kiss. Good old dependable Kieran. No matter what I say to him, no matter what I do to him, he's unchanged. He might have made weak boyfriend material, but as a friend he's unbeatable. If he can handle just being my friend, that is.

I tap out a reply.

Bar Chico, 7?

I decide against adding a kiss of my own. I think it's only fair that he doesn't get the wrong idea. Not right now.

His response is almost instantaneous.

Sounds good. See you there x

Tonight, I'm meeting Simon in a pub on the other side of town. I've never been there before, but it's near his place and he tells me it's good.

It's been my one ray of sunshine over the past day or so — the one thing to look forward to. I've already told myself I'm going to put the whole Gavin Armitage thing out of my mind — as much as I can, anyway — for the evening. I owe myself that much. Besides which, if there's any possible chance of anything happening between me and Simon, I don't want to go fucking it up at the first opportunity. Psychopathic-woman-who-thinks-she's-being-stalked isn't the most attractive personality trope for men, I'm told.

When I get to the pub, Simon's already there. He's talking to a middle-aged couple at the bar, and it seems he's well-known in here. Maybe it's just me being judgemental, but I wouldn't have expected a martial arts instructor to spend much time in pubs. You live, you learn.

We get our drinks and sit at a table in the corner. There's a roaring log fire going, and at first I wonder why no-one else has sat down near it. After a minute or so, I find out. The corner's something of a heat-trap, and I quickly find myself jettisoning layers. Simon, though, doesn't seem to mind, so I don't feel I can suggest we move.

'So how have things been?' he asks. It doesn't sound like he's fishing for info — he seems genuinely interested.

'Yeah, not too bad,' I lie. 'Well, I say that. I've not been too well recently so I've had a bit of time off work.'

'Nothing serious, I hope?'

'No, just a few dizzy spells and things. Doctor reckons I need to take it easy for a while. Not going to argue with that,' I say, smiling before I take a sip of my drink.

'Hence the absence on Thursdays,' he adds, before taking a mouthful of his pint.

'Yeah, sorry about that. I should have called or texted, I know. I've just been so scatty recently.'

'Honestly, don't worry about it,' he says. 'To be honest, most people tend to flake permanently and I don't hear a word from them again. The fact you got back to me is a good start.'

I don't know whether to be pleased with myself or not.

'So you come here a lot?' I ask him, trying to change the subject. I don't want to talk about myself; I want to find out more about him.

'Depends what you mean by a lot.' He shows me a cheeky smile, two dimples appearing at the creases of his cheeks as he does so.

'Breakfast, lunch and dinner?'

He laughs. 'Not quite that often, no. But I am partial to the odd pint a few times a week. Arrest me.' He holds out his arms towards me, wrists pointed skywards as he chuckles. I get flashbacks of being in the police station twice this week, but I try to force a smile anyway. 'Symptom of living on my own, I guess. Gets a bit quiet around the house in the evenings. There's only so much *Mad Men* a guy can watch.'

I smile, then realise it wasn't because of the joke, but because he mentioned living on his own. 'I've never seen it,' I say.

'Oh, it's brilliant. No question. But your brain starts to veg out after about six episodes.' He laughs again. 'Sign of the times, I guess.'

I leave it a moment before speaking.

'Do you not have a housemate or anything, then?'

He looks down at his hands and smiles.

'Sorry, I didn't mean it like that. I meant—'

'It's fine,' he says. 'Really. And no, I don't have a housemate. Nor a wife. Nor a girlfriend. Nor a boyfriend.'

I put on the best deadpan face I can muster. 'That's a bit presumptuous, isn't it?'

He looks at me for a moment, then smiles again as we both laugh. This is how it should be. This is what I like. I don't want danger, I don't want excitement and I certainly don't want woolly jumpers and yes-men. I want someone who understands me, who gets my style. Someone I can have a laugh with, someone whose company I can enjoy.

I think of Kieran, and how completely different he is to Simon. And how different they both are to previous boyfriends I've had. They can be likened to drinks. I've had my fair share of vodka shots and Jägerbombs in the past, but Simon is a quality glass of red wine. Kieran, on the other hand is... Well, he's tap water. Because he's decided it'd be easier and more convenient just to drive.

Listen to me. Going on about Simon as if there's something that's going to happen between us. This is the first time we've even seen each other socially, outside of the classes, and I'm comparing him to previous boyfriends. But I think that's exactly why. Even though this is the first social outing we've had, I feel completely comfortable with him. It's almost as if it's absolutely fine to see him once a week or every now and again. It doesn't feel as though there's that compulsion to keep meeting up with him every five minutes, either on my part or his. It strikes me that that's been the problem in more or less all my relationships up until now. And it's not always been the guy's fault.

But, most importantly, it's come at the right time. It's giving me hope. It's giving me something to hold onto. And I'm sure as hell not going to let go.

It's all I've got.

41

The one saving grace about keeping a friendship with Kieran is that I know I can rely on him if I need him. And right now I really need him.

The early morning sun streams in through my kitchen window, and I'm secretly quite proud of myself for getting up so early on a Saturday morning. But I know exactly why I have. I'm renewed with vigour. I've got a focus. A direction. A plan.

'This is going to sound really weird,' I say to Kieran, cradling the phone between my cheek and shoulder as I try to do the washing up, 'but do you still speak to your mate Danny or David? The guy who works for the police.'

'Darryl? Yeah sometimes. Why's that?'

I wipe my hands dry on my jeans and scribble *Darryl* down on the kitchen notepad, just under *bacon* and *bread*. 'Oh, just wondered. I thought I saw him in town the other day, but I've not seen him in years. Forgot all about him, actually.' Well, the last part's true. To be honest, I doubt I'd recognise him if he walked into my kitchen right now and introduced himself. But if my hazy memory is right, Kieran's friend could be the key to unlocking all this. 'He worked in IT or something, didn't he?'

'Erm, I think so, yeah,' Kieran replies. 'Something to do with their internal servers. He's civilian staff, though. Not actually a police officer.'

'Cool. I thought I recognised him. So how's things? I ask, changing the subject to make this sound more like a random, friendly call than a fishing expedition.

Unfortunately, Kieran tells me exactly how things are. He tells me about his week at work, the trouble he's been having with his boiler and his hunt for a new housemate.

'That reminds me. You still on for tonight?' I ask him, even though whatever he just said obviously didn't remind me of anything.

'Yeah, course. What's it all about?'

I shrug, even though he can't see me over the phone. 'Dunno. Just thought we should catch up.' I sigh. 'Call it me mending bridges. I was a cow the other day.'

'Don't worry about it,' he says. I can hear him smiling as he speaks.

'Hey, why don't you invite Darryl along? Be a good chance to catch up. If he's free, I mean.'

As soon as I say this, I realise how weird it sounds. I was actually thinking of looking him up on Facebook via Kieran's friends list, but I want to keep away from the digital world if I can. What if my online activities are being watched?

A thought hits me. Shit. What if *everything* I do is being watched? What if Gavin Armitage has put microphones or cameras in my house? Or bugged my phone? Fuck fuck fuck. It's too late now. I've had the conversation with Kieran. It's been said now. That leaves me only one choice. I need to put this plan into action quickly.

'Well yeah, I can do,' Kieran says, in the sort of voice that has a subtext of *But why the hell would you want me to do that?*

I laugh a little. 'This is going to sound so stupid. But if you can keep a secret... I'm thinking about writing a book. One of those things I've always wanted to do, you know. And there's this bit I'm thinking about which needs some research. When I saw—' I glance down at my shopping list. '—Darryl, it reminded me about it. I thought he might be able to help.

'Yeah. Sure. Sounds good. But why tonight?'

'Dunno. Just thought as we were meeting tonight anyway. No time like the present and all that. Besides which, I need to get started with writing it or I'll never do it. It'll be good for me. Therapeutic, perhaps.'

Kieran seems to consider this more favourably now. I thought he might.

'Alright. I'll send him a message, see what he says.'

'Great. See you tonight then,' I say, before we say our goodbyes and I end the call.

Instead of locking my phone and putting it back in my

pocket, I open up the *Photos* app and look again at the picture of Gavin Armitage — or whatever his real name is — and for the first time in a while I smile. Genuinely smile. And I think to myself: *Gotcha.*

42

It being a Saturday, Mandy's off work, so we arrange to meet for coffee. Somehow it seems healthier than a few drinks in the evening, but I'm not sure the overdose of caffeine from the super-strong coffees the local chain serves is going to be any better than getting shitfaced on wine. It eases my conscience a little, though. Until tonight, when I'll be meeting Kieran and Darryl.

I wonder if I can get away with ordering a decaf. I'd have to be the one going up and ordering, though, and I'd have to get Mandy to sit down. Otherwise she'd hone in on it like a guided missile and want to know why I wanted decaf. Was I pregnant? Ill? Hungover? Dying? The truth is my head is splitting. I stopped taking my medication yesterday.

I know. But I need to think clearly. *Properly* clearly. It's hard to describe, but it's impossible to pursue a clear train of thought when you're on those things. I know I've got the withdrawal stages to go through first. In the short term, it's going to be worse. But it'll be worth it for the long-term gains. And I'm currently feeling the full force of the initial short-term symptoms. Headaches, some nausea and that damn electric pulsing at my temples. It's not fun, but I'm determined to ride it out for the greater good.

Plenty of water, plenty of rest. Well, one out of two is a good start.

The coffee shop is busier than I expected it'd be. It seems it's not just me who's had the idea of the disingenuous health kick. Fortunately, Mandy's sitting on the other side of the room with a full cup of coffee, so I'm able to order my sneaky decaf and take it over to the table without being quizzed. I really don't think throwing caffeine into the mix with this headache is going to help. I'll leave that to the ibuprofen.

True to form, Mandy dives straight in with the question she's been wanting to ask me — the reason she invited me here — as if I didn't already know.

'So? How did it go?'

I take a deep breath. 'I think we might be getting somewhere.'

Mandy makes a high-pitched squeal and starts clapping her forearms together like a performing sealion, lifting her knees up and banging her feet down like a frenzied cyclist. It's not something I've ever seen her do before. It was almost feminine. Almost.

'I'm not getting my hopes up just yet, though,' I add.

'So what happened? Why the sudden change of heart on their part?'

I shrug. 'I dunno. Maybe they finally realised I was for real.'

'But you told them he was a copper, right?'

'Yeah.'

'And?'

'And I got the response I expected. I think. They weren't expecting me to come out with it, and I think they were skeptical, but at the same time they have to take those sorts of allegations seriously, don't they?'

Mandy murmurs her agreement as she swallows a mouthful of cappuccino. The froth clings to her upper lip like a moustache. 'So are they investigating him?'

'I dunno,' I say. 'I hope so. I had to go down to the police station again and look through a pile of photographs of police officers, to identify him.'

'And you did?'

I hesitate for a moment. I try not to, but it's unavoidable. I never have been a good liar. 'Yeah. Yeah, I identified him.'

'To the police?' she asks, as if she's rumbled me immediately.

'Yeah. To the police.'

She seems to accept this without question, and I realise I was perhaps just being paranoid.

'Wow,' she says, gazing off into the middle distance. 'That's some pretty fucked up shit.'

I flick my eyebrows upwards without even realise I'm doing it. 'That's one way of putting it.'

'So what now? They go in, arrest him, find out where he

says he was at the times he was following you? Fingerprint him? What?'

'I don't think so, no,' I say. I'm not lying. 'To be honest, I don't really know what happens next. I mean, they're not going to tell me, are they? I don't imagine they'll want to go in all guns blazing, though. They probably have set processes for things like this. Last thing they'll want to do is go wading in without the evidence.'

'Yeah, but in the meantime what's to say he's not going to creep into your house at night and try to... I dunno, rape you or something?'

Mandy can tell by the look on my face that she's said something really fucking stupid.

'Sorry. I don't mean that he'll—'

'Forget it. It's fine. And anyway, I've had all my locks changed.'

'Again.'

'To properly safe ones this time. I had the security guy round.'

Mandy says nothing, but I can tell exactly what she's thinking. She thinks I'm not safe in my house. She thinks I should leave for a while, go and stay at hers or somewhere else. After all, a couple of sets of locks on some doors don't seem to be stopping him. What's to say another set will?

And it's not the fact that Mandy is thinking these things that's worrying me.

It's the fact that – deep down – I think she might be right.

43

Kieran texted me to confirm that Darryl would be joining us tonight, but couldn't get there until 8.30. I'm quite pleased, actually, as it gives me some time to get Kieran on my own and prep him on what this is all about. I don't want the first he hears of Gavin Armitage to be when I tell Darryl.

And I don't want it to sound like I'm using Kieran, either. I mean, I need his help. Of course I do. But that's not the same as using him, is it? It's relying on a friend, a friend who has access to resources that no-one else I know does.

I know it's a long shot. I'm not expecting Darryl to say *Yeah, that's so-and-so. He's a known stalker. I'll get it sorted.* To be honest, I don't know what I'm expecting. But it's all I've got. I need help. And now I've got Gavin Armitage's picture, I can get something done.

Kieran turns up bang on time – predictably. Although I'm a few minutes early I've still not been served, so I get him a drink too.

We sit down at a table in the corner, near the window. It makes me feel slightly uncomfortable, but that's exactly why I'm doing it. I need to show Gavin Armitage – if he's watching – that I'm not afraid. He can take a photo of me in a bar if he wants. So what? I'm onto him. Bring it on.

Once we've got the pleasantries out of the way, I start to tell Kieran the whole story from the beginning. I tell him about the patisserie, the business card, the photoshoot. Then I pause before telling him about the photos I got sent.

He's shocked, to say the least.

'What? You can't be serious,' he says, his face showing me that he knows I'm serious, and he's seriously annoyed. I haven't seen him like this in a long time.

'Yeah, I am. But that's not all. He's been in my house. Twice, I think.'

Kieran just looks at me. 'You need to call the police. Now.'

'I have. I've been to see them. But I can't prove anything. That's the problem. This guy knows what he's doing. He's... Look, one of the times when I went to the police to give a statement, I saw him. He was standing in the office, wearing a uniform. He's a police officer, Kieran.'

Kieran's mouth hangs open. He looks like a dying fish. 'But... Jesus, you can't mean... So that's why... Darryl,' he says, not forming even half a sentence, but at the same time somehow managing to get everything across.

'Yeah. That's why Darryl.'

'Didn't the police believe you?'

I sigh. 'That's kind of a long story. Yes and no. But I know who he is. I mean, I don't know his name, but I have a photo of him.'

'You took a picture of him?'

'No. Well yes. Sort of. I took a picture of his picture. Look, can I explain this later? I just wanted to fill you in before Darryl came.' The truth is, I want a bit of time and space to think about how I'm going to approach this. Do I just come out and tell Kieran and Darryl I lied to the police and didn't recognise any of the photos? Or do I lie to them and say I did, but they didn't do anything? I'm sure Darryl will be able to find out anyway. It's probably on record or on a system somewhere.

For the next half an hour or so, we talk about anything but Gavin Armitage. It's the elephant in the room, but I really don't want to have to explain all this over and over again when Darryl arrives.

Shortly after 8.30, he does arrive. He and Kieran are immediately pally. Knowing Kieran, he's probably not seen Darryl for months – if not longer. He was never particularly very good at keeping in touch with his friends when we were together. Part of me wonders if it was *because* we were together. Perhaps he's one of those guys who doesn't speak to his friends much when he has a girlfriend. Or maybe he just doesn't speak to them all that much anyway. I don't know. I've not had long enough to find out yet.

'You remember Alice, don't you?' Kieran says, as Darryl sits down.

'Yeah I do. Hi Alice. I thought you two...'

'We did,' I say, putting him out of his misery. 'We're good friends, though.'

Kieran smiles at this. I can't tell if it's a real smile or a forced one. If it's a forced one, he's a good actor.

We talk about what we've been up to, how work is, what our current living arrangements are. And all the time Kieran and I keep looking at each other, conscious of where this conversation has to lead. Eventually, I take the plunge.

'I was wondering if I might be able to ask you a favour, actually, Darryl,' I say. I go on to tell him about Gavin Armitage and the photos. Kieran listens, entranced, even though he's heard the story already. I stop short of telling him Gavin Armitage is a police officer.

'That's so weird. Are you alright?' he asks. It's sweet that his first concern is for me.

'I'm fine,' I say. 'A little shaken at times, but yeah I'm alright.'

'Have you spoken to the police about it?'

I flick my eyebrows upwards and look down at the table. 'Not much they can do, apparently.'

'Always the way. What was it? Short-staffed? Not a priority?' The way he says it makes me think he's got a certain amount of dislike for the system at the moment.

'Not enough evidence,' I say.

He smirks. 'Ah. That old chestnut. Yeah, that's another one.' He pauses for a moment before the penny starts to drop. 'You said you wanted to ask me a favour, though. I mean, if it's to do with a crime that's been reported, I can't—'

'No, no. I'm not asking you to go behind anyone's back or

anything like that. It's all legal and above board, I promise.' I can't actually promise him that because I don't know what's legal and above board, but I can't imagine I'll be breaking any laws by showing him a photo and asking him the guy's name. 'Thing is, I managed to get a photo of the guy who's been doing this to me.'

'Do the police have it?' Darryl asks.

'Sort of... Here, I'll show you.'

I open up the *Photos* app on my phone, load the full-screen picture of Gavin Armitage's photograph and show it to Darryl. I'm careful to make sure I'm watching his face. Closely. He blinks a couple of times, and I think I see his eyebrows twitch. Without moving his head, he flicks his eyes towards me.

'That's him?' he asks.

'Yeah. Why?' I don't ask him if he recognises him. It's clear to me that he does. I need to hear him say it for myself. I need to know how open and trustworthy Darryl is. Kieran seems to clock this, too, and stays silent.

'Where did you get this photo?'

'I took it,' I reply. I'm not technically lying.

'Do you know who this guy is?'

All of a sudden Darryl seems to be the one asking the questions. I'm now surer than ever that he knows exactly who this man is. He is the person who can identify Gavin Armitage. He can help me. But I need to hear him say it.

'I don't know his name,' I say.

Darryl swallows.

'I do.'

44

'This is why you asked me here, isn't it?' Darryl says. 'This is a police staff photo. Where did you get it?'

'The police showed it to me. When I reported it. They showed me photos of some officers to see if I could identify him.'

Darryl blinks a few times. 'But I thought you said they weren't investigating? You said there was a lack of evidence.'

'There is. That's why I need you. That's why I need you to tell me who this man is.'

'But surely the police would've told you. I mean, when you identified him they would have... You didn't tell them, did you? You told them you didn't recognise any of the pictures.'

'It's not as simple as that,' I say. 'The fact is, this guy's covered his tracks so well they wouldn't be able to prove a thing. Besides which, the police will have two options. They can either speak to him and investigate him, in which case he'll be made aware and could turn dangerous, or they'll not do anything at all. Either way, I can't risk that. He'll get away with it no matter what.'

Darryl scrunches his eyes up for a moment before speaking. 'But what's the point?' he says. 'I mean, what's the end game? You find out who he is, and what? You going to go round there and arrest him yourself? Search his house for evidence? What?'

I sigh. 'I don't know. I haven't thought that far ahead. But all I know is we can't go through the police. He's one of *them*. I just... I don't feel like they can protect me. I did, but now I don't. I've lost all confidence in them.'

'You can trust them, you know.'

'I'd love to,' I say. 'I really would. But I can't. What if he gets word he's being investigated and decides to step things up? He's been in my *house*, Darryl. He's been following me. What if he does something else? Something worse?'

'There are units for that. Internally, I mean. For investigating serving officers without them knowing. Files they won't be able to access.'

'Without evidence? On the say-so of some random woman who points to a photo of a police officer and says "That bloke's stalking me"?'

'Well, no. They'd need a bit more than that.'

'Exactly,' I say. 'And that's why I need your help. You're the only one of the three of us who knows who this man is, Darryl.'

He looks up at me, as if he's just realised for the first time what I'm asking. 'What? Woah. No, no. No way. I can't go getting involved in this. I mean, don't get me wrong, it's shit what you're going through and I really hope they catch him – if it's him – but I can't risk my job by getting involved.'

I shake my head vigorously and place my hand on his. 'I'm not asking you to get involved. Seriously. Just tell me his name. That's all I'm asking.'

He looks uneasy. 'I dunno...'

'Oh come on,' I say, trying the other approach – firmness. 'If I walk up to an officer in the street and ask for their name they have to give it, don't they? It's hardly top secret. They go around introducing themselves to everyone. But I can't go up and ask him, can I? So I'm asking you.'

He seems to consider this. 'This didn't come from me, alright?'

I nod. I can feel my heart racing, the adrenaline pumping inside me as I wait in anticipation.

'He's PC Toby Sheridan. He works on the first response unit.'

I don't know what I expected, but I don't feel anything when I hear his name. Then again, I wouldn't. I've never heard it before. It means nothing to me. But this is the man who's been stalking me. This is the man who's been trying to ruin my life. And now I have his name. Toby Sheridan. Immediately, the name takes on all sorts of negative connotations. I'll never be able to look another Toby in the eye again. I'll never be able to read anything by Robert Brinsley Sheridan. Not that I ever did anyway.

'Do you know him?' I ask. I'm surprised to hear my voice

cracking slightly. I realise my throat has tightened.

'Not personally. I mean, I know of him. I know most of the people there. We aren't mates or anything, if that's what you mean. But I know who he is, yeah.'

'What's he like?' Kieran asks. It's the first time he's spoken since I broached the subject with Darryl.

'Erm. He's alright, yeah. To be honest, he's not the sort of guy I'd expect would be involved with something like this. Are you sure this is him? You're certain?' he says, pointing to my phone. 'I mean, he doesn't just look a bit like him or something?'

Him asking this makes me think for a moment. But yes, I'm certain. I know I am. I know it.

'No. That's him,' I say.

'Wow. Okay. Well I wasn't expecting that.'

A look passes between me and Kieran as we watch Darryl mulling this all over in his head.

'Listen, Darryl. I desperately need your help here. A name is great, but I need more than that.'

He looks at me for a moment, almost suspiciously. 'Why? What sort of thing?'

I swallow. 'I don't know. An address? Something about him? My head's in a right mess right now, but all I know is I need something. Some way of being able to prove he was in my house. Something that links him to it.'

'But I thought you said there *isn't* any proof? We can't just make something up.'

'No, but we can give him enough rope to hang himself with,' Kieran says.

I look at him and I recognise something in his eyes that I haven't seen for a while. It's determination.

Kieran looks back at me. 'I think I've got an idea.'

45

'Well it make sense to me,' he says, as Darryl and I exchange glances. 'You've got the connections, Darryl. It'd be stupid not to use them.'

Darryl shifts uncomfortably in his seat. 'Yeah, I don't think you quite get it, mate. This is my *job*. I rely on it to keep a roof over my head. How do you suppose I'm going to do that when they find out I've been abusing my position?'

'Simple,' Kieran says. 'You make sure they don't find out.'

Darryl makes to laugh. 'It's not quite as easy as that.'

'And what's the alternative? You can see what it's doing to Alice. Well, you probably can't, but I can. I know her. She needs your help.'

I'm not sure I'm keen on the way Kieran is talking about me as if I'm not in the room. 'Listen, don't worry about it. I'm sure we can sort something out. I don't want Darryl to risk losing his job.'

I imagine Darryl might seem placated by this, but he still

has an awkward look on his face. I take that as meaning he'd love to help, but he's stuck between a rock and a hard place.

'What sort of thing were you thinking?' he asks Kieran.

'I dunno. I hadn't got that far. But as I see it, we've got two options. We either try to gather some evidence... somehow... or we play the fucker at his own game.'

I raise my eyebrows. I don't think I've ever heard Kieran swear. I can see a passion in his eyes that I've never seen before – a fire, stoking him.

'What, you mean *stalk* him?' I say.

'Well I wasn't going to put it quite like that, no. But shit him up a bit. Let him know we're onto him. Let him know what it feels like to be scared, not knowing where the next threat is coming from.'

'I'm not sure I can do threatening,' I reply.

'No-one has to *do* threatening. It's all about him *feeling* threatened. Think about it. What's he done to you? He's taken a few pictures, managed to mess with your head by taking his studio away.'

'He's been in my house, Kieran!' I'm surprised by how upset I sound. It's as if Kieran just doesn't get it.

'I know, I know. And I'm not suggesting we do that, obviously...' He looks at Darryl, as if for reassurance or a nod that it might actually be possible. Darryl just stares him out. Kieran gets the message.

There's a long silence. Kieran's the first to speak.

'So what do you suggest we do? Nothing? I mean, you obviously want to do something, Alice. You took that photo of him for a reason. You lied to the police about not recognising him for a reason. You asked us both here for a reason. So why don't you tell us what you want to happen next?'

I guess it's a fair point, but I can't help feeling somewhat overwhelmed and under pressure. Whichever way I turn, the road seems to be blocked off. I can't just carry on as I am. I can't. How long will I have to live looking over my shoulder, checking every car window, never knowing if he's been in my house that day? I'll never feel safe, and I can't go through life like that. But I can't go to the police, either. That risks making things much, much worse. Without any evidence, they won't be able to charge him with anything and he'll know I'm onto him. He'll step up his game. Before I go to the police again – if I go to the police again – I need more. Much more.

But how? I don't know where he lives, and even if I did I couldn't just break into his house in the hope he'll have *Stalk Alice Jefferson* written in his diary. But there's no evidence at my end. He's taken it all. Except the emails, of course. The police said they were untraceable.

'What about the emails I received?' I asked Darryl. 'They're evidence.'

'They're pictures of you, Alice,' Kieran says. 'That's not actually illegal.'

'No, but surely it's harassment or intimidation? At the very least, if we can trace them we'll be able to see what computer he was using or something. It can't hurt, can it?'

'Didn't the police investigate the emails?' Darryl asks.

'Yeah. They said they're untraceable. Sent from a Gmail account through a... VP something or other.'

'VPN?'

I nod.

'Then there's nothing we can do,' he says. 'Not a chance, I'm afraid. Put it this way. The FBI find it impossible to track computer hackers who use VPNs. They tend to have to use some other trick, usually either impersonation, honey pots or some elaborate form of phishing. They need the bad guys to let their guards down, as the technology itself protects them like you wouldn't believe.'

I blink a few times, thinking. 'But couldn't we do something like that? Get his guard down somehow.'

Darryl shrugs. 'How?'

'I don't know. You know him. Well, you know more than I do anyway.'

Kieran interjects. 'This is all far too elaborate. We're not super spies, for Christ's sake. Either we break into his house and give him a taste of his own medicine, or we hire a group of thugs to go round and kick the fuck out of him.'

Again, I'm shocked at Kieran's language. He's clearly fired up about this. It's sweet in a way.

'Yeah, well I'm definitely not getting involved in that,' Darryl says. I don't blame him.

'You don't have to,' Kieran replies. 'Just tell us where he lives.'

I look at Kieran. So does Darryl. I can't see Darryl's face, but I imagine it's much the same as mine right now.

'No, Kieran. Just no,' he says. 'Not in a million years.'

'It'll sort everything out. No-one needs to know it was you.'

'Do you think they're stupid? Of course they'll know.

We're linked. And I'd have to use the computer system to find his address. That sort of thing leaves traces.'

'You're the IT guy. You can delete traces.'

Darryl looks up into the corner of the room and shakes his head. He doesn't deny the point Kieran just made about deleting traces, though.

'It's not happening, alright? End of.'

The look on Kieran's face is something I've not seen before. It seems as though this is starting to affect him almost as much as it has me. And I'm starting to seriously worry about what he might do. What he might be capable of.

46

I get home at a reasonable hour, and I'm quite proud of myself for not drinking too much either. I've felt somewhat safer since I've had Toby Sheridan's photo, and even safer now I know his name. He's no longer the anonymous figure lurking in the shadows. He's a man with a name, a job, a life. He's now human, and that makes him feel less threatening somehow. Besides which, I've heard nothing from him since seeing him that day at the police station. But even if he should decide to start up again, with the locks on my doors changed I now feel better guarded against him.

There's one thing I've been itching to do ever since I found out Toby Sheridan's name. All I've wanted to do is find out more about him, try to discover what makes a person like this tick. I boot up my MacBook and head to Facebook.

As it's loading, I wonder whether he'll even have an account there. And if he has, will it be under his real name? He's a police officer, so possibly not. I don't even use my real name on Facebook — I'm listed as Ali JaJa. Unoriginal, and inaccurate, too — it's a play on Ali Baba, for absolutely no reason at all, even though no-one ever called me Ali and it should strictly be JeJe, if I'm contracting my surname. I changed it a couple of years ago because I didn't fancy pissed-off former employees from work looking me up after being made redundant. So I can't imagine many police officers have an open and public Facebook account.

When the site loads, I ignore the dross in my newsfeed and type *Toby Sheridan* into the search bar at the top. A few results load immediately, but I hit the Enter key to take me to the full results page.

My heart jumps as the first result shows, accompanied by text that says:

1 mutual friend: Cindy A. Lennox.

I glance at the picture. It looks nothing like the man who's been stalking me. I then read the rest of the text.

Lives in King George, Virginia

Studied Marketing at University of Mary Washington '11

Thankfully, just a coincidence. Cindy's a friend I met on holiday a few years ago. She lives in Devon, but is originally from America. This must be someone she knows from back home who just happens to have the same name as my stalker.

I feel myself calm down slightly, and I carry on scrolling down the page.

Then something catches my eye.

Amongst the handful of Toby Sheridans who don't have a profile picture set, and instead are showing the default white-silhouette-man-on-grey-background, is one which is similar yet different. It's the same silhouette, except this one's wearing dark sunglasses. And next to the picture, under his name, is written:

Studied at Gardensview Upper School.

That school is in a neighbouring town, no more than three or four miles from here. What are the chances that there are two Toby Sheridans locally, with this one wanting to hide his identity just as much as the other? I click on his name and his profile loads.

It seems to take an age.

But when it finally loads, I wish I hadn't bothered waiting.

The profile picture is the only thing showing in the newsfeed. He updated that four weeks ago, apparently, but it doesn't show me what was there before. Even clicking through to his pictures, to the Profile Pictures album, shows me nothing except the one that's currently displaying on his profile. Four weeks ago. Not long before he entered my life. Coincidence?

In any case, it's all that's there. And it has to be his account. It has to be.

Either way, there's nothing I can do with it. There's no information. There's not even a picture.

But I have gained one thing. I've found him. The tables have turned, and I'm the one watching him.

47

Even though I know I'm dreaming, it doesn't help. I'm being chased down the street, but my legs can't carry me at the speed I want to go. They're slipping, as if on ice, like a cartoon character trying to run away at speed. The dark figure moves slowly behind me, stalks me. Although he's only walking, he's gaining on me. My heartrate increases as I panic more and try to run faster. But the more I try, the more I slip. The slower I get. The more he gains.

I feel his breath on my shoulder. I smell it. It's foul. His warm, moist breath sends cold shivers down my spine.

I physically jolt in my bed as I wake. The noise wasn't in my dream.

It was here.

It was in the real world.

I hear it again, but quieter this time. It sounds like a bang, followed by a faint rattle. It's almost like an open shed door banging in the wind, except I know there is no wind. Any time there's even the slightest gust, it whistles and hums under the eaves of the roof. It's like a wind early-warning system.

I hear it again.

I pull the duvet up over my head, willing it to stop, to disappear. But I know it won't.

I convince myself it's the sound of someone trying to get in my front door. Or maybe my back door. What does that sound like? I don't know, I've never heard it.

I tell myself not to be so silly. I'm imagining things. There are all sorts of noises going on all the time. What if I heard a couple of bangs during the day? Then I'd think nothing of it. But under cover of darkness, everything seems much more sinister. Needlessly. That's all that's going on, I tell myself. I'm being daft and—

There's a scraping noise. It sounds like someone dragging something solid along concrete. I try to think where the concrete might be. It could be my back patio, or the path leading up to my house.

I desperately try to work out which direction the sound is coming from, but I don't want to put my head back outside the covers again. It's the most pathetic protective bubble, but it's helping. A bit.

I hear the banging noise again. It's definitely coming from outside the front of the house. I think.

I take a deep breath and pull back the duvet. I wish to God I didn't leave my bedroom door open at night. The landing on the other side of the threshold is pitch black, although my bedroom is lit up slightly by the streetlight outside. If the door was closed, I'd feel much safer. But I never close it. Never have. When you live alone it seems kind of pointless, but that might have to change.

I make my way slowly over towards the window, making sure I tread carefully lest the sound of a creaking floorboard alert someone to my presence.

When I get to the window, I stand for a moment and steel myself before pressing the side of my face against the wall and pulling back the curtain slightly. I can't see much from this angle, so I try to push my head further into the window recess without disturbing the curtains too much.

I have a better view of the street now, but I can't see anything happening. Everything is still. The cars are sitting gracefully on people's drives, as if fast asleep themselves. Curtains are closed all along the road. A few wheelie bins are out, but that wasn't the sound I heard. And anyway, who puts their bin out at — I look at the clock — twenty-past-three in the morning?

Maybe it was foxes. Do foxes bang and scrape? I guess so, if they're trying to get into a bin.

But something tells me the sounds I heard weren't a fox. They sounded too deliberate, too human. It's hard to describe how I know, but I just know.

I can feel my heart rate increasing again as I begin to panic. Ever since finding out Toby Sheridan's name and having his photo, I've felt much safer. Almost as if the power was starting to swing my way. But now I know that was all a façade. It was just my brain trying to protect me, trying to stop me from going mad over it all.

How can the power be starting to swing my way when I get freaked out by the slightest sound in the darkness? How can I say I feel safer? I've never been scared by night-time sounds in my life. Even as a kid I tended to sleep right through. I never needed a night-light, never got up in the middle of the night and climbed into my parents' bed. But now that feels like something I definitely want to do.

What's happening to me? I'm regressing back past my own childhood insecurities, and developing insecurities I didn't have even in childhood.

I'm falling apart.

I turn with my back to the wall and lean back against it, allowing the cold surface to seep into my shoulders and kidneys as I slowly slide down the wall, scraping my buttocks on the skirting board as I come to a rest on the soft carpet.

I bury my head in my hands and press my fists into my temples. I just want it all to go away. I need it all to be over. Because until there's a solid, definite conclusion to all this, I'm always going to be on edge. I'm always going to be jumping at every noise, suspicious of every car, worried on some level at every minute of every day.

And in that moment, I realise Kieran might actually have a point. More than that. He's right. I can't just do nothing, even though there's very little I can do.

Except for one thing.

48

My head's still foggy from the lack of sleep last night. Well, in the early hours of this morning, anyway.

I couldn't get back to sleep after hearing those noises. My brain wouldn't let me. But it had come up with an idea, one which I needed to share with Kieran the moment I thought he might be awake.

I left it until six o'clock, knowing this is the time his alarm goes off for work. He still sounded groggy when I phoned, but I was anything but.

I told him he was right. I told him I couldn't go on like this, that something needed to be done. And I had an idea as to what we could do.

I got Darryl's phone number from Kieran, and sent him a text.

One small question. I promise I won't ask any more. Is he working today? A x

Darryl seemed to have worked out pretty quickly who I

was and what I was talking about — I didn't want to make it any more explicit in black and white — and he replied within a minute.

OK. Will look when in. X

I told Kieran my plan. I presented it as if it was based on his plan, though. I mentioned his idea about going round to his place and getting some evidence. I lied slightly and said that in hindsight that didn't seem like such a bad idea, but that there was no way we were going to be able to get his home address from Darryl, or from anywhere else for that matter. But there was a way we could find out for ourselves.

I suggested to Kieran that we find out when Toby was next working, then follow him home covertly at the end of his shift. Then we'd know where he lived. We'd know what car he drove. We'd have more information, more to work with. Even if we didn't use it. After that, who knows? I haven't got that far yet. But it gives us options.

It seemed like hours before Darryl texted me again, but it was only just over two.

Yes. Due to finish at 3. Might be later. X

I could see Darryl was trying to be deliberately vague, not wanting to put anything in writing that could incriminate him. I texted him back to thank him. I presumed the reason for possibly being later was that police officers could never guarantee being able to finish a shift on time.

Still, that didn't matter. I had time.

After what seems like the longest day in history, Kieran comes and picks me up at around two-thirty. The police station is only ten minutes away, even in traffic, so it leaves us plenty of time. There's a public car park opposite the police station's staff car park. That's where we'll wait for Toby Sheridan to finish work. Kieran's brought a pair of binoculars over with him. I don't ask why he owns binoculars. I don't think I want to know.

'You sure you want to do this?' he asks, at my front door before we leave.

'I'm sure,' I say. 'Are you?'

'Course. Anyway, you don't drive. You'd stand out like a sore thumb trying to follow him on a skateboard.'

I laugh, for the first time in as long as I can remember. I don't know whether it's optimism or just a release of tension, but I let it happen anyway.

We stand at the top of my front steps, in silence for a few moments before Kieran speaks again.

'So. You ready?'

I swallow and take a deep breath.

'Yep. Ready.'

49

We pull up in the public car park with a good view of the police station's staff car park. There are brown metal gates across the entrance, which whir open every now and again to let a car in or out.

You could cut the atmosphere with a knife, and I'm almost worried that Toby Sheridan might somehow be able to sense the tension from where he is and know something's going on. I can hear my heartbeat in my chest, the blood pulsing in my eardrums.

'You alright?' Kieran asks.

'Yeah. Fine,' I lie.

All of a sudden, this seems like a really bad idea. What the hell are we doing here? Even though I've had all day to think about this – indeed, I *have* been thinking about it all day – it's now real. I'm actually here, watching the entrance to the police station car park, waiting for the man who's made my life hell. And then what?

And then we start up the car and follow him home. But why?

I'm not entirely sure myself, but I know I need to do this. I need to know who he is. I need a hold on him. I need something. Even just knowing what car he drives will give me security. I'll be able to spot him a mile off if he's following me again.

But that's the thing. He's been silent for a while now. Maybe he's left me alone. What good would it do finding out that he drives a red Citroën, for example? What am I going to do with that? Become instantly suspicious of every red Citroën I see? Edge slowly up towards every red car I see parked on the street, getting closer and closer until I can be sure the badge isn't a Citroën one?

I worry that I might be torturing myself. He hasn't done anything since making eye contact with me that day at the police station. I didn't recognise any emotion on his face, but he could well have been as shocked as I was. Maybe he just hid it better.

Would that have been enough to scare him off? The realisation that I'd spoken to the police, that I'd recognised him. Knowing that if he did anything else, I'd be able to tell them exactly who this man is, despite how well he covered his tracks. But then again, he could only have so much confidence in how well he'd done so far. He could never be certain that I didn't have *any* evidence. All he could have is confidence in the covering up he'd done. He wasn't to know I had literally nothing.

Maybe seeing me at the police station that day made him

realise things were a little too close for comfort. But somehow I doubt it. Deep down, I think he's restructuring his whole approach. He'll be back, but in a different way. And in the meantime I'm left wondering why and how, if at all. And that wouldn't be great for anyone's mental health, least of all mine.

The gates to the police station car park begin to move apart, and Kieran raises his binoculars in front of his eyes.

The nose of a car appears – a big black 4x4 – a Range Rover, I think.

Kieran shakes his head.

'Blonde woman.'

He puts the binoculars back in his lap, and I try to stifle a laugh.

Again, nervous tension.

'What's funny?' he asks.

'This,' I reply. 'Us sitting here in a car park, spying on people with binoculars. It's just bizarre.'

Kieran looks at me as though I've hurt his feelings.

'I don't mean it like that,' I say. 'It's just... Honestly, I'm sorry. I'm just getting so worked up about the whole thing, it's put my nerves right on edge. I have to either laugh or cry.'

I see Kieran's jaw tighten a split second before he puts his hand on my upper leg and squeezes, before letting go. It's his way of trying to reassure me. The familiarity of the contact buzzes inside me.

I look at the clock on the dashboard. It's three minutes to three. Just as I go to look away from the clock, it ticks over onto the next minute. 14.58.

Realistically speaking, I know the gates aren't going to open at three o'clock with him pulling out in his car. Even if he finishes his shift on time, I presume he's going to have to change out of uniform, maybe have a chat with a colleague, grab his stuff. And that's if he finishes on time. What if he's out taking a witness statement somewhere? What if that takes him another hour or two? What if someone's tipped him off and he hasn't even come in today, but is sitting somewhere else, watching us?

I look around furtively, but I can't spot anyone else sitting in any other cars. There are people walking along the footpath, but none of them are him.

The time seems to take an eternity to pass, but pass it does. Slowly.

I watch every single minute tick past on the dashboard. There isn't a number between 14.57 and 15.21 that I don't see, but a few seconds after it ticks over onto 15.21, the gates open again. I know it instinctively, but Kieran peers through his binoculars and confirms it for me.

'It's him.'

50

Kieran fumbles to start the car engine, and I take the binoculars from his lap, putting them in the glove box. Finally, the engine starts and we pull away.

Sheridan's in a silver Volkswagen Golf. It won't be the easiest car to spot again if we lose it, but there's only one car between us as we all wait to pull out onto the main road.

I shuffle down in my seat slightly, feeling my feet press against the end of the footwell, trying to keep myself out of the line of sight. I rest my arm on the door and put my hand to my forehead as if shielding myself from the sun.

There's a gap in the traffic, and Sheridan turns left. The car between us turns right. Kieran goes to pull out to follow Sheridan, but I stop him.

'Wait. Go after the next one.'

'But the gap's huge. I can—'

'Just wait,' I say. I'd feel much more comfortable with another car between us again. If we're following right behind him, he's bound to spot us. He need only look in his rear-view mirror, which a well-trained driver – a police officer, say – would do often. This way, we're close enough and can keep him in sight without blowing our cover.

Kieran pulls out and we follow Sheridan at a two-car distance for the next two miles, out onto the country roads. My parents used to take me out walking in these hills when I was a kid. Every Sunday morning we'd wake up, have breakfast and head off in the car. We'd walk for hours, occasionally stopping at a country pub for lunch and a drink. It was almost a ritual. But now my memory of this area would be spoilt forever, eternally tainted by association with the scumbag two cars in front of us.

The line of traffic starts to slow down as we reach a roundabout. The turning to the left heads off to another big town about seven miles down the road; straight ahead and right leads to a couple of small villages. I keep my eye on Sheridan's car as it heads straight over the roundabout.

'Shit,' Kieran says, and I realise straightaway why. The car between us has turned right. 'There's nothing I can do,' he says. 'I'll have to slow down a bit, put some distance between us.'

I lean across and look at the speedo on the dashboard. He's doing a steady forty-five in a sixty zone already, and Sheridan's not exactly pulling away from us. If we go any slower, it'll look really suspicious.

'Alice, I swear he keeps looking in his rear view mirror.'

These are words I don't want to hear. I tell myself it's not true, and I tell Kieran, too.

'Don't worry. Just keep a distance. He probably won't be able to see anything from where he is. The sun'll be bouncing off our windscreen.' True enough, we're driving towards the low mid-afternoon sun, but I know I only made that comment to make myself and Kieran feel better.

Kieran slows his speed down a little. 42. 40. 37. By the time we're down to 35mph, we're still gaining on Sheridan's VW. Just as I start to wonder what's going on, a plume of thick black diesel smoke comes out of the back of his exhaust and the Golf takes off up the road.

'Fuck fuck fuck,' Kieran says. I've never heard him swear so much as I have in the past day or two.

He puts his foot down as far as it'll go, but his Hyundai doesn't have anything like the power Sheridan's Golf does.

'He's spotted us,' I say, stating the obvious.

'What now?'

I think for a moment. 'I don't know. Follow him.'

He's doing his best, but the VW is pulling further and further away. There's a sweeping left-hand bend that heads into a wooded area and we lose sight of him for what seems like hours but must only have been a couple of seconds. We reach the bend ourselves, though, and get him back in sight.

Sheridan's brake lights come on as he reaches the next roundabout, but he's not indicating. Still, he goes round the roundabout and heads off to the right. I have no idea where that road goes, but he's long gone before we even get as far as the roundabout.

'We've lost him,' Kieran says, the dejection clear in his voice.

'He wouldn't have led us to his house anyway. He spotted us miles off. Probably from the moment we left the car park. There's no way he's heading home. He's deliberately thrown us off the trail.'

Kieran goes right round the roundabout and back onto the road we've just been on, in the opposite direction. He stops a couple of hundred yards up the road in a lay-by.

We're both silent for a good minute.

'Now what?' he says eventually.

I don't know what to say. I shake my head, close my eyes and let out the tension I've been holding in all day.

If I thought there was any chance that Toby Sheridan might have given up tormenting me, I'm now as sure as I can be that I've only got more hell to come.

51

That was really *stupid.* Really *fucking stupid.*

I don't like having my hand forced, Alice. And that hand is now bouncing off my dashboard as I pound away at it, the windscreen misting up as I yell at the top of my voice.

This isn't the way it was supposed to happen. Not like this. It has to be done the right way.

Don't get me wrong. I admire your courage. You're finally stepping up to the mark. But you're not thinking for yourself. You're still beholden to that pathetic little weasel you used to call your boyfriend. That was all his idea, wasn't it? That's why you were in his car. The silver Hyundai Getz. FD06 TRG. I'd know it a mile off.

You see, I know a lot more than you think I do, Alice. I knew all about you before you even set eyes on me. Before I even spoke to you. Because that's how this works. That's how this has *to work. You do understand that, don't you?*

You've come so far. But that was stupid. She wouldn't have done that.

She knew how to play her hand. And she wouldn't have gone running to her ex-boyfriend for help. That is not the sign of a strong, independent woman, Alice. That is a sign of regression. You've gone backwards, slipped back to what you were before.

I'm disappointed in you.

I'm disappointed in myself.

I thought we could do better than this. I thought we were really heading in the right direction. You were following all the right moves, doing all the right things. All the things I'd predicted you'd do.

It's easy to predict what someone will do when you've studied them as closely as I've studied you. As closely as I've studied your behaviour, your patterns. And there's a hell of a lot of fucking patterns there, Alice. A lot of patterns. You're one big pattern. A creature of habit.

Deep down, anyway.

But I know there's something still deeper than that. Something that resonates. That's what's driving you, Alice. But only when you're in control. Only when you're making the decisions. Only when you're thinking clearly.

You haven't left me with many choices now.

I need to ask you a question. Is this the way you want to play the game? Because if it is, we can certainly play it that way. Absolutely fine with me. No problemo. You just carry on. But bear in mind I'll be playing the same game as you regardless. And you don't want to see me playing that particular game. I prefer it my way, and I think you will too.

I'm watching. I'm watching closely, waiting to see what your next move is. How you react. How you respond. Because that will steer this whole sorry saga. That'll show the direction we move in, where we go, what happens. It will define the endgame.

The choice is yours. You're the one in control, Alice. You have *to be the one in control. That's the whole point of all this. She was always in control. She always knew what was the right thing to do. She never wavered. And she never relied on other people to get it done for her.*

I know you can do this. I know you can kick out on your own. You have to. You have to prove me right and prove yourself right. I need to know her spirit lives on.

Because if I'm wrong — if her spirit isn't within you — I'm going to be very disappointed, Alice.

And you won't like me when I'm disappointed.

52

Kieran parks his car up outside my house and we just sit there. Minutes pass, but neither of us says anything. Both of us knows what the other is thinking, because that's what we're thinking too.

'What are you going to do?' he asks me.

'I'm going to go inside and get absolutely shitfaced,' I reply. And the weird thing is, it's not that I want to drink to forget, or drink to de-stress. It's because I no longer give a fuck. I want to down a bottle of wine and enjoy it. Because I deserve to. Because whatever comes next is not going to be enjoyable, so I might as well make the most of it.

'Are you sure that's wise?'

I shrug. 'Probably not, but when did wisdom ever do me any good?'

'When did drink ever do you any good,' he says, more as a statement than a question. He pauses for a moment. 'Do you want me to join you?'

Any other time, that would be an easy question to answer. But the truth is both yes and no. Yes, I'd love a drinking buddy. Especially one who knows what I'm going through right now. But I don't think it would be a good idea to have Kieran in the house when we'll both be drinking. That didn't work out too well last time.

'I tell you what,' I say. 'Why don't we go out? Got to be more fun than sitting at home on my own drinking. We can grab a bite to eat first, too.'

He seems to consider this for a moment. I can tell what's going through his mind. At least this way he'll be able to keep an eye on me, make sure I don't drink *too* much, ensure that I'm safe.

'Yeah, alright,' he says. 'I'll run back and get changed. Pick you up in an hour?'

'Nope,' I reply, as I get out of the car. 'You're not driving. You're going to enjoy yourself too. I'll meet you in town.'

I close the car door before he can protest, and head into my house.

Almost immediately, I feel less safe. I'm glad I'll be going out again in an hour. It sounds utterly bizarre that I should feel safer walking the streets than I do in my own home, but at least there's safety in numbers. Here, alone, I'm vulnerable. And he's been in here at least twice before.

The thought gives me the creeps, but with the new locks on the doors I feel safer. Still not *safe*, though.

I wonder what it will take to make me feel completely safe again.

And the scary thing is, I think I know the answer.

53

We opt for a pub dinner. Cheap and cheerful, with the added advantage that it won't look or feel like a date. Just two friends, out getting some food.

Afterwards, we head on to a couple of town-centre bars. I try to steer Kieran away from Zizi's, but we pay a flying visit to Bar Chico.

The alcohol makes me feel more comfortable. It gives me confidence. Don't get me wrong, I'm not an aggressive or loud drunk. I'm not someone who gets bolshy or arrogant after a couple of drinks. It's just not my style. But I worry less about stuff. Things wash over me. I'm happier, more confident.

The drinks start to flow, and before I know it we're doing shots. At the start of the night I was secretly half-tempted to take it easy, but that's out of the question now. The more I drink, the less I care. And the less I care, the happier I am.

Eventually, the bars start to thin out as people head home, and the time bells start to ring. Kieran walks me home, like the gentleman he is. I make a point of telling him I'm not going to sleep with him and I'm not even going to invite him in. I try to make it sound jokey and friendly, but I don't think he takes it that way. It's fine. He'll have forgotten I said it by the morning.

Like the gentleman he is, Kieran leaves me at the end of my front path and staggers off back down the road.

My head's swimming. I sit on the floor in my hallway, enjoying the cooler air at this lower level. The walls seem to be moving, and my wallpaper has an odd watery effect going on. I don't feel sick, but I can feel my heart racing. That'll be the shots. It's making me anxious. I know it's body feeding mind, but when did logic and common sense ever matter?

I pull myself up to my feet and walk through to the living room, with the intention of flopping out on the sofa. No, that'd be a bad idea. Then I'd fall asleep and wake up here in a few hours with a stiff neck and a raging headache. I need to stay awake, and for that I need to stay standing.

So I stand in the middle of my living room, thinking that I should probably go and down a couple of pints of water. But that would involve moving. Standing here is nice. I like it. I can get water after. I just need to stay awake. If I go to sleep now, I'll have one hell of a hangover in the morning.

As I stand in the middle of the room, my gaze is drawn back to the space on the mantelpiece where that photo frame stood. It's almost like a magnetic attraction. I can't avoid it. It's the elephant in the room.

Even though there's nothing there, the space still taunts me. Just knowing that he was there, that he had his grubby mitts on it. Before I can realise what I'm doing, I pick up the other two photo frames and hurl them at the wall. The wood cracks and splinters, and one of the frames breaks into two right-angled pieces. The glass smashes, and sharp fragments fall to the floor. The wallpaper is dented. I don't give a fuck.

It felt good.

The first thing I notice is the blood pumping in my ears as I bend down and tip the wooden coffee table over. Magazines and books fly through the air, sounding like a flock of birds taking off. The sofas follow, and everything ends up in a heap in the middle of the room.

I don't know why. But it works. It's a release of tension.

I don't give a fuck about how I'm going to sort it all out. It's a means to an end.

I stroll into the kitchen, walking in a straight line for the first time in a few hours, pull out the cutlery drawer and tip the whole lot out onto the floor. The knives and forks clatter onto the lino with a terrible din, a few of them bouncing and hitting my feet and legs. I don't care.

After a few seconds, I start to calm down a little. I look down at my feet, and I notice that a piece of cutlery — possibly a knife — has nicked the inside front of my leg, just above the ankle. There's a tiny rivulet of blood making its way slowly down towards my foot.

I snort loudly, grab a bottle of water from the cupboard and head upstairs to bed.

54

The thin shaft of light hits me right between the eyes, and I curse myself for not closing my curtains properly before going to bed last night. That's the least of my worries, though. Within a split second I pick up the vile taste in my mouth. It's a taste that tells me the previous evening was heavily driven by alcohol, as if the pounding headache wasn't a giveaway in itself.

Why do I do this? Why? I didn't need to drink. I could have just pulled myself together, got my head in the right place and enjoyed a nice quiet evening in front of the telly. Why did I feel the need to go out and get absolutely shitfaced?

I try to think back. I went out with Kieran. We got some food, hit a few bars, then I...

The anger rises up inside me again, almost like a Pavlovian reaction. Just remembering what I did when I got home last night allows all those feelings and emotions to resurface. But they're very quickly replaced by regret and the knowledge that I'm going to have to tidy it all up.

The house needed cleaning anyway. I've been letting things like that slip a bit recently. But I hadn't expected to be upending furniture and emptying out cutlery drawers when I got home last night. My head pounds as I remember the racket the knives and forks made as they clanged together and fell in a heap on the floor. Why did I do that? What was I hoping to achieve? I guess I was releasing tension, making myself feel better. But what have I become when the only way I can deal with stress is to destroy things? Then again, aren't we all guilty of that?

I roll over and look at my alarm clock. 9.36am. That's one hell of a lie-in. I probably didn't get to bed until about 1.30, though, so it's about right. Eight hours usually does me fine. But today I reckon I could quite easily stay in bed for the rest of the day. I've got a house to tidy, though, and I feel as though I need to punish myself by getting up and doing it now. I don't know if it's healthy for me to be guilt-tripping myself, but there we go.

Getting out of bed is a mission. I tell myself I'll go downstairs, tidy up the mess I made last night, then go back to bed. The rest can wait. Having a house that's a bit untidy is one thing, but if someone calls round and finds my furniture in a heap in the middle of the living room and my cutlery all over the kitchen floor, I'm going to have some explaining to do.

I pick last night's dress off the floor and put that on. It doesn't matter. I'll put it in the wash when I come back up.

It smells faintly of sambuca, as if I spilt some down it at some point last night. There's another smell too, which I can't quite define. Something musty, almost smoky.

I yawn, pick up the bottle of water from my bedside table and slug half of it back without stopping for breath. Then I set off on my long, torturous walk downstairs.

I decide I'm probably best off starting with the living room. But when I get in there, something isn't quite right.

I stand for a moment, my brain not making any sense of what I'm seeing. My sofas are exactly where they should be, at right-angles to each other, in the corner of the room, with the standard lamp and drinks table between them. The coffee table is in the middle of the room, magazines and books stacked neatly on top of it.

I rush through into the kitchen, expecting to see the cutlery all over the floor, but there's nothing. I fling the drawer open, and there it all is, neatly placed in the right compartments, as if nothing ever happened.

But I *know* something happened. I did it.

I go back into the living room and look at the mantelpiece. The picture frames are gone, but the dent is still there in the wallpaper where one hit the wall. I walk over and crouch down, looking in the pile of the carpet for any fragments of glass. I can't find any.

I push myself back onto my feet and head back into the kitchen, where I open the pedal bin. The photo frames are in there, a couple of large shards of glass nestled on top of them. This is exactly where I would have put them too, if I had tidied up. But did I? I don't remember doing it. No, I'm sure I didn't. I just grabbed a bottle of water and went upstairs.

I look down at my feet. I remember something catching the inside of my leg when the cutlery clattered to the floor. It drew blood.

Yes. It's still there. I didn't just dream the whole thing.

I follow my train of thought from that moment onwards. At that point, the living room was a tip and there was cutlery all over the kitchen floor. I can see that vividly. And then... Then I took a bottle of water from the cupboard – I can see myself doing it – and I went upstairs. The next time I came back downstairs was just now. I *know* it was.

So what the fuck has happened?

55

I rush over to the front door and pull the handle down. The door opens. It was unlocked.

Did I lock it last night? I must have done. I always do. I'm so security conscious at the moment. But then again, I'd had a lot to drink. Can I *guarantee* that I locked the door? To be perfectly honest, I can't guarantee anything. My memory has patches in it, as it tends to when I've drunk this much. I must have locked it. I'm obsessive about it. And I've been even more careful recently.

I rush back up the stairs and grab my phone from the bedside table. I fumble to unlock it, then call Kieran.

He seems to take an age to answer. I can only assume he's not feeling brilliant this morning either. Eventually, though, he does answer.

'Hey. What's up?' he says.

'Nothing. Listen, did you come in the house with me last

night?' I know he didn't — at least I think I do — but I need to check anyway.

'No, I waited at the end of the path. Why?'

'But did you see me go inside and lock the door?'

He hesitates for a moment as he thinks. 'Uh, I saw you go in, but I don't know if you locked it or not. How would I know from the outside?'

He's got a point. All I can do is rely on my own memory to be correct.

'How long did you wait after I went in?' I ask.

'Wait? I didn't. Why would I stand out in the cold looking at your closed door? Once you were in, I went home.'

'Did you see anyone around? Anyone walking down the street, sitting in a parked car, anything?'

'No, why?'

He answers a little too quickly for my liking.

'Are you sure?'

'I think I would've remembered, Alice. The streets weren't exactly thronging at that time of night. What's this all about? Has something happened?'

I swallow hard and try to think about how to word this. In the end, I avoid it completely.

'No, nothing. I heard some noises outside after you went and wondered what it was. Just scared me a bit, you know, with everything that's been going on recently. And after a couple of drinks my brain does some weird things, so I wanted to check everything was okay.'

Kieran's silent for a couple of moments. 'So why did you ask about the front door?'

Shit. 'Hmmm?'

'The front door. You asked me if I saw you lock it.'

'Oh. Yeah. I just wanted to check. Because I'd had a couple of drinks, and, y'know...'

'Did someone get in?'

'No. Why?'

'So why does it matter whether you locked it or not?'

I really don't know what to say. I've dug myself into a hole and I can't get out. 'I dunno. Just wanted to check, make sure I wasn't going mad. But it's fine. Really. You got any plans for today?'

I desperately want to get off the phone and disappear. I don't know where, but I need to go. At the same time, though, I can't just leave this conversation like this. I need to make it normal again.

'Getting rid of this bloody hangover, mainly. But you've got me worried now. What's this about the door?'

I sigh. 'I came downstairs this morning and it was unlocked. Don't worry about it. I'd had a few drinks and my mind's been in some weird places recently, so I probably just forgot to lock it. Honestly, don't worry.

'Right,' he says. He doesn't sound convinced, but has clearly noticed that I want to change the subject. 'You got much planned today then?'

'Nothing much,' I say, trying to sound as normal as possible. 'Got a bit of housework to do. Then I'll probably go back to bed, to be honest. I doubt I feel much better than you.'

He laughs, and I tell him I'll speak to him later.

As soon as I'm off the phone, I start pacing the living room. I can't escape the truth: I no longer feel safe here. Not only that, but I *can't* feel safe here. Even with the new locks, all evidence points to the fact that he's still finding a way in, or I can't trust myself to lock my own doors at night. I don't know which prospect is scarier. But right now I can't entertain either of them. He's been here. Last night. I know he has. There's no way in hell I'd be able to tidy up the kitchen and living room from the state it was in and not know about it. Not when I remember making the mess so vividly.

I'm sitting in a ball in the middle of the living room floor, holding my knees up to my chest. It's almost foetal.

My phone pings as a text message arrives. It's from Kieran. I read it without unlocking the screen.

Here if you need me. X

But I don't. I don't feel comfortable. I have no idea who I can trust right now. And when things get to that stage, there are only two people you can rely on. I unlock my phone and call their number.

'Hello, dear,' Mum says as she answers the phone. She always does. She probably even says it when she gets sales calls.

'Hi Mum,' I say, trying to ensure my voice sounds calm and not on edge. Mum's always been the first person to spot when something isn't right with me. Then again, that's a mum's job, isn't it? 'How's things?'

'Oh, fine, fine. Your dad's just out in the shed fiddling around with some motor or other. How are things with you?'

Dad's a retired engineer, but the bug has never left him.

The moment he retired he built an enormous outbuilding – affectionately known as 'the shed' – in the garden. It's almost the same size as the house, but calling it a shed somehow seems to make it more reasonable as an extravagance.

'Fine. Well, not ideal, to be honest. I've got a leak. Burst water main. They reckon it'll take a few days to fix it, and in the meantime they're moving us out. I just thought it might be a good opportunity to come up and see you guys for a bit, if you don't mind a temporary lodger.'

'Oh no! Of course not, sweetie,' Mum says. 'I hope nothing's damaged, is it?'

'Shouldn't be, no. They want to do some repairs and stuff, though, and I've got no running water so...'

'Don't worry, you can come and stay here. I'll send your dad over to collect you. He could do with getting out of the house.'

'No! It's fine. Honestly. I can get the train. It's only two stops.' I chastise myself for replying a little too keenly, and hope she hasn't spotted something's amiss.

'Don't be silly. You can't walk through town with all your–'

'I'm already in town,' I lie. 'They wanted us out sharpish, so I grabbed my bag and went. Thought I'd ring you on the way. But if you can't spare the room, don't worry, I can always–'

My diversionary guilt-tripping tactic appears to work. 'Oh no, sweetie. Of course we can spare the room. What time will you be arriving?'

I look at the clock and make a few mental calculations.

'Give it an hour and a half or so? I want to get a couple of things in town first. I'll ring you when I've got an ETA.'

Once the call's over, I run upstairs, grab the suitcase down from on top of the wardrobe and start packing.

56

They're lovely people, your parents. Richard and Linda. Richard John and Linda Margaret. Twenty-fourth of November 1954 and the eighth of March 1953, respectively. That surprised me. I never had your mother down as liking the younger man.

I'm sure you'll have a pleasant stay at 86 Sundown Avenue. Your father's replaced the crumbling old front wall with a new one. He had to move the rose bush to re-do the footings, but it looks great now. You're going to love it.

I must admit I got a little frisson of excitement when I heard you ask if you could go and stay with them. A change of location! We're going on tour! The thrill of the chase!

It matters very little to me where you are. Physical location means nothing. Because you're always here. And I'm always watching.

Just like I watched you coming home last night. Or this morning, I should say.

Just like I watched you forget to lock your door. Such a silly little thing, but what a huge impact it had.

Because that's the way the world works. Small actions can have enormous consequences. One person's decision or lack of care can change everything.

Have you heard of the butterfly effect? It's a critical part of chaos theory, but that's a subject for another day. Needless to say, chaos can be reined in or avoided with careful planning and forethought. We have the power to control the future, if only we care to use it.

The butterfly effect postulates that the smallest, most seemingly inconsequential action can have far-reaching and potentially devastating consequences.

Potentially devastating.

Potentially.

How often do you do things without thinking? I'd hazard a guess that it's far more often than you think. How many homeless people do you walk past on a daily basis? A couple? A few? Let's be conservative and say one. How many people do you think walk past him each day? And what do you think that does to a man, being castigated and ignored by his peers, just because he's fallen on hard times? What's to say your walking past him wasn't the straw that broke the camel's back, the one that convinced him to end it all? Because maybe he'd been counting to a hundred. Perhaps he told himself that he'd end his own life that day if one hundred people walked past without acknowledging him. One hundred people. But the person who inadvertently ended his life was you. Because you didn't think. Because you didn't care to think. Because you didn't think to care. What if that man had something burning deep inside him, a plan, an invention that could end world hunger or rid the world of nuclear threats? Not only did you walk past a man, and not only did you unknowingly condemn him to death, but you're now responsible for global hunger and the coming nuclear holocaust.

It's an outlandish demonstration, I know, but it bears thought. The theory is sound. It stands up to scrutiny. It is a thing. And one day there will be a tiny, seemingly insignificant event that leads to devastation and destruction. What if Alois Hitler had decided to pull out and wank over Klara's tits? I'm willing to wager he didn't consider that he was creating the greatest tyrant in modern history while he was grunting and groaning. Ja! Ja! Ja! Not a care in the world.

We should all have care and consideration. Everything we do affects someone. We aren't satellites; the whole planet, the whole ecosystem, the whole of human nature is congruent. It all feeds into the greater system, and we all get back what we put in. Carelessness and selfishness leads to... Well, I think you get the message.

The interesting thing is that the butterfly effect can be gamed, if you know enough about human psychology. Which is why every move I make is bringing you closer to me. You might not know it, you might not feel it, but it's happening.

Your little temper tantrum might have seemed out of the ordinary, but it was always going to happen. It had been coming a long time. Because you don't know how to cope with pressure. Yet.

I tidied up for you, by the way. But you know that already.

I had to be quiet so I didn't wake you. Do you have any idea how long it takes to pick up individual pieces of cutlery and put them back in the drawer without making a sound? And those sofas! They're pretty hefty considering they were only £798 from DFS. Picking those up and putting them back the right way round in silence wasn't easy.

Still, it's done now. And now we move on to the next phase, Alice. Because I need you here. I need you close. I warn you, I might have to go to quite some lengths to achieve that, but I'm willing to. Because you're worth it, Alice. You're worth every damn second.

57

The short drive home from the station to my parents' house is tinged with an odd atmosphere. It takes me a few moments to work out what it is, but I realise it's probably down to the way things were left the last time I saw Mum and Dad, when I asked them to leave after they turned up at my house out of the blue. The timing was dreadful, not that I've been having any particularly fantastic times recently.

'Look, I just wanted to say sorry about last time,' I say, punctuating the silence. I hate having to apologise for anything. Generally speaking, I try to avoid doing anything that means I'm going to have to apologise in the first place.

'Don't worry about it. I told your mum we shouldn't turn up unannounced. She wouldn't like it if someone did it to her.'

I can tell we're both thinking that's not true. Mum seems to think that people should spend their days visiting each other. She doesn't seem to understand that even if she's not busy working, other people are.

'How's life in the shed?' I ask him.

He chuckles.

'Peaceful. I'm reconditioning a vintage Atco 2-stroke. Off an old Suffolk Punch, the bloke reckoned.'

I nod, pretending to look impressed. It doesn't sound particularly peaceful to me.

'Your mum's worried,' he says, in a way which makes me think he's been wanting to say this since I got in the car. 'She tasked me with using the car journey to probe about your health.'

He accentuates this last word, and I know exactly what he means by it. That's what I love about Dad; he's open and honest, my ally against Mum's funny little ways.

'I'll tell her I reckon you're fine, of course. Stop her from harping on. But all I will say is if there's anything you want to talk about, anything you need, just shout. Alright?'

I put my hand on his knee and squeeze, without saying a word.

We arrive back at the house a few minutes later.

I've been thinking about what Dad said. I'm going to have to come clean to them about the non-existent water leak and tell them about the whole Toby Sheridan thing. But how much detail do I give them? I know what'll happen if I tell them everything. Mum will start to give me all sorts of suggestions or, worse, go behind my back and speak to the police or something. It isn't worth that sort of risk. I need to make out that everything's in hand, that it's all being sorted and I just need some space.

Oddly, as soon as I think about that, I realise that not telling them had never been an option. They're my parents. And not being able to talk about how I feel hasn't helped so far. That's what my counsellor is there for, but I've not been open and honest with her, either. Mandy's just... Well, Mandy's Mandy. She's great support; a fantastic person to cover your arse, but in terms of actually putting together a coherent plan of action she's probably not the best. Kieran's been wonderfully supportive, particularly since getting Darryl involved. But again, what can he do? The one set of people I should be able to rely on — the police — have been so completely unhelpful that Kieran's help and support unfortunately means very little.

Mum asks me how things are going, as she puts the kettle on to make a cup of tea.

'So so,' I answer. 'Seems that bad luck's a bit like buses. All comes at once.'

'Oh? What's wrong?'

'Well, there's the water leak,' I say, deciding it's probably best to keep that in there. If they think I've come here just because of Toby Sheridan, they'll only overreact. Mum especially. 'That's causing all sorts of havoc. And there's this weird thing that's been happening recently. There's a bloke who's been following me about and sending me messages and things.'

Mum stops and looks at me. I can see the concern on her face.

'Don't worry, the police are involved. It's being sorted.'

'What sort of bloke?' she asks.

'I dunno, just some bloke who's taken a fancy to me.'

Is that why Toby Sheridan's following me? I guess it's possible. But why the torment? Why not bunches of flowers or gifts left outside my house? Why break in and leave photos?

Mum puts the spoon back in the sugar pot and comes and sits next to me at the kitchen table.

'Alice, I want you to be honest with me. How long has this been going on?'

Great. Her mother's instinct kicks in.

'A little while. Honestly, don't worry.'

She's silent for a couple of moments.

'There's no water leak, is there?'

I look her in the eye, ready to lie to her, but I can tell that she already knows. She didn't ask it as a question; it was a statement that she wanted me to confirm.

'No.'

She nods. 'I looked on the water board's website. They always list any current issues. There's nothing mentioned.' My first instinct is to castigate her for checking up on me, for not believing me, but I realise it's probably justified. 'You came here because of this man, didn't you? You were all on edge when we saw you last, too. It's been going on a while, hasn't it?'

Dad comes into the kitchen at this point, and I let it all

out. I tell them everything. Right from the start, every single detail. Mum's brow furrows and I can see from the look on her face that she's feeling every word of it. Dad, on the other hand, leans against the kitchen counter, his jaw pulsating as he grinds his jaw.

When I finish telling them, it's Dad who speaks first.

'And what if he comes here?'

His voice is stressed. Generally speaking, he's the most placid bloke in the world, but he doesn't handle situations like this well.

'He won't,' I say.

'How do you know that? If he's managed to find out where you live and work, and has broken into your house, what's to say he won't rock up here and do the same?'

Mum stands and places a hand on his shoulder.

'Richard...'

'You need proper protection, Alice. If this guy is dangerous, you need to be somewhere where he won't find you. This is the first place he'll come and look.'

Although it might sound heartless when he says it, I can tell Dad's just scared. Mum's scared too, but she's stuck between a rock and a hard place.

'Richard, we can't turf her out onto the streets. He's very unlikely to come up here and—'

'How do you know?' he says, interrupting her. 'He could find her here easily. She isn't safe. It's putting us at risk too. Of course I want to help her, but what can we do? We're not bodyguards.' He looks at me, realising he's been speaking as if I'm not even in the room. 'Alice, we desperately want to help you and protect you. You're our daughter. But this man sounds dangerous. If you stay here, you're still at risk. We're all at risk. Surely there must be somewhere safer you can stay. We're only thinking of you.'

I can see his point, but I don't have anywhere else. 'Like where?'

He thinks for a moment. 'Well what about your Uncle George?'

'He's out of the country,' Mum says, reminding Dad that George and Sylvia live in New Zealand for six months of the year. Her tone says *And you should know that — he's your brother*.

I can see Dad trying to think of someone else, but there isn't anyone. I'm an only child, Mum's an only child and Dad's brother is on the other side of the world.

'We could ask Jack and Tara,' he says. I recognise their names as Mum and Dad's friends from the local ballroom dancing class. The four of them only ever went once, but were united in their realisation that perhaps that particular class wasn't for them.

'Don't be daft!' Mum says, scoffing. 'They've got a young baby. They don't want to be put under that sort of pressure.'

It's always lovely to hear your parents tell you that you're *pressure*.

'And what else do you suggest?' Dad asks her, challenging her. 'There's no way he'd be able to find her there. Besides which, they live on the top floor of a block of flats. He can't exactly just climb in through the window.'

'That's not the point, Richard. They don't want to feel unsafe with a young baby.'

'They won't be unsafe. There's no obvious connection between us and them.'

I feel as if I'm being passed from pillar to post.

'Listen, don't worry about it,' I say. 'I don't want to drag anyone else into this. I'm sure I'll be fine.'

'Nonsense. Your dad's just worried about you. We both are. We want you to be safe, but he's right. You won't be any safer here than you are at home. If he was able to find your address, he'll find ours very easily. Don't forget I was on the parish council for four years. Our name and address is everywhere.'

How could I forget? She never stopped banging on about it. That was probably part of the reason why she got voted off after her first term.

'What about Kieran?' Dad asks. 'Can't he stay with you? Bit of extra protection, I mean.'

'Richard, don't be stupid,' Mum says. 'They aren't together any more. And in any case, what's he going to do if this man breaks in and threatens Alice? Bake him a nice cake? Sit down and talk to him about the Crimean War?'

'You need an alarm and CCTV fitted,' Dad says. 'The full works. Anti-bump locks, window alarms, everything.'

'Richard, why should she have to live in a prison?'

'She shouldn't, but she should have the right to feel safe.' He turns to me. 'I'd do the lot here if I could, but...' He jerks his head in Mum's direction. She ignores it.

'I can't afford all that stuff,' I say. 'I've already had the locks changed.'

'Forget that,' Dad replies. 'We'll pay for it.' Before Mum can challenge him, he adds: 'Stay here tonight. I'll go out this afternoon and get all the gear. We'll go back to yours first thing and I'll fit it all. Should have it done by the end of the day.'

I smile and thank him.

I came here to feel more secure, to know that I was safe in the arms of my parents. But as much as they try to help, try to reassure me, I'm not entirely sure I feel any safer at all.

58

Dad went out yesterday afternoon and bought all the security gear as promised. I asked him to tell me how much he'd spent, so I could pay him back in time, but he wasn't having any of it. I can only imagine it was hundreds of pounds, if not more. The car boot is filled with cameras, alarm boxes, wiring and all sorts of stuff I don't recognise. Hopefully it'll be enough to dissuade Toby from coming anywhere near the house.

We got up at the crack of dawn this morning, ready for a quick breakfast and the drive back to mine. Dad wanted to start early to give him the best possible chance of getting everything in place for tonight. I woke up with an odd feeling of optimism. Maybe it was the act of getting up to watch the sunrise, having not had a single drop of alcohol the night before, or perhaps it was the recognition that I might actually be safer by the end of the day. Either way, I'm determined to embrace this positivity for as long as I can.

I try to get as much housework done as I can while Dad

fits all the security gear, but I feel as though I ought to take an active interest in what it all is.

I head outside and walk round to my front path. Dad's up a ladder, screwing a CCTV camera onto the front wall of the house.

'So how do these work?' I ask.

'They're wireless,' he replies, grunting as he tightens the screws. 'They'll run off your wifi router. It comes with some software that you install on your laptop or smartphone to view the images.'

This doesn't sound particularly secure to me. 'What about if the batteries run out? Or if my internet connection goes down?'

'It's plugged into the mains. Only the connectivity is wireless. And they have SD cards in them as well, so they'll still record even without an internet connection.'

'And if there's a power cut?' I ask.

'Backup battery. Trust me, they're safe. They're the best on the market.'

I trust him, but I'm living in a perpetual state of insecurity, so I'm not sure anything will ever totally convince me.

'What about at night? Do they have lights in case something happens in the dark?'

Dad, as always, entertains my silly questions without ever making me feel stupid. 'Sort of. They have infrared lights. It lights up the area as far as the camera's concerned. You can see the video footage almost as well as you can in the daytime, but it won't shine a visual light. Only the camera can pick up the infrared light. The human eye can't. So all a human would see is these little red LEDs around the camera barrel. They're what lights up the area for the camera.'

I make an impressed noise. 'I'm almost done with these. I've already put one on the back and one on the side of the house. That's all areas covered. Just got to set them up on the router, but I'll probably do the alarm next while we've still got light.'

I go to ask him if I can help at all, but I must have already asked a dozen times and he's not having any of it. This is man work, apparently.

'You'll have a box front and back,' he says. 'Both of them are full ringers. Most alarms only have a real one on the front and a dud one on the back, if that. Quite a few of them are dud on the front *and* the back, just to try and scare people off. They don't actually ring out. Both of these do. And if the alarm does ring out, you can set up to ten emergency contacts. It'll call them all and tell them your alarm is going off. I'll put mine and your mum's numbers in, and you should probably set it up for close friends, too. At least that way if it does go off you know there are people coming quickly. You can set it up with the emergency services, too, if you pay an annual fee. To be honest, though, we'd probably get here quicker than they would.'

He's got a point. The budget cuts in policing are all over the news at the moment. A lot of forces are merging their emergency services. Fat lot of good a fire engine will be if I'm pinned to the floor with a knife against my throat. What are they going to do, hose him off?

'I've also got sash jammers for your windows and magnetic bolts and a chain for your door. Always keep that on when you're opening it, just until you know who's there. Or, of course, you can look at the cameras on your phone.'

It all sounds very secure, I've got to admit. I feel more comforted. But there's still an uneasy feeling as to what happens at night. That's when I tend to feel most scared.

'Can you put a lock on my bedroom door?' I ask. 'It'd make me feel safer.'

'Sure,' he says, without questioning it. 'Although there's no way anyone is going to be able to get in the house after I've finished with it. They'd have more luck trying to break into Fort Knox.'

I doubt that somehow, but the sentiment's sweet.

A few hours later, he's finally finished and he heads home. I lock the doors, engage the magnetic bolts and put the chain across. I sit and watch the security cameras for a little while, panning, tilting and zooming to my heart's content, becoming familiar with their capabilities. They're certainly impressive.

I'm starting to feel hungry, so I think about having something to eat. I really fancy making a batch of pancakes. Quick, easy, and damn nice, too. I stand up and head back downstairs, before remembering that I don't have any milk. I used the last of it in a cup of tea before I headed out with Kieran the other night. With everything that's gone on since, I hadn't thought to replace it yet.

I go into the kitchen anyway, opening the cupboards and looking inside for inspiration for what I can have to eat.

Pasta? No. A can of soup? No. I open the fridge and look around in there too, and it takes a good few seconds for my eyes to register the significance of the plastic container of milk, sitting unopened in the door.

I never buy milk in plastic containers. I have it delivered in bottles by the milkman. It's something I've always done, probably because my parents always have.

My parents. I think about the possibility that Dad could've put it there. Maybe he thought he was helping me out. But wouldn't that have been a glass bottle, seeing as they have theirs delivered too? Not necessarily. They'll only have enough delivered for the two of them. Not enough to spare a bottle for little old me. Maybe he popped to the supermarket and left it there for me as a token that he's looking out for me.

I go to text him and ask, but think better of it. One thing I've realised recently is that sometimes it's better not to know.

59

I won't pretend I had a fantastic night's sleep, but it was an improvement.

First of all there was the milk incident. Even if it's the worst case scenario and it was a sick joke from Toby, he must've done it at the same time as he tidied up downstairs. When I left the door unlocked. Either way, the new security measures draw a line under all that. He's got no chance of getting anywhere near me now.

Secondly, I had to deal with my phone buzzing to let me know the motion sensor on my cameras had been triggered. The first time I almost shat myself, until I logged in and saw that it was just a couple walking past the end of my front path. I told myself I'd have to call Dad in the morning and ask him how to change the settings so it didn't buzz at me every time someone walked down the road, but it did twice more during the night. The second alert was because a cat had walked across my back garden, and the third was a car which had pulled up onto the kerb outside my house briefly to let another car pass on the other side of the road. The way people park around here, all sorts of car acrobatics are needed just to get down the road sometimes. Another reason why I don't drive.

By the time the sun's up, I'm downstairs and making breakfast. I go for scrambled eggs – without milk, having poured the plastic container down the sink last night. As I finish, I get a phone call. It's Dad.

'Bit of a strange one, actually,' he says, after we've done the usual hellos and how are yous. 'After I got back from yours last night, I set the door bump alarms on our front door. I don't usually bother if we're home, to be honest. Not at night anyway, as I always think we'd hear someone trying to break in at night. But for some reason I set them last night. Maybe I was in a security-conscious mood after being at yours. Anyway, about four-thirty this morning, the alarm goes off. Makes a right racket.'

I feel my blood turn to ice in my veins. 'What was it?' I ask, already knowing the answer.

Dad, to his credit, remains calm and gives me the simple facts, trying not to alarm me.

'We don't know. My first instinct was to go downstairs and switch it off, but your mum jumped straight up to the bedroom window. She says she saw someone jogging back down our drive and off down the road.'

I swallow, trying to force back the bile that's threatening to make its way up my throat.

'What did they look like?'

'A man, she reckons. Nothing else, though. He was in dark clothing, had a black cap over his head. She only saw him from the back. No chance of being able to do anything with that.'

Why is he telling me this? Is he trying to torture me on purpose? Make me feel guilty?

'Do you think it was him?' I ask.

'No idea. Probably not, to be honest. Probably just a coincidence. First night I had the alarm on, and all that. Who knows how many people try bumping people's doors open? If you don't have an alarm, you'd have no idea if someone had tried breaking into your house.'

Unless they leave a calling card, or a photo, I want to say.

'What, so you've called to tell me you were right and I was wrong, and that I've dragged you into all this now?' I reply, my voice cracking as the tears start to roll down my cheeks. I have. I've dragged them into this too. Perfectly innocent people, having to deal with being targeted by Toby Sheridan, through no fault of their own. All because I've fucked it all up, because I made the police think I was some sort of nutjob. Because I couldn't think clearly and handle my own emotions.

What have I done that's so bad? Why is he doing this to me? To my family? How did he know I was meant to be at my parents' house? Has he been listening in to my phone calls? Has he been watching their house? Maybe I'm just being paranoid. Maybe it was just a local kid trying doors. Either way, it's wrecking me. He's won. He's won.

'No, no, nothing like that,' Dad says. 'We don't think that

at all. At least I don't,' he adds, making the subtext perfectly clear. 'I just thought it was best to tell you. So you knew. In case it needed to come up at all. And anyway, look at the facts. My bump alarms are pretty cheap, basic things and they scared him off in seconds. He won't come within a mile of your place with all the gear we put in yesterday. This guy clearly isn't as big and clever as he thinks he is. If it's him, of course, which I don't think it is.'

That doesn't make me feel any better. If it wasn't Toby Sheridan trying to break into Mum and Dad's house last night – if it was just a kid from a local estate – that doesn't comfort me at all. It means Toby Sheridan could be perfectly capable of bypassing all the security measures Dad put in for me. We don't know. He hasn't been tested. It's local-yob-proof, but is it Toby-Sheridan-proof?

This was all meant to make me feel more secure. It doesn't. It's given me more questions than answers, when all I desperately want is answers.

Dad makes sure I'm alright, and says his goodbyes.

I put the phone down, sit down in the middle of the kitchen floor, bring my knees up to my chest and let out the most pained sobs I've cried in years.

60

It's almost midday, and I've already had four missed calls from work. I say missed calls; I mean avoided calls. I didn't actually miss any of them. The fact of the matter is that I can't face going to work. I don't care if they sack me. I'll find another job. I really don't care. Work's the least of my worries right now. I can't even face leaving the house.

But I'm going to have to. I called Maisie Haynes about an hour after Dad rang this morning. I didn't know what else to do. I can't even understand my own thought processes right now, so I need someone who can. I need the therapist to untangle the threads, make sense of the spaghetti mishmash that is the lines of thought currently going through my head.

Maisie said she could fit me in at 12.30. That's the best she could do, unfortunately. She was completely booked up until then. The wait is torturous. By the time I'd rung Maisie, I'd just about managed to psych myself up and convince myself that I could leave the house, only to find out I was going to have to wait another few hours.

I've been sitting in the living room with my shoes, coat and hat on for the past hour. I figure I can leave now. It'll only take me three or four minutes to walk to the clinic, so I'll probably arrive about half an hour early. I don't care. I just want to get there, get it over with and get back home. I need someone to tell me I'm not going mad, but that at the same time I don't need to panic and worry myself over what this man's doing to me. I need someone to put it in proportion, to make it all okay.

Easier said than done, I know.

I do the walk in record time. I don't fancy hanging about or walking slowly, and by the time I arrive I'm somewhat out of breath. Fortunately I've got enough time to get it back whilst I wait the best part of half an hour for my appointment time.

The waiting room is empty, except for me. It's only small, but wide – probably eight feet deep by about twenty-five or thirty wide. It's more of a partitioned-off section of Maisie's main consultation room, but it's eerily silent. There's the occasional scraping of a chair that makes its way through the walls, or a particularly loud cough. But, generally speaking, it's still. Tranquil, almost.

Until there's a loud bang over my right shoulder that has me leaping up out of my seat, yelping like a small dog whose tail has been trodden on.

'Sorry,' the pensioner says as he enters the room, closing

the door behind him. 'I thought it was a "push" one. Turns out it's a "pull" one.'

'Don't worry about it,' I say, hoping he didn't spot that he'd frightened the life out of me.

We sit in silence for a minute or so, before I start to think. There's about twenty-five minutes until my appointment, and the sessions tend to last forty-five minutes to an hour. I'm stupidly early myself, so what's this guy doing here?

'What time's your appointment?' I ask him, hoping that Maisie hasn't cocked up the appointment times.

'Oh, I don't have one. I'm here to pick up my daughter. She should be finished soon,' he says, checking his watch. I can tell by the look on his face that he's realised he's got here far too early as well.

The rest of the wait happens in silence. The old man sits scrolling through his smartphone while I read a magazine from the table to the left of me. I have great fun browsing through the TV listings from eight months ago and the adverts for sales that have long gone. Some of these companies are probably long gone by now, too.

Eventually, the door to the main consultation room opens, the man's daughter greets him, they leave and I enter the room.

'So how are you?' Maisie asks me as I sit down.

I sigh. 'I would say fine, but I'm guessing you wouldn't fall for that.'

'Well, most people who are fine don't tend to book emergency appointments with me, no,' she says, smiling. 'Has something happened?'

Where do I begin? 'I'm having a bit of trouble. Paranoia, mostly.' I feel disingenuous telling her this, because I know damn well it's not just paranoia. But I need to work on the assumption that it is, because the alternative doesn't bear thinking about.

He's got into your mind, Alice. He left you alone when you saw him in the police station. You tidied up the house yourself but you don't remember because you were too drunk. Either that or Kieran let himself in through the unlocked door and did it for you, but doesn't want to admit it because he doesn't want you to feel ashamed. And it was just a local kid trying doors at Mum and Dad's last night. Toby Sheridan has got into your mind and every little thing that happens now is fucking with you. You can't live like this.

I tell myself all this – and more – but me telling myself doesn't work. I need Maisie to re-wire me, to get me thinking sensibly again.

'There've been times when I hear noises in the night, and my brain tells me someone's trying to break in, or someone's trying to get to me. And occasionally I feel like I'm being followed or watched. I can't... I can't seem to handle the thought processes. I know I'm being daft, but it's taking over my life.'

Maisie nods and scribbles down a few notes as she nods. 'And is there anything that's caused this?'

Why can't I just tell her the truth? Why can't I open up and tell her everything, tell her about Toby Sheridan, about the fact he's a police officer, about what he's been doing to me? I don't know. Maybe it's pride. Maybe it's not wanting to sound like I'm insane. Or maybe part of me doesn't quite believe it myself. Right now, I don't know what I'm thinking. I don't know who I am. And that scares me.

'There was an incident I had, yeah. I wouldn't quite say "stalker", but that's about the gist of it.' Yeah, I would say stalker. I'd say a lot fucking worse than that, actually.

'Was this recent?' Maisie asks, her eyes narrowing, the subtext being *Why am I only just hearing of this?*

'Yeah. Last couple of weeks. It's all sorted now, but it's just left me with this paranoia.'

'That's understandable. So what is it you're thinking and feeling when these things happen?'

I tell her, as best I can. I tell her about the insecurity, the fright, the sheer dread. But I'm not expecting her to say what she says next.

'I think, if I'm honest, we probably need to recommend you for some additional treatment. You've been down the medication route, and you've done the talking therapies — very well too, I must say — but they don't seem to be working. With your permission, I'd like to recommend you for further evaluation.'

I sit for a moment, stunned.

'Further evaluation? What do you mean?'

'Just so they can evaluate what other treatment options might be open to you,' she says innocently.

'So *who* can evaluate?'

'Medical professionals.'

'You mean shrinks.'

'I mean medical professionals.'

There's a stand-off in which neither of us says anything. She can see I'm not happy with this suggestion, and I'm making no secret of that fact.

'Alice, I do think it's right to look at other avenues of treatment. I'm going to be completely open and honest with you now. I had a call from someone who said they were worried about some of your behaviour recently. They weren't sure how much was coming out in our sessions, and they wanted to ensure that you were able to get all the help you needed.'

I can't believe what I'm hearing. 'Are you serious? Our conversations are private! You're not meant to—'

'I didn't divulge anything that was said in any of our sessions, Alice. I didn't even acknowledge that there *were* any sessions. I just listened to what they had to say, that's all. I promise you absolutely nothing was said or shared in the other direction.'

I suddenly feel like everyone is ganging up on me. Who would call Maisie? I think of who knows that I go to see her. As far as I know, it's just my parents, plus Kieran and Mandy.

'I can't believe this,' I say. 'What the hell's going on?'

Maisie tries to calm me with the tone of her voice. 'Alice, people are worried about you. They want to help.'

'Well this isn't fucking helping! Someone phoning you and grassing me up for acting weird? How the hell am I meant to feel?'

'He just wants to look out for you, Alice.'

Maisie stops as she realises what she's said. She tries to backpedal, but I get there first.

'He?'

'Or she,' she says, unconvincingly.

I shake my head as I stand up to leave. 'Don't even bother, Maisie. Don't even bother.'

61

I feel completely and utterly betrayed. I give myself a headache as I start to walk home, my teeth grinding together as I think about the burning injustice of what's just happened. How dare he go behind my back like that? What right does he have to call Maisie and speak to her without letting me know about it? What was he hoping to achieve?

And when did he make that call? Was it before we tried following Toby Sheridan home from work? Between then and our night out? Was he happily enjoying a few drinks with me, knowing that he'd already grassed me up to my therapist? Or was it something he did afterwards, having decided that I was too nutty to hang around with after all?

As much as I try to force it from my mind, I keep playing through the conversation in my mind, imagining what might have been said.

Don't tell her I said any of this.

Whatever you say to me will remain confidential.

She'd kill me if she knew I was talking to you.

I must admit I've been having concerns myself.

Between you and me, I think she needs to go into an institution.

I'll keep a close eye on her next time she's in.

I'll speak to her parents. They might have some information too.

What do we do about Alice?

I hate people talking about me at the best of times. I hate being the centre of attention. I just want a quiet life. I don't want hassle. I want to be able to get up, go to work, come home, watch TV, go to bed, rinse and repeat. Why is this all happening to me? What have I done? Who have I upset? Where did I go so wrong?

I fumble with my phone as I try to navigate my way through to the *Contacts* app, the adrenaline coursing through my body, making my hands shake uncontrollably.

Eventually, I find Kieran's entry and tap the screen to call him.

I don't even wait for him to answer; I start talking as soon as the call connects.

'What the hell have you done, Kieran?'

'Sorry?'

'Maisie Haynes. My therapist.' I can hear the adrenaline in my own voice. I sound like I'm sitting on top of a washing machine.

'What about her?' Kieran asks.

'Did you call her?' I don't know why I'm phrasing it as a question. I know damn well he did. But there's something in his tone that tells me he hasn't got a clue what I'm talking about.

'Call her? No, why?'

There's a woman walking towards me, giving me an odd look. I cup my hand around my mouth and the bottom of the phone as I speak, trying to keep my voice down.

'Don't treat me like a fucking idiot, Kieran. She told me she had a call from someone expressing their concerns about my "recent behaviour". But she slipped up and referred to that person as *he*.'

'And? That narrows it down to fifty percent of the population. How did you leap from there to me?'

'Because who else would it have been, Kieran? Only a couple of people even know I go to see Maisie, and one of them's you.'

Kieran sighs. 'Alice, I didn't call her, alright? I'm not the only bloke you know, am I? You must've told someone else at some point. For all I know you met someone else while you were drunk and told him.'

Kieran's response takes me by surprise. What the hell is he talking about?

'What's that supposed to mean?' I ask.

'Well I don't know, do I? You've been flitting about all over the place recently, making weird comments and doing strange things. Half the time, I reckon you don't even know yourself what you've been doing. How can you honestly say you can guarantee that I'm the only male who knows about your therapist? You can't.'

I let out something approaching a laugh. 'That's what this

is all about, isn't it? You've totally changed since we split up. And now I can see why. These silly little comments about other blokes, about me getting drunk. This is all about you trying to get me back, trying to make me dependent on you again.'

'For God's sake, don't be so—'

'No, I'm serious, Kieran. That's what you've always wanted, isn't it? Your safe, comfortable little life with the dutiful wife or girlfriend always where you know she is. Reliant on you.'

'Alice, you're talking rubbish and you know it.'

'How far would you go to make me reliant on you, Kieran? Hmmm? I mean, you wouldn't go so far as to get someone to pretend to stalk me, send me a few weird photos, try to break into my house? That'd get me running back to you, wouldn't it? Straight into the safe arms of Kieran, happily ever after!'

I'm now aware that my voice is very loud and my arm movements are exaggerated. I'm getting a few odd looks from passers-by, but I don't give a shit.

'Jesus Christ, you're paranoid,' Kieran says.

'Am I? Am I? How else did he get into my house that first time? You had a key. You had one for ages.'

'I gave it back when we broke up, Alice. You know I did.'

'Yes, you did, but what's to say you didn't have a copy made before then? Maybe when you started to realise things were coming to an end and you were going to need to go out of your way to make sure I came running back to you? How else did he find my address? How did he know where I work?

Somehow he knew my routine, he knew where my parents lived for crying out loud!'

'Alice, please. This is getting out of hand.'

'Is it? Is it really? Or is this all one big, sick ploy to win me back, Kieran?'

Kieran's silent for a moment, then I hear a sigh.

'Alice, I don't want you back.'

Even though I had absolutely no thoughts or intention of ever getting back with Kieran, this news still hits me like a ton of bricks.

'What?'

'I can't handle you like this. Besides, you've got your new bloke now. Simon, is it?' The tone of his voice is pure venom.

'How do you know about Simon?'

'Mandy mentioned him. Nice to know I was just being used, as per usual.'

'What the hell are you talking about?'

'Well, there's me thinking you wanted us to spend time together. You came to *me* when you wanted help finding this guy. You came to *me* when you wanted to follow him home from work. Why not Simon? Because I was *convenient*? Or because you didn't want Simon to know what a nutcase you are?'

I expect Kieran to fall silent after saying that, as if he'd just realised what he'd said and immediately regretted it. But he doesn't. He continues.

'Seriously, Alice, I didn't call your therapist, but I completely agree with whoever did. Your... condition... is affecting your reality. You don't know what's what any more.

You don't even know what reality is. You've got to stop this, before innocent people end up being hurt by your accusations.'

'What? Which innocent people?'

Kieran sighs again. 'Who knows? Maybe Toby Sheridan's innocent.'

I stop dead in my tracks, even though I'm only yards from my house. 'What did you just say?'

'I said maybe Toby Sheridan's innocent. Maybe you're imagining the whole thing. Who knows? You don't know what's real any more, and I'm starting to struggle as well.'

The feeling of anger and complete betrayal is now overwhelming.

'In that case, maybe you should have nothing to do with me any more, Kieran.'

I'm not expecting his response.

'Yeah. I think that would probably be a good idea.'

62

Even though I wasn't technically with Kieran, and even though we've broken up before, this feels a whole lot worse. Before, I was prepared. It was my decision. It was mostly amicable, too. This is completely different. This time, I feel betrayed. I feel victimised.

How could Kieran say that he doesn't believe me, that I'm making it all up? How could he even consider that as a possibility? He *helped* me track Toby Sheridan down. He knows he exists. He, of all people, should be the one who's there to support me. But, instead, he goes and throws it all away.

I've only been home a couple of minutes when my phone rings. My first instinct is it's Kieran calling me back to apologise, but I know in my heart of hearts that's not going to happen. I look at the screen. It's Darryl. Great. So Kieran's called him and told him what happened, and now I'll have Darryl on my back too.

A thought crosses my mind. Darryl works for the police. Does that mean he's ringing to let me know they're investigating me or that Toby Sheridan has reported me for following him home the other afternoon? I tell myself it can't be that. Darryl's a member of civilian staff working in IT, for a start.

I answer the phone.

'Hi, Darryl.'

'Hi. Listen, I can't talk long as I'm on my break, but I've been having a closer look at our mutual friend.'

Darryl's method of trying to disguise what he's talking about makes me feel reassured that I can trust him, but there's still the Kieran factor.

I keep silent, waiting for him to continue.

'There was another case just over a year ago, not too dissimilar to this,' he says. I can hear he's cupped the phone and is talking quietly to avoid being overheard. 'Another woman, living locally, who reported being stalked. That's not the weird thing, though. We get hundreds of stalking reports a year. This one stuck out in my mind for a reason. When I saw you the other night, it jarred something in my memory. I couldn't work out why. But this morning I realised what it was. You look exactly like that girl that was being stalked last year, Alice. You're a dead ringer for her. It stuck in my mind because she only lived a few doors up from me. Wait. Give me two secs.'

There's a pause as I hear some fumbling and tapping noises. He comes back on the line.

'Right. Check your messages.'

As he finishes saying that, my phone vibrates and dings to let me know a text has arrived. I take the phone away from my ear and open up my messages. I tap Darryl's name, and a picture appears. It's the woman. And he's right. She looks just like me. It's so accurate, it's scary.

'Bloody hell,' I say, putting the phone back to my ear.

'I know, right? Listen, there are a couple of cases like this. Possibly more, I don't know. I'd have to look at different records and things and I'd risk being caught doing it. It's just lucky I was doing some maintenance work on that particular database this morning. I don't know when that chance will come up again, but I took it. This girl, she reported things just like you did. Not a photographer, though; this was a guy she met while she was working on her dad's market stall. One day a week she used to man the stall for him, and this guy came to buy stuff three weeks in a row. They used to chat about various things, and on the third week they swapped numbers. That's when it all started going weird. He never visited the stall again, either. But get this. The description the girl gave the police was identical to how you described Sheridan.'

I can't quite believe what I'm hearing. So this guy is a serial offender, but the police still didn't think they should do anything about it? They must have known I wasn't going mad or making it up. They must have realised this had happened before to another woman and that we couldn't both be imagining the same fictional stalker.

'To be honest, I reckon there's more,' Darryl says. 'When

I next get the chance to have a poke around, I'll take a look. But in the meantime, you need to stay safe.'

'Thanks, Darryl. But why would he be doing this? What do me and this other girl's looks have to do with anything?'

Darryl exhales loudly. 'Could be anything. I'm not a profiler or a criminal psychologist. But my best guess would be that you remind him of someone. Perhaps an old girlfriend who treated him badly. For stalkers, it's all about control. That'll be why he needs to keep showing you he's been in your house and that he knows where you are at all times. It's his way of showing you he's in control and that whatever you do, he's there.'

'But why?' I ask. 'Does he think it's going to make me go running to him or something?'

'Who knows. Maybe. He's obviously sick in the head, so I wouldn't expect any of it to make sense, but it might be a punishment thing. Perhaps he's convinced himself that you don't just look like someone he used to know, but that you *are* that person. Maybe that person needed punishing, in his mind. If that person isn't around any more, you're the next best thing. Perhaps he feels as though punishing you is somehow making him feel better, because in his mind he's punishing that person who hurt him before. If you see what I mean.'

To be honest, I don't. It's all confusing the hell out of me. 'Like projection?' I ask.

'I dunno. Kind of. Like I said, I'm not a psychologist. This is just my own opinion.'

I sigh. 'So what do we do now?'

There's silence for a couple of moments before Darryl speaks.

'I dunno, Alice. I really don't know.'

63

The rest of the day passed in a haze, and I felt exhausted by the end of it. Mentally more than physically. Sleep helped to clear my head a little, and I woke up this morning trying to figure out the ramifications of what it meant for me that Toby Sheridan has clearly done this to other people before.

Does it make me feel any better? No, of course not. If anything, it scares me a little. This isn't just someone messing about — the guy does this regularly. But, at the same time, the possibility remains that he could lose interest in me the same as he did with the other girl and move on to someone else. Of course, that doesn't help either — no-one should have to go through what I've been through — but my main priority right now has to be to keep him well away from me and to hope for an end to all this.

Darryl was hazy with the details, as I imagine he probably has to be. He didn't tell me the girl's name, and I didn't ask. I figured he wouldn't be allowed to tell me, and in any case I'm not sure I want to know. What would I do with it? Try and track her down on Facebook, see if he's either completely ruined her life or if she's happy and healthy and free of him? Which would I prefer? Which would make me feel better? The answer is neither. So what's the point? Why would I want to torment myself?

The ideal outcome would be for the police to get involved, find some evidence that they can use to charge him and somehow manage to tie that up with this previous case. That way, he could be charged and convicted for stalking us both. And there might well be more. I imagine there probably is. Who knows how many women he's tormented over the years? How many of them managed to get away, and how many met other, grizzlier ends? Does this man become violent when he doesn't get what he wants? Or does he just torment them to the point where they get so desperate to be free of him that they end their own lives?

As these thoughts all cross my mind, I get up and make myself some breakfast, listening to a documentary on the radio about the fight for women's rights in South Sudan. Programmes like this sometimes make me wonder if we aren't so different after all.

With breakfast made, I take my mobile phone out and go to check my emails while I eat. There's the usual junk – newsletters from companies I once bought something from four years ago, a message from my credit card provider to let me know my latest bill's ready and an email from Simon letting everyone know that the kickboxing class will be starting half an hour later than usual this week. The usual collection of things that really aren't very interesting at all.

But as I scroll further down, there's another email which stops me dead in my tracks. My heart skips more than a beat or two as I take in what's on the screen in front of me.

Gavin Armitage | *01:13*

(no subject)

I know I should delete it. Swipe the screen, tap *Delete* and forget all about it. Ignore him. He's playing for attention, and he needs to know he's not getting it. But I feel compelled to open it. What if he's got some sort of tracker on there and he can see whether it's been opened? Sure, opening it would feed his ego, but not opening it might enrage him somehow or make him do something worse to try and get my attention. He's already been in my house, so I dread to think of what he might resort to next. I quickly decide it's best if I open the email, see what it says, then delete it.

I open the email, which takes a second or two to load. I quickly realise this is because it's got a photo embedded in it. The picture loads slowly, from top to bottom, gradually revealing its subject matter like an ancient theatre curtain.

It's another picture of me, but this one was taken very recently. Yesterday, in fact. I recognise the clothes I was wearing when I went to see Maisie, and in the picture I'm on the phone, looking particularly upset and angry. I realise that this is when I was speaking to Kieran, having the argument about him telling Maisie he thought I was going mad.

When I see this picture I'm not shocked. I'm angry and confused. How the hell did he manage to take another photo of me? Where *was* he? I look more closely at the picture, and it looks as though there's a slight glint of reflection on it, as if it's been taken through a pane of glass. He was waiting in his car, I realise. But it can't have been *his* car, because I would have recognised it. I've suspiciously eyed every single Volkswagen Golf I've seen since that day Kieran and I followed him home from work. There's no way I wouldn't have spotted his exact same car parked outside my house, is there? The photo's a bit grainy and out of focus, so I guess he could have been parked quite a way down the street when he took it. But still, I'm sure I would have seen it. Unless I was too wrapped up in getting angry at Kieran and brooding on what Maisie said...

I lock my phone and put it back on the kitchen table, face down. And in that moment I realise something that I had been hoping I wouldn't have to think about. Far from having left me alone, far from being scared off by seeing me in the police station that day, Toby Sheridan is still following me. He's still taking pictures of me. And he's still after me.

But it's what else this means that frightens me. It raises the chances that it was him who tried breaking into Mum and Dad's house the other night. It raises the chances that it was him who broke into my house and tidied up the mess I made after being out with Kieran. Despite knowing I've been to the police, despite knowing I know who is he, despite knowing that I've tried following him to his home, he's still not relenting. He's still out there, closer than ever, more determined than ever.

And I don't know what I can do about it.

64

There's only one person I can call. There's only one person who has more information than I do, who has ways and means of getting things done. And I don't want to get him into trouble or cause issues for him at work, but I really don't have any choice. As far as I'm concerned, my life could be in danger. The police don't think so – there's been no threat to my life – but I know when I feel intimidated, and that word doesn't even cover it right now.

I'm shaking as I call Darryl, two of my fingers bleeding from how far back I've bitten the nails. But I don't care. The blood and the physical pain is actually a nice release from the mental anguish and distress I'm feeling.

I don't even let Darryl speak when he answers the phone, instead leaping straight into trying desperately to let him know what's happened.

'I received another email. From Toby Sheridan. Another

picture of me, outside my house. It was taken yesterday. He's back, he's still doing it, he's not going away.'

'Can you forward the picture to me?' he asks, going straight into analytical problem-solving mode. No interrogation, no asking questions. Just plain action.

'I can try, but I don't think there'll be anything you can use. He's been really careful before.'

'All criminals slip up at some point,' he says. 'If there's nothing, there's nothing. But it's worth a try. I'm at home today, so I can take a look on my personal laptop. You'll need to forward it to me with the full header information, though.'

He explains to me step by step how to do this. Apparently just forwarding an email wouldn't send him all the original sender's information, but if I forward it with the full header information, Darryl can view the digital footprint of the original message. I don't really understand what this means, but if it's going to help me to prove a case against Toby Sheridan, I'll do it.

Darryl keeps me on the line as he looks through the forwarded email.

'Yeah, doesn't look like there's anything usable here. Sent through a proxy in Taiwan.'

'What does that mean?' I ask.

'Well, unless he's nipped over there for a holiday, which I know for a fact he hasn't, he'll have used a VPN or something to trick the email server into thinking he's in Taiwan. Truth be told, he's probably hiding behind multiple layers like that, so getting the original source of the email is going to be nigh-on impossible. At least one of those layers will be heavily encrypted, or the server will be owned by an offshore VPN provider who won't release the logs. They don't legally have to, many of them. Some don't even keep logs, for that very reason.'

'So, again, there's nothing we can do?'

Darryl sighs. 'Not really, to be honest. By which I mean no, nothing at all. Like I say, it's a case of waiting for him to slip up. Everyone does eventually. And when he does, they'll be able to pin the lot on him.'

'But what if he doesn't slip up?' I ask, hearing my voice rising in pitch as I start to feel more and more desperate. 'What if next time he does something worse? What if it's physical? I'm scared, Darryl.'

'I know you are. Listen, you need to report it to the police. They can deal with it.'

'How? You just said yourself that the email isn't traceable. What are they going to be able to do?'

'Well, nothing straight away. But they can log it as evidence. If they get to the point where they find evidence they can use to charge him, the email will count towards it. Or they might be able to link it to other crimes, maybe other emails being sent to other people. It'll all go onto HOLMES – the Home Office Large Major Enquiry System. It's designed to spot patterns and things, and for forces to collaborate and share information. Without information, the police can't do anything.'

'They're not doing anything anyway!'

'I'm sure they're trying,' he says, clearly trying to placate me but also sounding slightly defensive. That tells me he's probably got the same concerns that I have, only he doesn't want to voice them.

'Darryl, if there have been previous cases involving this guy, he's obviously dangerous.'

'We don't know for a fact it's the same guy,' he says, unconvincingly. 'Besides, no-one's ever been interviewed, arrested or charged. He can't be that dangerous. There were no reports of violence or even threats of violence in the other case.'

'And how do we know that was the only other case? What's to say there weren't more? You and I both know the odds are that there were more. What percentage of crimes actually get reported? I mean, what's to say he didn't stalk another woman — maybe more than one — who didn't report it to the police, but ended up getting kidnapped? Or worse, killed.' As I say the word, it shoots through me like a bolt of ice. 'What if they just went down as a missing person? Or if he's been doing stuff out of the area?'

'HOLMES would link it all up. It's nationwide.'

'You're missing the point, Darryl. Any computer system is only as good as the information that's fed into it.'

'Which is exactly why you need to report all this and ensure it's on the system,' he says.

As far as I see things, I've only got two rolls of the dice left. I go for the kinder option first, trying to appeal to his human sensibilities and emotions.

'Do you agree that this guy could potentially be dangerous?' I ask him. 'That he could pose a physical danger to me or other women?'

I hear Darryl sigh. 'It's possible, but from a legal point of view there's no—'

'Sod the legal point of view, Darryl. I'm asking for common sense here. Could you live with yourself if something happened to me – or to another woman – and you knew you could have done something to stop it?'

'Alice, I really don't think that's fair. You're asking a lot of me here. And most of it is based on a hunch.'

'You've seen the evidence,' I tell him, before realising I'm going to have to play my last card. 'I understand you could potentially lose your job, but I could lose my life. And in any case, I'm pretty sure the information you've already given me would land you in a lot of hot water as it is.'

I leave that hanging in the air for a moment.

'Are you trying to blackmail me, Alice?'

'I'm asking you for help. And pointing out that you're already in over your head, whether you like it or not. You can either finish the job properly or bail out and risk the consequences for both of us. But either way, I need Toby Sheridan's address.'

My heart's hammering in my chest. I never start a confrontation like this, nor have I ever issued anyone with a threat. It makes me feel slightly sick, but I'm acutely aware that I need to do it. I have no other option.

Darryl is silent for a few moments before he finally speaks.

'Whatever happens, Alice, if anyone asks, you didn't hear this from me. Alright?'

65

I didn't need to write down the address that Darryl told me. I know it'll be indelibly printed on my memory forever. It's not the sort of thing I'm likely to forget.

142 Runsmere Avenue.

I'm shaking as I put the phone down. I have everything I need. I have his name. I have his address. I just don't know what to do with it.

I know exactly what I *want* to do with it, but the thought scares me. I want to go over there, confront him and show him who's in charge. I want to let him know that he won't win, that I'm stronger than he thinks I am and that he's not going to go free after what he's done to me.

I'm not going to lie – I want him gone. He's made my life an absolute living hell, and the adrenaline coursing through my body and the blood pulsing at my temples has me thinking only one thing: I want him dead. I don't want him escaping justice, wriggling and crawling his way out of it just because he knows the system. Just because he thinks he can stay one step ahead. Maybe he can. But can anyone stay one step ahead of death?

I don't know how much I mean these words. What would happen if I killed Toby Sheridan? And why am I even considering it? It's far too drastic a response for me. I'm not a violent person in the slightest. But I'm running out of options. I'm desperate. I just want him gone.

I'd be arrested, of course. Charged. Probably found guilty. Would there be mitigating circumstances? I presume his reign of torment would be taken into account on some level. I'd still go to jail. I've no doubt about that. But how is that any different from my position now? If Toby Sheridan is still walking this earth, I'll be living in my own private prison for the rest of my life. At least this way I'll come out eventually, and when I do he won't be there. I'll be free again.

Even if we were able to get enough evidence against him to get a conviction, the maximum sentence for stalking is five to ten years, according to my research on the internet. Even if he got the maximum sentence, which is unlikely, he could be out within five years if he managed to play the system well and had a record of good behaviour. Every single one of those days over that five-year period would get increasingly more depressing, knowing that it was getting closer and closer to his release every single day. I don't think I could bear that. I don't think I'd ever really feel like I'd got my life back — only that I was borrowing it for the best part of five years.

But there's still a huge stumbling block, something that's stopping me from driving over there in the middle of the night and setting fire to his house. It just isn't *me*. And in all this, despite what he's been doing to me, I can't let him change who I am inside. I can't let him win. If he affects me to the point where I become a shell of my former self, a violent person, then he'll have won. I can't let all this evil have consequences. I can't allow him to have been a success and to change my core values and beliefs.

Which is why I need to have hope, even in the face of utter despair. Easier said than done. With some sort of evidence – *something* – we might be able to ensure that he feels the full force of the law. The police would have to throw the book at him, wouldn't they? Anything less would make them look complicit, especially as he's one of them. And there's always the chance that having the spotlight thrown on him would encourage others to come forward. And I know there have been others. At least one, anyway. If we could somehow manage to stack up four or five charges against him, he could be put away for a long time. He's probably in his forties now, so – what – another forty or fifty years inside, just to make sure he's too old and frail to do anything when he gets out? That's going to mean ten guilty verdicts, plus the judge ordering that they're not served concurrently.

It's when I have these realisations that I feel complete and utter despair that the system is so heavily stacked against the female victim. He can make my life absolute hell, yet either avoid justice completely or have his life back inside five years. Yet if I were to retaliate in any way or try to ensure that I could live a normal life – despite having done nothing wrong – I'd be the one arrested and charged. I've never seen myself as a radical feminist or champion of social justice, but I'm starting to wonder if this whole episode might have changed me irrevocably, whether I like it or not.

But for now I have to play things by the book as much as possible. Kieran's right. I need to find something that we can use against him. And there must be something. Maybe the business card will be at his house, or his camera equipment. Perhaps there'll be copies of the photos he took. Surely, if TV and films are anything to go by, he'll have all this stored somewhere. He's probably got some sort of warped shrine to the women he stalks. The thought sends a shiver down my spine.

I put my shoes and coat on, wrap my scarf around my neck and go to leave the house. As I do so, I pause, my feet planted to the ground as I look at the knife block. Without further thought, I pull the largest carving knife from the block and slide it into my inside coat pocket. Just in case.

66

I don't know what I imagined Toby Sheridan's house would look like. I suppose I thought it'd be some grubby little bedsit, like a crazed serial killer's damp old dungeon. But, in reality, it's a very nice-looking house in a leafy suburb, hidden by tall hedges at the front, as are many of the houses along this stretch. They're all detached, and I reckon they must be four- or five-bedroom affairs.

What are policemen paid? Thirty grand, maybe? Nowhere near enough to be able to buy a place like this on their own. Which raises the odds that he lives with someone else. A wife, girlfriend perhaps. Someone completely oblivious to the real personality of the man she lives with. Someone else who's going to get irreparably hurt when they find out what Toby Sheridan is really like. I just hope there are no kids involved. To find out your husband or partner is a stalker is one thing, but your own father? It doesn't bear thinking about.

I feel an electric jolt in my temples, which shocks me for a moment, even though I know exactly what it is. The withdrawal symptoms from my medication do this occasionally. I had something similar about fifteen minutes ago when I was at the taxi rank a few streets away from my house. It happens when I mix medication with alcohol, too. And now it appears to be happening when I mix no medication with alcohol. I can't win.

As I get to Toby Sheridan's house, I walk a little slower. I don't have many choices here. I can either carry on and keep walking, and come back again once I've had a chance to case the scene, or I can head straight down his driveway. Either way, I can't just stand here looking at the place. That'll look far too suspicious.

The journey here has calmed me down somewhat. At one point, shortly after leaving my house and thinking about the hell he's put me through, I was completely ready to turn up here and shove the knife through his neck, but having to walk to the taxi rank and get a cab over here has taken the edge off my anger a little. Not too much, though. Besides which, I'm here now. And I need to put an end to all this. One way or the other. Because otherwise I'm going to go insane.

I take a deep breath and walk between the tall hedges, before heading to the right and walking down the inside of the hedge line. There are no cars on the driveway, and certainly no sign of Sheridan's VW Golf, so I can only assume that he's out. At work, perhaps.

There are no security cameras on the front of his house,

that I can see. There's an alarm box on the front of the house, but the 'armed' lights aren't flashing. From what I remember Dad telling me when he came round to install mine, that means it's not switched on. I think. I'm not certain enough to want to test that theory, though.

As I get to the house, I look behind me. From here, all that's visible through the front of the hedge line is some trees across the road. So far as I can see, no-one in any other houses will be able to see me from here.

My heart's hammering in my chest as I peer in through the front window on the right-hand side of the house. There are vertical blinds — slightly open — and the sun's directly behind me, but I can just about make out that it's a study of some sort. There are a couple of bookcases, and a desk up against the window. I can't see a laptop or computer of any sort — I imagine being a policeman he'll know not to leave anything like that on show near a window.

If there's going to be any evidence of some sort, it'll be in that room. Where else would he keep business cards? Or printed photographs? As I look in through the window, my heart starts racing even more as I think about what I might find in there, if only I could find a way in. What if there are other pictures? Not just of me, but of other girls too? This isn't just about finding justice for myself now, but for the other girl Darryl was talking about and for any other women who've had to live through the sort of hell that Toby Sheridan has put me through recently.

I'm not the sort of person who willingly or readily breaks the law. I don't do confrontation. Even the act of coming here, of being here, isn't me. But then I wonder if I ever really knew me. Because I know I *need* to be here. I need to find out the truth. I need something that will end all this, whether that's damning evidence from inside his house or the large, sharp knife from inside my jacket pocket.

I pull the zip down on my jacket a little further, giving me ready access to the knife should I need it.

The front door's not an option. That'll be in full view of the street if I head over in that direction. Instead, I carry on round the right-hand-side of the house, putting my hand through the not-very-secure wrought iron gate and unlatching it, before walking through and pushing it closed again behind me, the gate creaking on its hinges as I do so.

A few steps further along, there's another window, this one on the side of the house. I stand with my back against the wall before leaning over and peering through the very edge of the window. It's a kitchen. A large kitchen. But there's nobody in it. I keep my eyes very much on the window as I begin to walk past, keeping my gaze on the room inside to make sure there's no movement or signs of life. My hand is hovering near my now-open jacket, the knife tantalisingly just centimetres away from my fingertips, the cold winter air diving inside and chilling my torso.

Until something stops me.

I pause and hold my breath, and I swear for a moment my heart stops beating as I narrow my eyes and look closely at what I'm seeing inside the kitchen.

The back door is open. Not just unlocked. It's open. In

December. That can mean only one thing. This house isn't as empty as I thought it was.

Panicking, I step back from the window and turn back towards the gate. Before I can move in that direction, though, a large hand clamps over my mouth as an arm comes around my chest from the other side, lifting me off my feet.

67

Hallelujah, it worked!

I knew you'd come to me eventually. I knew you'd come back. You just needed a little help finding your way, didn't you?

We've still got a long way to go yet. I know that. I wouldn't be so foolish as to think otherwise, but this is a huge step. The biggest step. Everything now is just detail.

You've proven yourself to me in a way I thought I could only ever dream of. I knew it was there. I could see it right from the very start, and now so can you.

I knew you hadn't left me. I knew you'd be back. Because we know each other so well, don't we? No-one has an understanding or a connection quite like we do. You can't beat that bond. It's unbreakable. We're unbreakable. Which is why I knew you'd be back, and it's why you knew you'd be back too. You just needed a way, didn't you? And when you found that way you needed my help. Just a little nudge in the right direction.

Because if you'd come back with full knowledge, it would've been doomed from the very beginning. It had to be this way. I know that now. And I know I was impatient at the start, but I just wanted you back here with me. You should never have left in the first place.

I don't blame you for that. Of course I don't. It wasn't your fault. There's no way you could have prevented the cruel hand of fate throwing the dice in that way. Snakes eyes. And there are plenty of snakes in the world, believe me.

I still remember when you first told me, like it was yesterday. It took me a while to believe it was real. Things like that just don't happen to people like us. Another sign of the injustice in the world, I remember you saying. Whatever we do, it's all stacked against us. People like us. The chemical imbalance of the world means we have to fight harder, have to push to make our voices heard. But shouting isn't always the best way to make your voice heard. Not if everyone else is deaf.

What's the use in yelling at a deaf person? You can't. You have to show them instead. And when the whole world's deaf by choice, you can not only show them the truth but enable them to hear again. And that's a gift that not everyone can give. That's something special. Extra special.

I'm not going to lie: it's been hard doing it on my own. I've had to live a different life. One you wouldn't recognise. But I needed the stability. I needed the cover. I know you're going to forgive me. I did it all for the greater good. That was what you always said. The Greater Good. It's allowed me to stay under the radar, too. I've been a great actor. You would've been proud of me. You will be proud of me.

Because you're back. You're here with me again. And this time I'm going to make sure no-one — absolutely no-one — takes you away from me.

I've learned a lot since you went away. I come into contact with every far-flung corner of human nature every single day. I've seen it all. And every day, every hour, every minute, I've seen just how right you were. I've seen the greed, I've seen the jealousy, I've seen the complete contempt for the fellow human. And it makes me sick as much as it did you.

It's not that I didn't know it then — I did — but this has just reconfirmed everything for me. It's made me realise that you were wiser than I thought. And I thought you were the wisest person I'd ever met. I adored you. I never stopped adoring you. But now I can adore you all over again.

Because you're back.

You're with me.

You returned.

Welcome home, Mum.

68

My neck hurts like hell as I pull my head upwards. It feels like I've slept on it funny, and it creaks slightly as I move. I wince with the pain.

I roll my head and try to open my eyes, the light searing through my eyelids as I try to focus on what's around me.

The first thing I see is the clothes I'm wearing. I've got loose-fitting trousers on, grey, with huge flared legs. They look like some sort of soft cloth, the sort of thing display boards in schools are backed with. Or a grey snooker table.

My feet are uncovered, but I can see that my toenails have been painted. I never paint my toenails.

I groan and look down at my arms, but they aren't there. They're tied behind my back, attached to the chair I'm sitting on. I'm wearing what looks like an orange blouse with a flower pattern on it. It's not an item of clothing I recognise, and for a moment I wonder if I'm even looking at myself or at someone else.

I can't make any sense of what's going on.

I hear footsteps on the floor shortly before I see the feet that make them. A pair of black, heavy duty, steel-toecap boots. I look up as I hear his voice.

'You're awake.'

I grunt in response. I can't yet force any words out. But it's him. It's Toby Sheridan.

'Don't try to talk. It's okay. You'll be groggy. But I had to do it. I had to make sure you couldn't go anywhere. Not until we're completely there. Not until I know you're fully here again. We need to make sure every part of you has returned.'

I have no idea what he's saying, what any of this means, but he's speaking calmly, as if he knows me. There's not a hint of malice in his voice whatsoever. It's almost as if he's helping me. Helping me by knocking me out, tying me to a chair and dressing me in strange clothes.

'What are you doing?' I say, forcing out a hoarse whisper.

He bends down in front of me and smiles.

'Exactly. There's still some of Alice in there that we need to expunge. That'll happen naturally, over time. But meanwhile I'm going to need to keep you where you are. We've got so far, we can't possibly be taking any backward steps now. You understand that, don't you?'

I look at him and nod. It seems like the sensible thing to do. Just until I've worked out what he's going on about, at least.

'Do you like what I've done with the kitchen?' he asks. 'I noticed the look on your face when you peered in through the window. I could see what was going through your mind.

"What happened to my cupboard fronts!"' he says, chuckling to himself as he waves his arms in the air in mock shock. 'Looks good, though, doesn't it?'

I nod again.

'My head hurts,' I say.

'Don't worry. That'll clear soon. It's a side effect of the sedatives.'

'Sedatives?'

'Yes. Sorry. Like I said, I need to make sure you're fully back with me first. I couldn't risk you disappearing and everything going back to square one.'

He leans in and takes my face in his hands. They feel like ice, and I shudder as he touches me. This man who's made my life hell, who's been in my house, who's been taking photos of me. 'You forgive me, don't you Mum?'

I understand the words he's saying, but the meanings of them make no sense.

'What do you mean?' I say, my voice still hoarse. 'I'm not your mum.'

His face drops immediately. The friendly smile has disappeared, almost as if those words have jolted him into another personality altogether. It's like someone's flipped a switch.

Slowly, he pushes himself back to his feet as he takes his eyes off me, and walks over to the other side of the kitchen, rubbing his chin with one hand, the other planted on his hip as he walks. When he gets to the other side of the room, he leans on the counter, his head bowed, before turning back towards me, leaning back against the counter with his arms folded.

When he speaks again, his voice is low and serious.

'I had worried you might say that. Don't get me wrong, I hoped you wouldn't. Because that makes things very difficult. Very difficult indeed.'

There's a look in his eyes that tells me things are about to get a whole lot worse. It's like the calm before the storm.

'I should have seen the signs,' he says, before pushing himself away from the sideboard and walking back towards me, slowly. 'I should have known.'

He's now barely a foot or two away from me. I try to stay calm but it's difficult. He leans over me, reaching behind me, and I hear the sound of something scraping against a wooden surface.

'I should have realised when you turned up with this.'

He waves the knife in front of my face. I recognise it immediately as the one I brought from my kitchen earlier.

He nods. 'Yes. I should have known that meant we still had work to do.' He walks back away from me. 'Although what we're going to do, I don't know. I really don't know. I don't want to have to hurt you. You know that, don't you?' he says, turning back towards me, waving the knife just inches from my face.

I nod vigorously, even though I'm not at all sure he doesn't want to hurt me. The evidence appears to show otherwise. For some reason, my response appears to anger him further.

'Then why did you bring this with you?' he says, his voice

raised. Then he begins yelling, his face pressed up against mine so our noses are almost touching. 'Why did you say you weren't my mum? What is wrong with you? Why would you say that? Why?'

I'm desperately trying to think of something to say, feeling as if my life is only seconds away from ending.

'I don't know,' I say. 'I'm sorry. I was confused. This is difficult for me too. It's a lot to take in. But I'm here. I'm here for you. I'm back.'

His face seems to settle slightly.

'Say that again.'

I swallow. 'I'm back.'

'The other bit.'

'I'm here for you,' I say, my voice choking – solely because I'm certain I'm about to die, but hopeful that it might sound like it's because I mean it.

He cocks his head slightly, as if watching my face and eyes for signs.

'It's the sedatives,' I say. 'They confused me. I'm sorry. I didn't know where I was. And I don't like being tied up. I don't like being restrained.' I hope to God this is the right thing to say.

'You never did,' he says eventually. 'You were always a free spirit.'

I latch onto this. 'Yes. Yes, I still am. I'm not myself when I'm tied up like this. I can't be.'

He nods. 'I've locked the doors.'

'That's fine.'

He raises the knife slightly, just to show me that he's got that, too. He looks at me for understanding, and I nod.

He walks behind me to untie me from the chair, and a shiver of terror runs through me. I can't see him, I don't know what he's doing. For all I know, that knife could be running across my throat within half a second, with me bleeding out here on his kitchen floor. This'd be the last sight I'd see. Toby Sheridan's formica worktops.

A few seconds later, I feel the bounds around my arms begin to loosen, and I move my hands, the blood rushing back into them painfully.

'Thank you,' I say, as he comes back into view. 'You've always been good to me.'

I feel sick saying this, but I know I need to. Playing along is the only way I'm going to be able to survive. I need to go with it, just until I get the opportunity I need. Until then, I'm going to need to suck it up and make him think I'm on his side. Make him think I'm his mum.

I can see tears starting to well up in his eyes. He believes it. He truly believes I'm his mum.

'I've missed you,' he says, through his tears, his voice breaking.

I take his face in my hands, every fibre of my being trying to swallow down the bile that's rising in my throat as I do so. I look him in the eyes, and force myself to mean every word I say.

'I've missed you too.'

He pulls me in for a hug, and I let him. I have to. If he feels any sort of resistance or tension in me, it'll be game over.

He holds me for a good twenty seconds or so, and sobs on my shoulder.

His next words take me by surprise.

'Would you like a cup of tea?'

I'm not sure whether this is a trick question or not. Did his mum have a particular aversion to tea? But I look in his eyes and I can see that this is just a regular, normal question. He's actually asking me if I'd like a cup of tea. Like nothing had just happened. As if this is all completely ordinary.

'Yes please,' I say.

He puts the kettle on, leans against the sideboard and looks at me, smiling. I smile back.

He takes two cups out of the cupboard above the kettle, puts a teabag in each of them, then takes a milk bottle from the fridge and a bag of sugar from another cupboard, putting them both on the sideboard.

'Here, let me help,' I say, thinking I've spotted a chance to get myself out of this. 'Do you have a spoon?'

Without saying a word, he opens a drawer, takes a teaspoon out and hands it to me. I deliberately fumble, and drop it.

There's a moment where I think he's not going to do it. Where I actually think he's going to stand there and look at me, forcing me to bend down and pick it up. It's probably only a fraction of a second, but it feels like an age. But, finally, he bends over and reaches for the spoon.

I take my chance, pull my leg back and deliver a solid roundhouse kick to the side of his head.

He grunts and falls backwards, the spoon clattering to the

floor, and I have a split second to make a decision: Deliver another kick or get the hell out of here.

I opt for the latter, and make a dash for the door, fumbling for the handle before I remember it's locked. I run back past him, groaning on the tiled floor, and head in the direction of the front door. When I get there, that's locked too. I look around for keys — there must be keys somewhere — but I can't find anything.

I head to my left, into the study room at the front of the house. Maybe I can get out of the window. I tug at the handle, but it's not shifting. It's locked. It's only one of those silly little window locks, with the keys that are as tiny and flimsy as anything, but it's stuck fast, and feels like trying to break into a bank vault.

I scour the windowsill for any sign of the key. No. Of course not. He's a police officer. He's not going to leave a window key lying around near the window.

I pull the desk drawers open and rifle through, feeling inside the corners, desperate to hunt for this key.

I look down into the drawer and see the photos. One of me catches my eye at first.

It's one I've not seen before — one of me sleeping soundly in my bed. I've never seen myself sleeping before — of course I haven't — but I recognise myself immediately.

He's watched me sleeping.

There are photos of other women in here, too. There must be a dozen different people. All shots taken seemingly without their knowledge. One woman walking her dog, another putting shopping into the boot of her car. All taken with a long lens.

I force myself not to look at any more, and instead pull them all out of the drawer and dump them on the desk. I pull the whole drawer out, struggling with its weight, before turning it upside down on the floor.

I hear the clatter of the small key bouncing on the exposed floorboards.

I bend down to pick it up, and that's when I see the black boots.

69

I retch and gag continually at the pair of dirty socks stuffed in my mouth as Toby Sheridan manhandles me towards the bottom of the stairs. When we get there, he takes a huge handful of my hair and tries to drag me up the stairs by it.

I go to scream, but I can't. It's muffled by the socks.

I scrabble to my feet and try to walk myself up the stairs but I keep slipping, feeling an agonising jolt of my scalp tearing away from my skull every time I do so.

Eventually, we reach the top of the stairs and he drags me into a bedroom. He picks me up and throws me onto the wooden bed. I hear something snap – maybe a strut or leg from the bed. He looks around and goes through a couple of drawers, as if looking for something. Then he stands, appears to have an idea, grabs my arm and yanks me up from the bed. I feel my shoulder pop in its socket.

He pulls me over towards a walk-in wardrobe, opens the door and throws me inside. Before I've even hit the back wall, the door has slammed behind me and I hear the sound of him dragging the wooden bureau across the floor and putting it in front of the door. I know there's no way in hell I'm going to be able to get out of here, so I don't even try. I fall to the floor in the complete darkness, and sob.

A few minutes later, I hear footsteps again, followed by the sound of the bureau moving. The door opens and the light streams in, hurting my eyes. Toby leans in and grabs my arm again, yanking the same shoulder as I squeal in agony.

He throws me down on the bed, and climbs on top of me, pulling the ball of twine from his pocket and tying it around my wrists and ankles, before binding those to the bed frame. The twine is cold. I presume he's kept it in the shed over winter.

When he's finally done, he pulls the dirty socks out of my mouth and leans over me, his legs still astride me, and looks into my eyes.

'How dare you,' he says, more as a statement than a question. 'How dare you take her name in vain? How dare you pretend to be her? Who do you think you are?'

It feels as though these are questions that don't need answers. And in any case, what can I say? It's all over. Whatever I say now isn't going to make the slightest bit of difference.

'You fooled me, Alice. You tried to make me look stupid.'

'You were in my house,' I say. It's the only thing I can think of. I need answers. I need to hear him tell me why he's been doing this. Why he picked me.

'Yes. Yes, I was,' he says, eventually. Just hearing him say it makes me sigh with relief. As if I hadn't just been imagining it all along. Hearing your stalker tell you he broke into your house shouldn't flood me with relief, but it does. It vindicates me.

'Why?'

'Because I could.'

I'm not sure what this means, but before I can ask, he tells me.

'You made it too easy, Alice. Especially the last time. Those new locks were good. Solid. Your locksmith knew what he was doing. But it doesn't make a blind bit of difference if you forget to lock the door.'

'But why?'

'Why what? Why all this? Why any of it?' I nod. 'Because I had to. Because I really, truly believed it. You let me believe it. Even today, downstairs,' he says, spittle flying from his lips as I see him getting angrier and more emotional at my betrayal, 'you led me to believe you were her. You *told* me you were her.'

The look in his eyes is something I've never seen before. He doesn't look angry. Just deeply, deeply hurt.

'I'm sorry,' he says, his eyes turning to sorrow and regret. 'I didn't want to have to do this. But I haven't got a choice.'

He leans back for a moment, freeing his hands from supporting his weight, before placing them around my neck and squeezing tight. He puts his weight back on his arms, pushing my neck backwards, the force crushing my windpipe, stopping any air from getting into my lungs as I make a deep gurgling noise.

My vision starts to turn watery, the edges swimming as I begin to see twinkling flashes of light and darkness encroaching from the sides. I hear nothing other than my own gurgling, until the sound of the floorboard creaking and the familiar sight of Kieran stepping into view, just as Toby Sheridan looks round and sees the heavy wooden rolling pin connect with his own forehead.

70

'Kieran, stop!' I choke helplessly, as I flail around on the bed and plead with him not to carry on caving Toby Sheridan's head in. He pulled him off of me after the first impact, then carried on hitting him. The thuds are sickening, each one reverberating around my head.

Kieran straightens up and looks at me, his chest heaving with emotion and physical exertion as he pulls a strand of hair from his eyes and tucks it back behind his ear.

'Is he...?'

He shakes his head. 'Not yet. His chest is moving. But he isn't getting up.'

'Call the police,' I say. 'There's evidence downstairs. Photos. Loads of them. There's got to be more stuff, too. Enough to convict him. Enough to end all this.'

He looks at me with something in his eye that I've never seen before.

'I can end it all right now, Alice. Another couple of blows to the head and he's gone. Or a knife through his fucking throat,' he yells at Toby, who's lying on the floor at the side of the bed, out of my view.

'No, Kieran. Please. You can't. You'll go to prison.'

'Self defence,' he says, not taking his eyes from Toby.

'That won't work if you beat the life out of him or stab him. One hit to get him off me, maybe. Bludgeoning the man to death won't do anything but get you a life sentence.'

He seems to recognise the sense in this, and I start to recognise him again as the Kieran I know and loved.

'Untie me,' I say, my arms and legs throbbing and my back tight. Kieran does as I say. 'How did you get here? How did you know I was coming?' I ask him, surprised that this hadn't crossed my mind sooner.

'Darryl told me. He was worried about you and said he'd told you his address. I thought you might do something stupid so I went over to yours. You weren't in. I figured you'd come here.'

'But the doors were all locked.'

'Yeah, they were. Until the stupid bastard went out to the shed,' he says, delivering a kick to Sheridan's ribs. A thought crosses my mind. The twine. 'So much for slating you for not locking your door.'

There are a few moments of silence before he speaks again.

'So what now?' he asks, as if I've got all the answers.

'We call the police.'

I look at Kieran for a sign that he agrees, that he's not going to kill Toby.

He looks back at me and nods.

71

Jane McKenna's tone is conciliatory as she sits in my living room and explains what they've discovered in the days since Toby Sheridan was arrested. She still hasn't apologised for not believing me, but at the same time she hasn't questioned me about why I didn't tell her I recognised his photo that day in the police station. The unspoken agreement is that we're even.

'His mother died when he was thirteen,' she explains. 'Cancer. It's an impressionable age to go through the pain of your mother dying. By all accounts, she doted on him. She was a campaigner for social justice. She'd been very active in the sixties when she was younger, and that vibe had never quite worn off. She'd obviously made an impression on him, more so than most mothers do. Toby was an only child. His father disappeared before he was born. He never knew him. I don't even know whether his mother did. It seems as though he never quite got over her death.'

She leaves that hanging in the air, as if it's meant to mean something. As if it's meant to explain why he did what he did to me.

'I don't get it. What's that got to do with anything?' I ask.

She looks at her sergeant before speaking, as if they'd hoped I wouldn't ask for more information and would just accept that it happened and that was that.

'Ever since she died, it seems he's been convinced she would come back. He's not said much – he's not really able to – but he mentioned something about her spirit being too strong. About knowing she'd return. We turned his place upside down, as you'd expect, and we found quite a few photos of her hidden under the bed. By all accounts, Alice, you're a dead ringer for her. We reckon that's what he spotted. He saw that you looked like her, and wanted to mould you into becoming her.'

'What about the other women?' I ask.

'Some of them were the same. They looked similar to her in many ways. Some didn't. We aren't sure about those, but we presume there must have been something that he spotted, something that made him think they resembled her. Maybe something in their personalities.'

'I don't get it, though. Why wasn't something done about them?'

McKenna looks at her sergeant again. 'Honestly? A few reasons. Lack of evidence in many cases. We never had him down as a suspect in any others, because he was so careful. He hid in plain sight. And the other cases just sort of fizzled out. He left the women alone.'

'Why? Why not me?'

She shakes her head. 'I honestly don't know. Maybe he really thought you were the one. Perhaps something you did – completely inadvertently – made him escalate things to this level. We might never know.'

I don't know what else to say. Maybe I'll never get all the answers. I guess it must all make sense in Toby Sheridan's mind, but I also know we might never get access to that mind.

'But what I don't get is how he had access to that building where he had his studio. The cleaner told me there was no-one in that office space upstairs,' I say.

McKenna cocks her head. 'We can't be sure, but it looks as though there's a link between him and the firm of architects downstairs. He went in for a meeting a couple of months back, apparently. Something about plans for a new build house. While he was there the intruder alarm went off. The rear entrance to the building was permanently alarmed. He came out of the toilet next to that entrance just as one of the staff members went to investigate and shut off the alarm using the keypad. They didn't think much of it until we went in to ask about him a couple of days ago.'

'He watched them shut off the alarm and memorised the code?'

'Looks like it. Whether he picked the lock on the door first when he went in that weekend to set up his photography stuff, I don't know. We might never know.'

'Is he still in hospital?' I ask.

'Yeah. Probably will be for a while yet. I've got to tell you, it's looking like he'll be in a wheelchair for the rest of his life at the very least. His brain injuries are pretty severe.'

'Is he talking?'

'Not much. A bit, but we're struggling. Hopefully we'll get there eventually.'

I don't know what to feel. Part of me is pleased, although I know that sounds bad. How can I be pleased that a man who's clearly mentally ill has ended up having to spend the rest of his life confined to a wheelchair – and possibly worse? But the truth is that at least he won't be able to do this to anyone else. Even when he's out of prison – if he ever gets sent there, or ever gets out again – he'll likely have to be in a home for the rest of his life.

'But how was this allowed to happen? How did he manage to get a job working for the police if he was that mentally unstable?'

'Psychological testing's only as good as the the person taking the test is honest. He gave all the right answers. Nothing was flagged up at any level. To all intents and purposes, he came across as a totally normal person. He's a good actor.'

'Well. It's over now,' I say.

'I'm obliged to tell you,' McKenna explains, 'that due to the way you've been treated throughout this investigation, you're entitled to lodge a complaint with the IPCC.'

'What does that mean? For you, I mean.'

She shrugs and tilts her head. 'I don't know. If they investigate and find that we were negligent in some way, then it's possible there'll be some form of disciplinary action.'

'Would you lose your job?'

'It's not likely,' she says, seeming to become a little defensive. 'I followed procedure to the letter and did everything I could with the information we had available. It's not an easy job and I believe I did everything I could.' She pauses for a moment, before calming slightly. But if I was you? I'd be on the phone to them right now.'

It's not an apology, but I can tell it's the closest I'm going to get. It's a tacit admission that the way she treated me was diabolical, and that she feels remorse for it. I don't see the need in throwing salt in the wound by putting in an official complaint. It's over. Sheridan's life has effectively ended and I can start to rebuild.

'You'll let me know when you have more news?' I ask, making it clear that I want to be kept informed of what's going on. No more concealing information, no more hiding the facts from me.

'Yes. I can promise you that much,' she says. 'And in the meantime, you call me any time you need to ask anything, alright? Personally, I'm keen that we do right by you. We should have done earlier. If it's something to do with the case and the prosecution, though, you'll need to go through DCI Cosgrove. He's leading the case now.'

'They took you off it?'

She nods, a sad look crossing her face. 'Yeah. Standard procedure when they think there might have been some sort of operational cock-up. It's understandable.' She rises to her feet, and her sergeant does the same. 'You take care, alright?

You're free now. You don't need to worry about him any more.'

I nod and watch as they make to leave.

'Jane?' I call after her.

She turns back to look at me.

I smile. The first genuine smile I've smiled in a long time. 'Thank you.'

EPILOGUE

I exhale heavily as I walk down the stone steps at the front of the courthouse, the summer sun warming my skin. There are journalists waiting as we leave, but I've already told my solicitor I don't want to make any comment. Besides, the Chief Constable has far more to say than I do. She'll have the press hounding her for explanations on officer vetting, public safety and the integrity of their detectives. Me? I just want to get home.

Sheridan tried pleading insanity at the trial, but that was quickly jumped on by the prosecution. After all, how could someone who was clinically insane manage to hold down a job as a police officer? Or even get the job in the first place? Rumour has it, according to my solicitor, that he retracted that plea after Sheridan's own solicitor – under pressure from the police – convinced him that it would be better to accept his punishment rather than try to wriggle out of it and potentially get a longer sentence. The cynic in me thinks this was just damage limitation by the police force. After all, if the court accepted that he was clinically insane, what would that say about their staff vetting procedures? The shockwave that would send through the general public would be enormous.

I squeeze Simon's hand, and he looks at me and smiles. He's been an absolute rock since he found out what had happened. I had to tell him – he would've found out eventually, anyway. The story's been all over the news since Sheridan was arrested. I was worried at first that it might scare Simon off, but it had the complete opposite effect. He's been my constant ever since, looking out for me and allowing me to take my time, never pressuring me into telling him any of the details.

We're taking it easy, seeing how things go. When people ask, I tell them we're a couple. Deep down, I'm fairly sure this will be long-term. I can't see any other way, and I'm certain he feels that too. But as things stand I'm cautious about making any predictions for the future. I've seen how quickly things can change.

I thought Kieran might have reacted badly when he found out about me and Simon. I tried telling him as soon as I could, as soon as I felt sure that Simon and I were an item. He looked at me for a couple of seconds before breaking out into a smile – a smile I knew was honest and true – and telling me he was happy for me. I could see in his eyes that he meant it. I think he knew we would never be able to be together and that Simon was good for me. I hope I can prove him right.

Mandy jogs up behind me as we walk to Simon's car, and punches me playfully on the shoulder.

'You coming for a celebratory drink?' she asks me, before looking at Simon. 'You're invited too, Karate Kid.'

I look up at him, feeling safe and secure, but still wanting to gauge his opinion.

'What do you reckon?'

He shrugs. 'I don't mind.'

I look back at Mandy.

'I dunno. We've got a few bits to sort out at home.' I call it home, but it's not my home; it's Simon's. I stayed a few nights with him after Sheridan's arrest and we took it from there. When I realised I couldn't go back to my own place – that I still didn't feel safe there – Simon said I could stay with him for as long as I wanted. The long-term plan is to put my house on the market and move in permanently. Perhaps he'll sell his flat too and we can get a place of our own. Start afresh.

'Oh yeah, because I forgot it's just an everyday occurrence to see your stalker sent down for ten years,' Mandy says, pulling a sarcastic face. 'So. Zizi's? If you run home and put some proper clothes on we might just make happy hour.'

I laugh. 'Proper clothes? It's a dress suit. I was just in court, in case you hadn't noticed. We can't all turn up in jeans and trainers.'

'Hey, these are new,' she says, sounding offended.

Simon smiles at me. I smile back, then look at Mandy.

'How does six-thirty sound?'

GET MORE OF MY BOOKS FREE!

Thank you for reading *In Her Image*. I hope it was as much fun for you as it was for me writing it.

To say thank you, I'd like to invite you to my exclusive *VIP Club*, and give you some of my books and short stories for FREE. All members of my VIP Club have access to FREE, exclusive books and short stories which aren't available anywhere else.

You'll also get access to all of my new releases at a bargain-basement price before they're available anywhere else. Joining is absolutely FREE and you can leave at any time, no questions asked. To join the club, head to adamcroft.net/vip-club **and two free books will be sent to you straight away!**

If you enjoyed the book, please do leave a review on the

site you bought it from. Reviews mean an awful lot to writers and they help us to find new readers more than almost anything else. It would be very much appreciated.

I love hearing from my readers, too, so please do feel free to get in touch with me. You can contact me via my website, on Twitter @adamcroft and you can 'like' my Facebook page at facebook.com/adamcroftbooks.

For more information, visit my website: adamcroft.net

THE PERFECT LIE

What if you were framed for a murder you didn't commit?

Amy Walker lives the perfect family life with her husband and two young sons. Until a knock at the door turns their lives upside down.

It's the police. Her father-in-law is dead and they're arresting her for his murder.

The evidence against her is overwhelming. Forensics and witnesses place her at the scene. But there's only one problem:

She didn't do it.

With her family destroyed and a murder sentence looming, Amy must discover who murdered her father-in-law – and why they're so hell-bent on framing her as the killer.

HER LAST TOMORROW

Could you murder your wife to save your daughter?

On the surface, Nick Connor's life is seemingly perfect: a quiet life with his beautiful family and everything he could ever want. But soon his murky past will collide with his idyllic life and threaten the very people he loves the most in the world.

When his five-year-old daughter, Ellie, is kidnapped, Nick's life is thrown into a tailspin. In exchange for his daughter's safe return, Nick will have to do the unthinkable: **he must murder his wife**.

With his family's lives hanging in the balance, what will Nick do? Can he and his family survive when the evil that taunts them stems from the sins of his past?

TELL ME I'M WRONG

What if you discovered your husband was a serial killer?

Megan Miller is an ordinary woman with a young family – until a shocking discovery shatters her perfect world.

When two young boys are brutally murdered in their tight-knit village community, Megan slowly begins to realise the signs all point to the lovable local primary school teacher – **her husband**.

But when she begins to delve deeper into her husband's secret life, she makes discoveries that will make her question everything she knows – and make her fear for her young daughter's life.

Facing an impossible decision, she is desperate to uncover the truth. But once you know something, it can't be unknown. And the more she learns, the more she wishes she never knew anything at all...

ONLY THE TRUTH

He's not the perfect husband. But he is the perfect suspect.

Dan Cooper has never been the perfect husband to Lisa. He travels for work and plays the carefree bachelor when he can. But now, on a solo business trip, in a remote coastal hotel, he's surprised to find Lisa in his bathroom. She's dead.

He has no idea how she got there but one chilling fact is clear: everything points to Dan having murdered her. Someone is trying to frame him. Someone who might still be watching. In a panic, he goes on the run. But even as he flees across Europe, his unknown enemy stacks up the evidence against him.

Dan is determined to clear his name and take revenge on

Lisa's killer, but the culprit is closing in. And then there's the agony of his own guilty conscience. No, he didn't kill her—but is it all his fault?

Click here to buy it now.

ACKNOWLEDGMENTS

Any book has a much bigger team behind it than many people imagine, and this one was no different. My thanks, therefore, go to many people, some of whom I've remembered to name here.

The first thing you likely saw was the cover, and for that I have to thank James Ryan, who's designed my last few book covers and has done a sterling job.

Enormous thanks go to Lucy Hayward for her eagle editing eye and her honesty and clarity in letting me know what I've done wrong and how to fix it.

To my advance reading team, who offered their advice and spotted the remaining errors (I hope).

To Louise (LJ) Ross, Jay Stringer and Mark Dawson for their encouragement, friendship and words of advice that helped me to make a series of decisions about this book and many more. To the other fellow authors who made excellent sounding boards around the same time, thank you also. You know who you are and, hopefully, why I've omitted your names here.

To Joanne, my wife, who is always my first reader and does her very best not to laugh when I kill off a character in one chapter, then have him sitting in the pub three chapters later.

To Laura Dalton for casting her eye over an early draft, helping me ensure that Alice's decisions were sound and logical.

To Bob Daws for his encouragement and input, including his excellent work on adapting HER LAST TOMORROW for television. Watch this space for more on that... Thanks must also go to Will Peterson at Independent Talent for his encouragement on this front.

To Mark Lefebvre, Shayna Krishnasamy and Taylor Kaisaris at Kobo; Isabella Steel, Ami Greko, Kristen Freethy and Jessica Hanak at Apple iBooks; Julie Braunschweiger at Barnes & Noble; and Andrew Rosenheim at Amazon, for their advice, expertise and hard work in helping to get my books to sale and promote them afterwards. I'm excited to be able to once again offer all my future full-length books across all digital platforms, as well as paperback and audio.

To Diane Capri, Fleur Camacho, Jenna Bennett, Seeley James, Helen Hanson and Rebecca Cantrell for their advice and assistance in crafting the sales blurb for the book.

To all of the members of my VIP Club. Although there are now tens of thousands of you, every single one of you plays a huge part in making each of my books a success.

And to anyone else, if I've forgotten to mention you here, don't blame me; blame my four-week-old son for the sleep deprivation.

Lightning Source UK Ltd.
Milton Keynes UK
UKHW011808070419
340625UK00001B/158/P